THE GILDED CAGE

Sarah E. England

Copyright © 2024 S. E. England
All rights reserved.

No part of this book may be used or reproduced in any manner whatsoever without written permission of the author, except for brief quotations used for promotion or in reviews. This is a work of fiction. Names, characters, places and incidents are used fictitiously. Any resemblance to actual persons living or dead, business establishments, events, or locales is entirely coincidental.

ISBN:979-8-3217-8385-6

1st Edition
www.sarahenglandauthor.co.uk

About the author

Sarah England is a UK author with a background in nursing and psychiatry, themes which creep into many of her stories. At the fore of Sarah's body of work is the bestselling occult horror trilogy, *Father of Lies, Tanners Dell,* and *Magda,* followed by a spin-off from the series, *The Owlmen*. Other novels include *The Soprano, Hidden Company, Monkspike, Baba Lenka, Masquerade, Caduceus, Groom Lake, The Droll Teller,* and *Creech Cross. The Witching Hour* is a collection of short stories; and *The Gilded Cage* is her first international psychological thriller.

If you would like to be informed about future releases, there is a newsletter sign-up on Sarah's website. Please feel free to get in touch – it would be great to hear from you!

www.sarahenglandauthor.co.uk

Part One

'All that glisters is not gold. Often have you heard that told. Many a man his life hath sold. But my outside to behold. Gilded tombs do worms enfold.'

The Merchant of Venice, Shakespeare

Chapter One

The Golden Triangle
Chiang Rai, Northern Thailand
September, 1992

Louise still can't believe it sometimes. Gazing at Vic across the breakfast table high above the river, her heart swells at the sight of him. Is she really here? With him? And in such exotic surroundings? It's a dream. Surely, it's a dream?

Along the top of the balcony rails are carved wooden elephants shouldering lamps in the shape of orbs. At night they light the entire periphery of the hotel, a necklace of pearls in the black velvet forest. At eight in the morning, though, a layer of soft, ethereal mist shrouds the scene. The air is still cool, but in a couple of hours it will be hot, sticky and humid. Already the vibrating chorus of cicadas has begun. But, according to local information, the mountain villages have once again become accessible, as the rain tails off and the wet season turns to dry.

Vic is staring across the valley into the jungle, his expression far away, when the shadow of a lone eagle with black, hunched wings soars and circles high above, and she looks up. A serpent eagle, its call high-pitched, persistent – *Kek kek kwee kwee* – is searching for snakes, as the veil begins to lift and the sun lasers through.

Vic Landry. However on God's green earth, did she

come to be married to a man like him? She wasn't the only one who'd asked the question. Others couldn't understand it either, one of his colleagues voicing his astonishment on their wedding day.

You really are incredibly lucky, you know?

There is a pang in her chest at the recollection.

The holiday is almost over – just five days – a short break from where they currently live in Singapore, after leaving England over six months ago. She finds Singapore stifling, a blanket of oppressive heat that never lets up, day in, day out, month in, month out, and is reluctant to think ahead, to the day after tomorrow, to the prospect of returning to their high-rise apartment and the hum of air-conditioning, to being there alone, always alone. But that is not yet. There is today. And tomorrow. With Vic.

"Big day ahead," he says, draining his coffee and standing up. "Come on, let's go."

They're heading into the mountains to see the hill tribes, the expedition booked.

After that, there'll be one more road trip in the Jeep. They plan to go east to the town of Nan, along a notoriously hair-raising single track from Chiang Rai, which winds through the mountains towards Laos. It's exciting. Exhilarating. The whole experience has taken her breath away. Even the hotel is astonishingly surreal – a hillside resort deep in the jungle, with Lanna architecture, using local teak wood and bamboo. Chiang Rai was the first capital of the Lanna Kingdom in the days when the country was Siam. She sees the timelessness of it everywhere here. It is in the elegance of the people, in the beauty of the golden temples, or wats, and the majesty of the great statues of Buddha, which rise from fields and mountain glades, dominate entrances to caves, and even sit atop boats. Buddhas are everywhere, in meditative pose, palms pressed together, blending with the mystic land.

The walkway back to their room skirts a series of infinity pools fringed with palms. Here, there are tropical lotus ponds, lush gardens, and outdoor spas. The hotel offers Lanna fire massages and hot volcanic stone treatments, and the air is fragrant with sweet, white ginger lilies. Not enough time, Louise thinks. It would have been nice to have spent a day idling here in paradise, to float in the pool… Although once, a mangrove snake had slithered into the water while they were leaning over the balcony watching. It had to be scooped out in a huge net. The incident had plagued Louise's dreams that night – there'd been a woman swimming in the pool at the time. And just as the memory resurfaces, there's a quick rustling movement at the side of the path and she jumps.

Vic stops dead, grabs her arm. "Look, a skink!"

It's shiny olive-brown, quite big, a snake with legs.

"Oh, my God!"

"Don't be silly. He won't hurt you."

The skink is motionless, frozen mid-movement.

"He's far more scared of us than we are of him."

She nods, trying to quell the panic, which she knows is ridiculous but can't help.

He looks at his watch. "Come on, we'd better hurry."

Their bedroom has a view of the jungle-covered hills on the opposite side of the river. White mosquito nets surround a four-poster bed, the sheets now crumpled beneath a whirring ceiling fan. Every night they fall asleep to unfamiliar sounds, to the eerie, wailing screams of fish owls, the *kweek kweek* of savanna nightjars, an occasional cacophony of shrieking macaques, and other, more mysterious sounds – of rhythmic drums from within the tar-blackness, and the distant yet ever-present sound of tinkling wind chimes. Each day has been action-packed though, and after a few minutes of lying perfectly still, listening out for mosquito buzzes beyond the nets, they've both slipped quickly into sleep.

In the morning, it is the clatter of crockery that wakes them, breakfast being set below, on verandas still swathed in mist. The staff move around noiselessly, swift as cats, and should they pass one, there is a smile, the *wai* greeting of pressing the palms together, and a slight bow. Courteous, respectful, silent. She loves it here. Has even become used to the tiny geckos spreadeagled on the walls, with their beady-black eyes and miniature hands.

They've had a good time these past few days. And her heart aches a little because of it. Quickly now, they gather together what will be needed for the day. The guide is meeting them at the travel office in Chiang Rai at eight-thirty. It will take several hours to climb the mountain track, and they probably won't be back before dark.

"Have you got the gifts?"

Louise nods. "Yes, I've put them in the backpack. And…" she reels off a checklist, "bottled water, fruit, biscuits, first-aid kit, torch, cash, map…"

"Long-sleeved shirts? Deet?"

She flings her cross-body satchel on. "Yes."

The whole area is quinine-resistant, even around the hotel once the sun has set. But other than contracting malaria, the ominous buzzing of a lone mosquito after dark a haunting sound, they have few concerns. Credit cards and passports are locked in the safe, Vic's office in Singapore is apparently aware of their flight times and where they're staying, and a local guide is booked for today's trip.

"Do you think there's any danger?" she asks, as he locks the room behind them.

"In what way?" He's striding ahead of her, hitching the backpack over one shoulder. "Come on, get a shimmy on, we don't want to miss the whole damn thing."

"Because it's the Golden Triangle."

"These are hill tribes – seriously impoverished people."

"Who grow opium."

"Only a few of them. Besides, they wouldn't run tourist treks up there if it wasn't safe, would they?"

"No, I don't suppose–"

"If you must know, we were in the most unsafe area the day before yesterday when we drove up to the Burmese border. And you had no idea."

They run to catch the hotel's tuk-tuk, a kind of covered pick-up truck with two benches for sitting passengers in the back, and bars to cling onto for those standing. Several local men jump on at the last second, and it rattles off, quickly building up speed, haring downhill, pitching alarmingly in and out of potholes, winging round blind bends in the middle of the road.

Louise holds onto the seat with both hands. "What do you mean, the most unsafe area?"

"A French couple were shot there last week, apparently. I didn't know. Don't blame me. It's a drug-running area."

Apart from a few disused military checkpoints, the mountain roads had been completely empty, the open-sided Jeep they'd been riding around in pretty flimsy.

"Now you tell me."

She hadn't even thought about being unsafe here, not

once. But then again, she'd only studied the tourist brochures – working out the best places to go, the language, understanding local customs, history, food and culture – not the drug and gun trade. In the three days they've been here, they've visited temples, waterfalls, hot springs and tea plantations. They've been to the Royal Villa on Doi Tung Mountain, and the border town of Mae Sai, where they walked to the halfway point on the bridge to Myanmar. Later, they had their photographs taken with hill tribe children and an old woman smoking a fat cheroot. The days have been hot, a burning blue sky, the air smoky, aromatic and spicy. There's been a river trip on the Mekong, and a strenuous trek up to an observation point where all three countries can be seen at once – Myanmar, Laos and Thailand – a golden haze of bamboo forests, rice fields, and mist-shrouded mountains. It is hard to believe in a dark side.

He shouts above the noise of the truck, "Don't worry. Stick with me, you'll be fine."

"As long as we don't see any snakes!"

"I hope we do, they're fantastic creatures."

She grimaces. "I can't even stand the thought of them. Seriously."

The tuk-tuk hurtles down what is little more than a dirt track into town. More people run and jump onto the back of it, hanging on the bars, swinging precariously by one hand.

"Actually, it's extremely unlikely. Besides, you'll be on the back of an elephant, and we won't be tramping through swamps. That's where the pythons are. Some of them are about twenty feet long. They can swim and climb up trees…"

The sun is breaking through the steamy haze of early morning, and as the tuk-tuk finally, thankfully, clatters into town, she pushes the image of a giant, pulsing, muscular Burmese python swimming alongside the boat they're taking later, out of her mind. It's the stuff of nightmares, hers anyway, the worst.

Groups of tourists are filling up the streets, partly distinguishable by the way they're dressed – shorts, trainers, sunglasses, hats, cross-body bags, and cameras – but largely by the fact they're in organised clusters. Mostly they're Chinese, some American. Motorbikes whizz up and down the main street, along with brightly coloured songthaews and tuk-tuks. Already the smell of frying chillies, garlic and ginger fragrances the air, along with stalls heaving with exotic fruits – mangoes, water melons, durian, jackfruits, and papayas. Life seems to have burst out like a cuckoo from a clock, a stage-set cacophony of colour and noise.

Louise scans the main street for the travel office as they hurry along, hand in hand, wending in and out of the crowds.

"Where is it?"

"Down here."

At the far end is an alley leading to a jumble of dimly lit shops in a quiet, deserted square.

"Is this what the hotel recommended? Are you sure?"

"Yes." He checks the directions jotted on a piece of paper. "Definitely."

The travel agency is unlit, and the door pushes open. In the dark cave of an office at the back, a man is talking to an elderly woman. Spying Vic and Louise, he takes the cigarette from his mouth and raises one hand in greeting. Right place. Good, he's expecting them. His name is

Narong, and according to the staff at the hotel, he speaks some of the tribal languages. Each tribe, they've been told, has their own language, none of it written down, and the people don't speak Thai. There are many different tribes and sub-groups, some originating from Tibet, others from China, many having migrated from neighbouring countries for reasons of war, politics or repression. Even here, however, they do not settle, but keep moving, adopting a slash and burn culture as forest is cleared and new villages built.

Photographs of tribal people, and tourists posing with them, just as they did in Mae Sai, adorn the walls of the agency – women of the Karen tribes with heavy rings coiled around long skittle necks; others with elaborate embroidered headdresses adorned with silver, bells, feathers, monkey fur and beads; and smiling children with red sashes tied high over white blouses, and decorative skirts wrapped over pantaloons.

But the remote mountain tribes they're going to see today are very different from those integrating with locals, those in the lowlands selling wares and posing for photographs with tourists. They do not take children into these remote areas, or the elderly, or anyone with a medical condition. It will be an arduous day; they must take gifts of thanks, be respectful, know what they can and cannot do, and not cause offence. They are not to touch anything in the village, Narong reminds them, especially the gates or the altars, and must refrain from taking photographs or ever walking inside a house without invitation. He will speak for them, they will stay silent, he will lead the way. Louise should put on a shirt, cover her arms.

She takes the backpack from Vic, pulls on her white

linen shirt and buttons the cuffs, while Vic pays. Narong, cigarette balancing on his lower lip, passes the money to the old woman, who begins to count it out. She is tiny, and wears the chut Thai, a full-length narrow skirt and a blouse buttoned to the neck.

Louise doesn't understand a word of their rapid-fire exchange and is pretty sure Vic doesn't, either. Not that you'd know that, she thinks, from how confident he looks. He towers over all of them, sunglasses on, obviously keen to get going.

The tribe they're going to visit are the Akha, Narong says, fastening his backpack. They're taking a songthaew to base camp by the river, from where they'll trek by elephant to the village, and leave the elephants there.

"Four hours," he says, holding up four fingers. "Four hours."

"How do we get back again, then?" Louise asks. "I mean, from the mountain top down to the river for the boat?"

"Walk."

Immediately, she envisages a sweat-soaked machete-trek through spider-infested jungle, and a gauntlet of snakes – cobras in the undergrowth, whipsnakes flying from tree to tree, giant slithering primeval pythons three or four times longer than her own body...

"Um... What, through the jungle?"

But Narong is running through a list of what they should have with them, his English staccato, their attempts at speaking Thai dismissed with a shake of his head.

They think we're stupid, fat and rich, Louise thinks, wondering what she can do about her terror of snakes. Hopefully, Vic's right and they will keep out of the way, more frightened of people than the other way round. And even more hopefully, they won't cross paths with one today. But there's something else bothering her now, too. All at once, she's conscious of how they're going to appear to these remote hilltribe people, and it's a thought that, now formed, cannot be unformed: stupid, fat, rich tourists arriving on the back of an elephant with cameras and money round their necks.

In fact, neither of them is overweight. Louise had always been considered thin back home, at a hundred and thirty pounds and five foot eight, until they moved to the Far East and a shop assistant in Singapore told her they stocked nothing in Extra Large. Nor is she rich, far from it – she really has nothing – although Vic is undoubtedly very well paid. However, to the hill tribe people, they will probably appear to be both. Stupid, though? Perhaps they are. And perhaps this is a very foolish thing to do?

The smoky office suddenly feels gloomy. Why are they in this back-alley office, anyway? Why not one of those on the main road with brightly coloured posters in the windows? Just for a moment, the street outside seems glaringly bright by contrast, and oh-so-far away. It's just a moment. A heartbeat. A feeling she can't quite pin... but for the first time since they've been here, a prickle of unease creeps up her spine.

***

Chapter Two

A flimsy wooden seat, no more substantial than a tea-tray, is strapped onto the elephants' backs. They wobble precariously from side to side, sliding back and forth, as the elephants, two of them, the one in front carrying their guide, rise from the ground and begin to head towards the mountain path.

"Doesn't this hurt their backs? I don't like this one bit! It feels unstable. I want to go back. I want to get off!"

There is nothing to stop them falling. No safety belts, nothing to hold onto except the narrow edges of the seat. With the river and base camp soon behind them, the steamy, dense jungle closes in, and the elephants begin to climb steadily, slowly and methodically up a precipitous muddy track pitted with stones. The noise of screaming cicadas is building. Heavy, wet branches brush their faces, and gigantic spiders' webs glint in the early morning sunlight. There is nothing she can do but push the foliage out of the way with her hands, appalled; but the most urgent and overriding fear, the one making her feel physically sick, is that the slope is almost vertical. The rickety seat is now tilting so far backwards, she has a vision of shooting straight off the back, falling hard onto the stones below and hurtling all the way down the slope. They have no helmets, no padding, nothing to break the fall.

Another branch crashes into their faces, and as they push it away, she catches a flash of viper-green.

Clinging onto Vic, she cannot keep the panic from her voice. "No. I want to get off. I'll walk. Please! Stop! I have to get off!"

The mahout, sitting on the elephant's head, glances over his shoulder, glowering eyes squinting into the sun. She looks behind. With every step the drop below is magnified. It's like an Alpine ski-run. She hadn't realised, had somehow had in mind a gentler journey than this. Instead, it's terrifying. Occasionally the elephant stumbles and the seat tilts not only further backwards, but also alarmingly over to one side. They have to adjust, carefully re-balance bodyweight.

"It's all right, calm down," Vic says. "Remember, they do this all the time."

"They haven't done it in months – look how overgrown it is. It's wet and slippery too, covered in mud. This is lethal."

The mahout pushes back a heavy tree branch with his stick, and they duck as it snaps back in a spray of showery leaves.

"Oh, God! This is horrible. There are snakes in the trees. And giant spiders. They could be poisonous. I want to walk. Tell him, please! I have to get off."

There's a sudden eruption of shrieking macaques, swooping from tree to tree in a great, gleeful gang. As if they're laughing at them.

"Well, it's too late now." He seems at ease, perusing a map, slinging an arm around her as they slide from side to side on the seat. "Look, this is where we are. About here."

She doesn't look. Panic is beginning to consume her.

"Oh, God – look! There's a massive snake in the tree. Look!" Her voice sounds different to her own ears, childlike, breaking. "Coiled up round the branch!"

"Louise! For goodness' sake, calm down."

He continues to scan the map, unperturbed, swaying gently with the momentum, while Louise, instead of screaming, turns inward. She is sheet-white, mute, rigid.

After about an hour, the path begins to level off, and the elephants plod heavily from out of the trees onto a flat cliff edge. On one side, her side, the drop is sheer. Without moving her head, she casts an uneasy sideways glance from her unnaturally lofty height, over the top of the forest canopy, to the valley far, far below. Miles and miles of table-mat-sized plains stretch out as far as the horizon. They're going to fall. The elephant will slip and they will fall. Briefly, there's a premonition of being propelled over the top of the trees, of flying through the air, and she checks herself, looking straight at the back of the mahout's head, grimly holding onto the seat. When suddenly the elephant's head turns to the side, the tea-tray seat wobbles slightly, and her heart thuds sickeningly. His giant feet are just inches from the edge, and it seems to her he has a yearning to leap over, to crash through the forest, and run for freedom. She sees him hurtling across the plains below. To the rice fields, to where tiny stick figures dot the landscape.

"He's going to run off, he wants to be free."

Vic folds up the map.

"Louise, you've got to stop this. Look how laid-back the mahout is – he's nearly asleep. The elephants will be fed when we get to the top, and you saw them bathing in the river. They're looked after. They're not going to run off.

Now, try to calm down, darling."

But the elephant's enormous head turns once again and his pace has slowed. She's right, she knows it, instinctively. Can feel his hesitance, his call to the wild. She would feel the same. Why should he cart tourists up the mountain? It must hurt his back. Rub the bones of his spine. Her fear is palpable and beginning to escalate out of control again, a Vesuvius eruption.

"Stop! Hey! I want to get off. Stop and let me down! Now! Stop! I mean it!"

This time the mahout swivels around fully. "Lady! No!"

Vic has hold of her arm, is saying something about getting a grip, making a fool of herself, being silly, ridiculous.

Shamed into silence, she is instantly alone with her terror, the cold plunge of it in her stomach. Automatically clutching the pearl cross around her neck, she closes her eyes, praying. It would take one slip of the elephant's foot, a crumbling of earth beneath the enormous weight... or a snake to slither across the path... But she vows not to speak again. What good would it do?

"Fantastic view," Vic says. "That must be Laos in the distance. See the hills?"

She steels herself to look. It is, as he says, a fantastic view. What is the point of fear, she wonders. What good does it do once it's informed you of danger, if you can't do anything about it? It's either her turn to die or it isn't, and no amount of worrying is going to change that. It's just that there's a deep well of terror inside her, always waiting, always there, threatening to engulf.

"Try to relax, Lou," he says again. "There's a long way to go yet."

Her heart is like lead, thudding dully. "Yes, I'll try."

Eventually, the troop veers away from the cliff face to begin the next stage of ascent, the trail winding ever higher and deeper into the mountains; tree branches, as they push them aside, still wet from mist. The clouds are lifting now though, the day warming rapidly, and what was a quiet morning is now becoming a shrieking cacophony of cawing, clicking, and a near-deafening buzz of cicadas. It's as if they're vying with each other for attention, building up to a feverish crescendo, thousands and thousands of them, like an electric sawmill.

After a little while, she's able to talk normally again.

"Do you think they practice Voodoo up here? Only sometimes at night, I can hear drums and haunting music, like pan pipes or flutes."

"Some of the tribes are Buddhists, actually. But I think the Akha mostly practice ancestral worship, honouring the land, shamanism, that kind of thing. They respect spirits, nature and animals."

"Like indigenous people everywhere."

"Exactly. We're the heathens, if you think about it. I don't know anyone who's spiritual or even thinks about it. They'd laugh in your face."

She nods, finally feeling calmer inside. Her grandmother, Marion, was spiritual. She'd tell her to take a long walk on the moors because that's where she'd hear her soul. "Get quiet," she'd say. "Stop talking and get quiet. That's when the answers'll come to you. No point frettin'." Fleetingly, homesickness washes over her. For the wide-open Yorkshire moors. Sunlight filters through the canopy, dappling on the path, and she takes a series of long, deep breaths.

"It's called the Akha Way," Vic's saying. "They pass knowledge down through generations by word of mouth – memories, myths, ancestors, tribal law and so on. That's their education. Nothing written. And then there are spirit gates to the village, demarcating the border between the two worlds, spiritual and physical. Physical being the carnal world of man within the village confines, while the forest is where spirits and animals reside. That's why Narong said not to touch the spirit gates."

She smiles. He's well-read, had travelled extensively before they met, and with him being older and a lot more experienced, she's having the kind of life she would never ordinarily have had. God, she's been so embarrassing, so… she searches for the right word… gauche, unsophisticated.

"There's a leader, usually the shaman, and a protective village spirit they worship and thank. They have daily rituals, and sacrifices are made to all living things – trees, river, mountain, ancestors, dragons and heaven. Even rice. They have rituals for the rice crop."

"Dragons?"

"Think Chinese dragons, I suppose."

"Maybe they once existed? I mean, there's St George who slayed the dragon in England. And a dragon on the Welsh flag. Maybe, they were real, after all?"

"Could be. There are Komodo dragons in Indonesia, don't forget. And monitor lizards. You've seen those in Singapore Zoo."

"Yes, of course. Well, who's to say the bigger ones didn't die out? Or were killed? I often think herons look a bit prehistoric, actually."

"I suppose they do. And cormorants. And pelicans."

"And hornbills."

They're quiet for a while, rocking from side to side with the movement of the elephant, occasionally gripping the seat tighter when the climb lurches more sharply upwards. A further half hour passes, maybe more, as each is lulled into daydreams, snapping alert at times, not so much at others.

"I wonder what shamans do?" she says, not really expecting an answer.

"Preside over rituals, treat illnesses, astral travel, drive out evil spirits. Apparently, tribal funerals are three days long, and the body's buried in the forest with no marker. Spirits can't exist in the carnal world of the village, so the dead now belong to the other side, in the forest, returning from whence they came."

"How did you find all that out? I couldn't find any books other than tourist maps, where to stay and what to see. I never found anything on spirit gates and shamans."

"Oh, it was years ago when I worked in Bangkok. There was a woman called Katty, and she told me."

"I didn't know you'd worked there, you never said. Was she a colleague?"

Vic shrugs. "Just a woman I had, in my long, dark, distant past. Don't worry, it was ages ago, long before I met you, darling. But she was rather fascinating, I have to say. She had this weird-looking amulet on a chain, with letters on the front that she was always touching. Sometimes I'd look up and she'd have her eyes closed, holding onto it, murmuring something. So, you know, I asked what it was and she said for spirit protection."

"An amulet?"

"Apparently, and this will probably spook you out – it contains the ground bones, teeth and bits of hair from a human sacrifice. And the symbol on the front binds the wearer to a spirit entity. It's done with a ritual, a contract. Same with the tattoo I got."

She nods, ever so slightly shocked, processing the new information. She'd never given much thought to the ink tattoo on his chest. It was something he'd had done on a holiday to Bangkok, he said. A holiday. He'd definitely said holiday, not work. And she'd always pictured a back street tattoo parlour, and a group of drunken lads egging each other on. Not an occult ceremony with a sacrifice and spirit-binding ritual.

"So, what did you have to do, exactly?"

"It was ages ago, now. I can hardly remember. Her brother did it in the back room of his house, really late at night, probably about one in the morning or something. It was pitch dark and there were lit candles, joss sticks, all this incense floating around; and the table was set out with offerings, food and drink, that kind of thing."

"Weren't you scared?"

He glanced at her and laughed. "No, of course not. It was nothing."

"So, what happened next?"

"He put a gold mask on and started chanting, pounding on this little drum, summoning what they called the grandmaster."

"Oh, my God. I'd have run for the hills."

"I think I went into a trance or even fell asleep, because it went on so long. Then all of a sudden he stopped and I woke up. I do remember a thump to the heart, like I'd been out cold. I had to say out loud who I was and what I wished for. As in, stating my name and exactly what my deepest desires were. After that, there was more chanting to bring a spirit through for me. Then I had to drink a potion, which I knocked back. Only to find out later, it was the juice of a recently deceased corpse."

"What? Are you serious?"

"Absolutely. It's well known, and of course, completely illegal. Corpse oil in a little vial made from bodily organs. So, after I'd consumed the sacrifice, he said to keep repeating the particular words I'd been given, and then he left me in the dark to keep chanting them, over and over, and not to resist whatever came."

"And what happened? Anything? No, of course not."

"Exactly, darling. Nothing happened. He came back in, put the lights on, I kept saying the same words, and he inked the tattoo. And that was it."

She glances at his profile. And for the first time, it occurs to her to wonder how well she really knows him.

"And what did you ask for? Or does that break the spell?"

"Nothing can break the spell, although I suspect what I asked for is what most guys ask for. Mind you, there are consequences. You might get what you want, but sooner or later you have to pay a price. Karma and so forth. Load of tosh, isn't it? But highly amusing."

"I thought you said you'd got it on holiday. I didn't know you'd worked in Bangkok."

Sighing, he reaches for her hand. "I did have a holiday there, but it was while I was working in Bangkok for the bank, many, many years ago. You'd be bored if I talked about Futures trading in Asia, darling."

"Hmm. So, you think it's all superstitious nonsense then? Nothing in it?"

He shrugs. "Same as anywhere else in the world, isn't

it?"

She's quiet for a while, reflective, considering passed-down tales in the small northern English town she grew up in. There was a woman who worked in the school kitchens who made bracelets, charms and poppets, said to be dark magic. She used to ask for locks of hair or fingernail clippings. Everyone was terrified of her.

"I guess. It wasn't that long ago the whole of Britain, Europe and North America was locked in a witch-burning frenzy, whether people were witches or not."

"Frenzy's the word," he agrees. "And terrified people acting en-masse don't stop to ask questions. Something takes them over."

"Like a tulpa?"

Abruptly, he turns to face her, eyebrows raised, and she's struck anew at how startling his looks are. Clear, deep brown eyes as keen as a fox, russet-chestnut hair that's thick and wavy, swept back... a high-bridged nose and very white teeth... wide smile...

"You know about tulpas?"

"Not really. I must have read it somewhere. It's when there are more than a few people all believing the same thing, wearing the same badge or symbol, same club, same thoughts. A kind of separate entity is formed, a presence that's the sum of the whole. It's how cults work. Individuals are weakened because they conform to the greater will of the group, and it can take over. Like with a mob. A pitchfork mob, for example."

"Indeed. You surprise me."

"Well, there you go. Not as stupid as I look."

"Hardly possible."

"Gee, thanks."

For the first time that day she laughs, and when she laughs she laughs properly, from the core of herself, head thrown back. People do think she's stupid. She's blonde, with pale, freckled skin and blue-green doe eyes – a wide-eyed, startled creature emerging from underground, blinking in the dazzle of daylight.

"You're just a little girl really, aren't you?"

Is she?

But there's no time to answer.

"Hey, look. I think we're here."

She doesn't know what she expected as the elephants plod along the path into a clearing, but it wasn't this: dingy rags hanging on a line, a couple of skulking, hungry-looking dogs, and a rusty moped propped up against an oil drum.

"You've got to be kidding. Is this it?"

The guide, Narong, has dismounted and is hurrying towards them, motioning to the mahout. There's no sign of life in the village, no noise at all. No one in sight beyond an arched wooden framework, gates strewn with grotesque images and small animal skulls on poles.

"Yes," Vic says. "I think it could be."

***

Chapter Three

The village is a semi-circle of houses on stilts, each with a bamboo roof and a sheltered area for animals and storage below. Led by Narong, Vic and Louise walk through the spirit gates, past a couple of women pounding rice in a giant pot. There are no children around, not so much as a baby's cry, the air smoky, earthy, strangely sweet, and absolutely still. Even the cicadas seem to have reached their peak, and stopped.

As if a storm is coming.

Louise hangs back.

"You come," Narong says, beckoning them to the largest of the houses. He speaks to someone inside, words exchanged sharply, loudly, before beckoning them again. "Yes, yes. Come. Is okay."

Every instinct Louise possesses tells her not to go inside, and so she lingers in the doorway, in the shadow of Vic's broad back. A man is lying on a rickety straw bed covered with filthy rags, his eyes hooded and glazed. Beside him on the floor, a long clay pipe smoulders, the remains of a dark, resinous substance in its bowl. He's utterly wasted, a thin bundle of bones, borderline unconscious; and as her eyes become accustomed to the gloomy interior, she sees through the smoky haze that there are others. What were grey heaps of cloth on the floor, are men staring up at them; and on the other side of the bamboo partition walls, shadows move, swaying, silent as ghosts. There's a small fire lit in a tin caddy in the centre of the room, and it is this she focuses on. Nothing else.

One of the men speaks to Narong, who nods and hands over a packet of cigarettes from his shirt pocket. The exchange is fractious, and he appears to be placating, gesturing towards Vic and Louise. What is he saying? Asking if they can take photographs? That they've paid for a full experience or something? Frankly, that's the last thing she wants to do. But the conversation doesn't seem to be going well. And suddenly he has his hands in the air, is shaking his head, taking a step back.

"We have to go," he says to Vic. "Day wrong."

The man glaring at Narong suddenly shifts his attention to Louise, and her heart almost skips a beat. For the second time that morning, her hand reaches for the pearl-adorned cross around her neck. It's the only precious possession she has, left to her by Marion; and she holds onto it more protectively than ever. In a flash, her grandmother is there before her, just as she'd last been, in her best Sunday hat and coat, with the pearl cross around her neck – on a bright, breezy, moorland day, the front garden at Spring Bank Heights full of shivering daffodils. A few days later, she'd fallen to the floor with an aortic aneurysm. No time to even say goodbye. How stupid she's been to wear this today. Why did she not think?

The man is staring at her hand, and what it might be covering.

Stupid… stupid…

The awareness of where they are, of the situation they're in, is as sharp and shocking as a bolt of lightning. How isolated they are! There's no one around for miles. No one to call for help. They've trusted the guide implicitly, a man they don't know. And how gloomy his back street office was, not on the main road like the other tourist agencies. Who had recommended Vic to go there? Was it someone at the hotel? Could they have been set-up? She tries to remember. But Vic had fixed it all up. Someone at Reception, he'd said. Oh God, they were going to be robbed. Maybe worse…

All this races through her mind in less than a second, as the man's eyes burn into her throat. She pictures herself and Vic running out of here, tearing through the jungle, stumbling, running, out of breath. But there's no way they'd be able to find their way back to town – the route had twisted and turned, sun on their backs one minute, on their faces the next. Now it beats down on the bamboo roof, with the piercing cacophony of cicadas building up once more, the day heating up, opium smoke drifting into her senses. For a fleeting moment she can taste it, the bitterness nothing like the promised sweetness in the air – but a thick, pulsating serpent of smoke oozing into the tunnels of her mind, flicking at the edges with seductive promise, snuffing-out all coherent thoughts.

Give up, relinquish, give in, goodbye…

The man's amber eyes are now on hers.

The moment is drawn out, time standing still. And then abruptly, they're all three back outside, walking smartly across the silent village towards the gates. As they pass through them, she glances at the monkey skulls on poles. Not a word is said, the atmosphere brittle, urgent, as eyes burn holes in their retreating backs. They speed up. At any given moment, their worlds could shatter like glass into a million fragments. Part of her expects the crack of a shotgun. A bullet. The thud of hard earth on her back, and the swirl of the canopy overhead.

Narong is heading swiftly towards the elephants and the waiting mahouts. There's an undercurrent, an undertow, his back rigid. He's angry, she thinks. Almost as if something had been planned but it didn't work out.

***

Chapter Four

From the moment the man with amber eyes had focused on her hand clutching Marion's necklace, life was on hold, their collective fate held in a white, timeless waiting room. She doesn't even remember breathing again until they were through the gates and back on the elephants, tramping heavily, but definitely, away from the village.

"They were going to rob us."

Vic doesn't reply, but stares straight ahead.

Perhaps it's the aftermath of danger, delayed shock, but she's shaking quite badly, her skin glossy with sweat. She'd have let those men take everything except Marion's cross. And for that she'd have fought like a wild cat – maybe even lost her life in the process. Anger shudders through her now, perhaps with the realisation that to others she's nothing. Less than human. Just someone to rob for the next fix.

"Why the hell did he take us there?"

Still, he doesn't reply.

"Weren't you worried, though? I mean, that was seriously hairy – didn't you think?"

She finds she wants to shake him, to incite some feeling, a reaction that would make her feel less alone.

"Not really," he says eventually. "They just didn't want us there, that's all, Louise."

She stares at his profile, askance. Oh no, it was a hell of a lot more than that. There'd been a prickly energy, an air of menace. The situation could have flipped at any moment, their lives at risk. This is an opium trading area and those people are desperate.

"It was dangerous," she says. "That was bloody dangerous."

A cool river rushes between them, a fresh gulf. The elephants are trundling at a good pace now along the flat path, and for a while they all rock steadily to the rhythm of the journey, in sync with the solid thudding on turf. Moving rapidly away.

There haven't been many times she's felt as immediately threatened as that. Once, a friend had become involved with another student, a man barely out of his teens, who she'd had down as a weed-smoking nerd, but was actually using heroin. She hadn't known, could never have guessed. But one night there'd been a row at a party when almost everyone else had gone home. Louise had made the mistake of supporting her friend, when the man had turned on her instead, index finger jutting at her face. Briefly, there'd been a flash of intense, deeply unnatural hatred in the yellow fire of his eyes. Someone nearby had gasped, the moment crystallised. Could have gone either way. Funny how she thinks of that now.

It is well past midday and an oven-hot sun pierces the canopy.

Narong turns around and gestures to the road emerging ahead, a shimmering mirage.

"Next village," he shouts. "Is good village. You can buy!"

"Buy?" she shouts back.

"You go shopping! Shopping!"

"Okay." She hesitates, then shouts back, "Narong?"

He turns around.

"Can we stop to drink water, please? And…" She mimes eating, as well. If they don't eat soon, she'll faint.

He gives her a thumbs-up, then lights another cigarette, leaving it in his mouth.

The road they're approaching is a dirt track, wide enough for trucks and rutted with tyre marks. Glimpses of it appear through the trees like a shiny brown river and her heart lifts at the sight. Finally, they emerge from the jungle, to where a huddle of villagers and their children are waiting on the corner of a hairpin bend. For a few moments there's mutual confusion, as the group seems to be facing uphill, looking up the road as if expecting their visitors to come down the mountain. Then, spying the troop exiting the forest, one of the children shouts and everyone turns the other way.

This is how Louise had expected today to be, how she'd visualised the trip. They are helped down, the elephants led to a long trough of water under the trees, and the people are in flamboyant, stunning traditional dress, smiling red-stained, betel nut smiles.

"You can feed elephant," says Narong. "They want to show you."

These people are also Akha, he explains, but different. No poppies.

"See, Louise?" Vic says. "He was just showing us the difference. You really do need to relax. Enjoy the day, for God's sake."

She nods, still uneasy, but he's right. And she doesn't want to be the kind of person who always needed reassurance, or to spoil his holiday, especially when he has so few days off.

"Sorry!"

The children are feeding the elephants bananas, eager to show them how to do it, and laugh when Louise's elephant grabs the whole bunch from her hand and she shrieks.

She roots in the rucksack for bottles of water, and the children gather round.

"Here," she says. "Soap. Pens!"

They mimic her words and dance around, the group beginning to make its way towards the village. Here, the spirit gates are more substantial, although the carved effigies are outrageously pornographic.

"Human inside gate," says Narong. "Spirit outside." He points to the somewhat grotesquely erotic effigies. "Scary to spirits."

Some of the villagers giggle behind their hands at Louise's surprised face.

"Ah, yes. Kind of like gargoyles."

Narong smiles, shrugs, shakes his head.

"Ugly things put on churches to scare away evil?"

"No one's going to understand that, darling," says Vic.

She bristles slightly at his tone. Something's changed between them, although it's difficult to pinpoint what. Is he angry with her for being scared? Whatever it is, it feels isolating. Hurts. He seems such a long way away from her. What can she do to put it right? The whole thing is now over. Her fear was an intense wave, unexpected, but it is, quite definitely, over. Taking a deep breath, she closes her eyes for a second, resolving to let it go, yearning for him to take her hand instead of stalking ahead with Narong.

This village is so markedly different from the last, it's difficult to believe they're less than an hour apart. Chickens run around squawking and pecking, there's a pen for pigs, and a huge swing in the middle, similar to a children's playground, although no children play on it. Narong lights another cigarette and leads them to where women are weaving cloth using looms made out of bamboo. They wear blue embroidered jackets, and high sashes over full skirts and pantaloons, with elaborate headdresses adorned with a variety of beads, silver, feathers and fur.

"They dye cloth. Weave. You watch."

It's skilled and quick, but there's no language between them and the women, other than smiles and nods.

Narong points to his chest. "*Nga.*" Then to Louise. "*Naw.*" Then, spotting a chicken scurrying past, he points to that. "*Za!*"

"Oh, I see." She points to the chicken. "*Za!*"

And everyone laughs, the funniest joke. The children, she thinks, look so happy – they giggle and chatter, want to show her things, their eyes dancing, sharp, bright.

"You buy now," says Narong.

Vic laughs. "Of course. We buy."

Along with cloth, there are carved elephants, baskets, and instruments. So, she hadn't imagined the haunting sound of wind chimes coming from the mountain forests, or the drums and tambourines? She buys as much as the rucksack will hold, everyone nodding and smiling. And the afternoon is a glimmer of joy, its brilliance obliterating the morning shadows. Sunlight has settled on the village, the sky deep azure – a clearing surrounded by a gilt-edged forest buzzing, clicking and humming with thousands of hidden creatures.

In the main house, built on stilts like the last one, there are no window openings, and with the eaves hanging low on both sides, it's gloomy inside, with a shoulder-high partition dividing the men's quarters from the women's.

Narong shakes his finger at them. It sounds as if he says, "*A poe paw law.*"

Louise shakes her head until she realises he is showing them an altar.

"No touch," he says. "For ancestor. Rice ritual. Planting ritual. Evil spirit ritual. Many ritual. For good luck and wealth."

He then motions for them to sit, and the head of the village sits with them. Small cups of boiled water swirling with herbs are brought, along with tiny bowls of rice.

It is, however, only after they've left the village, said their good-byes, and passed back through the spirit gates, that Louise suddenly realises they haven't taken a single photograph.

The moment happens in slow motion.

Behind her, Vic and Narong are deep in conversation. She swings around, and at the exact moment she's reaching for the camera around her neck, her attention is caught by an elderly woman on the opposite side of the road. Standing with her back to the jungle, the one they'd emerged from less than an hour before, the old lady is dressed entirely in black, her headdress a coil of cloth, like a turban, her face as wrinkled as a walnut, eyes glinting dark beads in the sun.

Too late, it occurs to her, as she's lifting the camera to take her photograph, is already looking through the lens, that this woman is not like the others.

Something wrong. No face. Just a blur...

A stab of shock contracts her stomach.

Instantly she drops the camera, the straps pulling on her

neck as it rocks into her chest.

She peers into the forest.

There's no one there.

"What are you taking a picture of, Lou? Did you see something?"

The road is empty in both directions, the forest path illuminated.

She shakes her head. Silent. There had been a woman there in the dappled shade of the trees. Small, powerful, staring directly at her and her alone. The effect that of a shadow passing across the sun. Like an omen.

***

Chapter Five

Vic points at the jungle. "We were just saying we have to go back the way we came on foot for a while, then head down to the river."

She had not imagined the old woman in black robes. She was definitely there, the image seared on her mind.

"You were both looking at the path while you were talking just now, weren't you? You were facing that way, while I held the camera up to take a picture?"

"Yes, why?"

"But you didn't see anyone?"

"No." He shrugs. "Hundred percent sure. Maybe it was a trick of the light?"

She nods, latching onto that explanation, soothing herself. She's seen a ghost, is all, had a bit of a jolt. Or maybe it really was a trick of the light? But her heart's still galloping ten to the dozen, and the woman's face lingers.

"Where's Narong?"

"Gone for a pee."

The midday heat is intensifying, and they sink to the ground to wait, re-packing their purchases – a wooden elephant and a small bowl, a piece of woven cloth, a bamboo wind chime – after retrieving water bottles and biscuits.

"I love what we've bought," she says. "A reminder of our

travels for when we're back home."

He pours water down his throat.

"So, where's the path down to the river, then?" Louise says.

"I told you – back the way we came." His T-shirt is soaked, face beaded with sweat. "It's going to be quite a trek. Fuck, it's hot today."

"I'm too hot already. It's getting hotter by the minute. Even the cicadas have gone quiet." She has a vision of hacking through the jungle with machetes. "We must be stark, staring mad."

"Mad dogs and Englishmen out in the midday sun."

"Well, we're certainly the only ones out here."

She downs half a bottle of water, then dabs at her face with a tissue.

"I'm glad we've seen the village, though," she says, determined to be upbeat, not wanting to annoy him like she clearly did this morning. "The one we've just been to, that is. Just wish I had a magic carpet to take us back to the hotel."

"Oh, for a cold beer, and that heavenly swimming pool."

"Maybe there's another way down?" she says hopefully. "Or we could tell Narong we'd rather keep to the road?"

"I think you'll find that takes you in the opposite direction, miles and miles north."

When Narong appears, a fresh cigarette balancing on his lower lip, he squats beside them. The cicadas are revving up again, the jungle a sawmill of industry. It will be three hours to the river.

"Where's the track downhill? Is it far along the path?" Louise asks.

He looks at her. "You can cover arms, un?"

She puts the linen shirt back on and fastens the cuffs. "What about snakes?"

"Stop worrying about snakes," Vic says. "I've told you, they're shy, they'll keep out of our way. You'd have to actually step on one."

Narong holds his thumb and forefinger a few inches apart, smiles. "Leech. Many leech." Points to her feet. "Keep shoe tight."

The prospect of leeches hadn't even occurred to her, and a fresh wave of alarm washes over her as she copies the two men, tucking jeans into socks, lacing walking boots over the top.

Finally, Narong stands up and they do the same, snapping on rucksacks. They must go. It is not good to be in the forest at dusk. And minutes later, the smiling villagers are little more than a postcard memory, as the steamy forest closes behind them.

Narong takes the lead, Vic in the middle, Louise behind. Strangely, the heat does not abate in the shade but seems to increase, racking up by degrees, until sweat breaks out all over them, soaking through their clothes.

On constant alert, Louise determines to push from her mind any number of scenarios, from camouflaged snakes in the trees, to armed robbers. Instead, as the path steepens and the jungle thickens, she pictures the aqua cool ripples of the resort's pool, fluttering palm fronds around the edge, fruit cocktails clinking with ice, and a lantern-lit dinner on the veranda that evening. This will come to an end, she tells herself. It is temporary. And she will not complain, or cry, or give up. The heat is almost at the point of intolerable, and in a very short time her head begins to pound, as they slip and slide down the muddy slope, branches snapping into their faces.

With each spring of leaves, she quickly scans the foliage for snakes, afraid to put out her hands to steady herself, frequently stumbling. At one point, Narong stops abruptly, and waves them past, holding back a branch around which a pale grey viper is swathed like a coil of rope. One glance. A lightning-fast glimpse of its flicking tongue and arrow-shaped head. Inches from her face. In a blind panic, she hurries past so quickly she slips and skids several feet down the slope on the heel of her boot.

Vic stumbles after her, hauling her up by the elbow. "For fuck's sake! You could've broken your ankle."

Her white linen shirt is now ripped, her side smeared with mud, and her hip and the palms of her hands have already begun to sting. But the main concern is leeches, and spiders. Frantically, she dusts herself all over.

"Oh God, no. Is there anything stuck to me?"

"No. Nothing."

"Are you sure?"

He checks her hair, assures her she's clean, that there's nothing to worry about, and with Narong standing further down the slope waiting, there's no choice but to keep going.

"Okay now?"

She nods.

After that, the trek is methodical and determined, no one talks. Narong speeds away, occasionally hacking at branches. And the sounds are like nothing she's ever heard – invisible birds with their strange calls, increasing in volume and frequency like the cicadas, competing with each other – *Kek kek kuck kuck, kweek kweek… chit chit.* It is a deafening, insistent mill of industry, a workshop of machinery that reaches a crescendo before it breaks. Then restarts. There are sudden wild bursts of activity, followed by splintering cracks and bouncing branches: creatures flying between the trees, hidden in the dense green foliage, as Narong hacks through, and they follow, stumbling and skidding all the way down to the river.

Eventually, the smell of water, a swampy, swirling freshness, permeates the smothering blanket of heat, and the atmosphere changes. The sun is still high above the canopy, interplaying with the shade of the forest, but the temperature is no longer intensifying and seems to be abating, at least levelling off.

"Watch out, lady!"

Both men duck suddenly, and caught unaware, Louise barely avoids walking straight into a spider's web. Has no time to react. It's only when she's past it that her mind replays the moment of near-impact in all its Technicolour glory – of a spider at least eight inches in length, with bright yellow joints appearing like dots in a web large and strong enough to net a hawk.

A split second too late and it would have been on her face, stuck over her nose and mouth like the infamous scene in *The Alien*.

Stunned, appalled by the horrific image of trying to pick it off, the spider in her fingers, running down her chest, the web in her hair, she has no choice but to keep on walking. Soon they will be at the river. On the boat. Going home. Her legs are weary now, weakening, her stomach a hollow cavern. Oh, to be already on the boat, to feel the freshness of the river breezes on her face. It can't be much further, surely? Already, the sun has begun to drop behind the hill.

But first there are mangrove swamps and mudflats, and a trek through sucking mud pitted with hundreds of tiny holes. Ahead, a longtail boat is waiting on the bank by a river flanked with trees. It's now within reach, and an elderly man who's smoking next to the petrol engine, a length of ash perilously hanging over the tank, spots them and raises a hand as, with a last surge of effort, they push on towards him.

"How long back to Chiang Rai?" Louise calls to Narong.

Vic turns around.

"He said one hour."

One hour. One hour and it will be dusk. They lunge for the boat, sagging with relief and fatigue, climbing in, as the old man and Narong wade into the river and push them out.

"Look out!"

With disbelief, Louise looks to where Vic is pointing, in time to see a long snake wiggling and winding its way alongside the boat, a ringed python perhaps twenty feet long.

Incredibly, the two men wade past it and jump into the boat, as calmly as if they'd just hopped onto the last bus, and ease it into the main current. The older one pulls the cord to ignite the engine and, with a fan-shaped ripple in their wake, they're quickly into the middle of the muddy river, with the much-longed for breeze in their faces. Narong and the old man light cigarettes and shout to each other, laugh, joke. Vic undoes the rucksack, swigs from the remaining bottle of water and offers the rest to Louise… who sits gripping the side of the boat, trying to push from her mind what she's just seen.

She would not have missed this day, it's been like no

other, but a deep undertow of terror she didn't know she had, has surfaced today, and now it lives with her as a companion. It has, she thinks, caught up with her like a stalking shadow. And now they are one.

The river is deep and dark in the middle, its breadth a wide mouth. On the opposite shore, in the mud, is a sprawling village of bamboo houses on stilts. And children are running down to wave. She lifts a hand to wave back. They look so happy, it lifts her spirits. At once they are in the water, doing a fast crawl to reach the boat.

"They're swimming out to us. Have we got anything left to give them, Vic?"

They're really fast, closing the gap quickly, shouting, racing, calling from the water.

"We ought to give them something! Vic?"

But suddenly there's a lurch of acceleration, the boat pulls away rapidly, and Louise is thrown sideways in surprise. The old man has it on full throttle, and both he and Narong have oars poised to hit the children.

Louise shouts, "Hey! What are you doing?"

It is then, however, that she sees a small hand had reached the side of the boat and had been about to grab her bag with one hand, the rucksack with the other. The sudden acceleration, however, has thrown the child off and he falls away. Within seconds, the children are small dots in the water, and only then does she realise they were going to rob them.

"Pirates," Vic says. "They send the kids out to rob tourists on the boats. Narong says a couple were robbed here last week."

The rest of the trip is uneventful, and by the time they're helped from the boat at a small mooring bay on the edge of town, she's just dirty and bone-tired.

Miraculously, Narong still has a cigarette balancing on his lower lip, and they tip him and the old man the baht they have left.

"Thank you," Louise says. "I'm sorry I got scared today."

A shadow crosses behind Narong's eyes. He bows slightly, presses his palms together.

"Fantastic day," Vic says. "Really enjoyed it."

There's a look between the two of them, between Vic and Narong, that she sees but doesn't understand. She won't understand it for a long, long time yet, but notes it all the same. There is something off, she's as sure of that as she's ever been about anything. Or is she imagining something where there's nothing?

Fantastic day…

There are creatures in the mud, with tiny black eyes, gills and flippers and she hurries up the small jetty. They've no cash left and will have to walk up the hill to the resort. Maybe twenty minutes. Her legs are like jelly, head light with hunger and fatigue. What wouldn't she give for fish and chips, wrapped in paper and sprinkled with sea salt and vinegar?

"Quick shower and then dinner," Vic says, catching her up.

He likes the Lanna food – the sticky steamed rice in bamboo baskets, the khoo soi, and fish heads with tamarind and ginger. But since they've been in Asia, she's lost ten pounds in weight and suspects she's doubled the void today, having barely enough energy to shower and wash the sweat from her hair, which is now kinked and plastered against her forehead. For the first time since they've been out here, she has a painful yearning to go home, to the small Yorkshire town she grew up in, to the wind-blasted moors and rows of stone terraces lining the streets. There would, at this time of year, be a smell of wood smoke in the crisp night air.

"Nearly there," Vic says, as the lights of the hotel come into view.

"Do you mind if I go in the shower first? Only I've got to blow-dry my hair. I can be doing that while you shower."

He slings an arm around her shoulder, leaning on her with full weight, dragging and heavy, and she's forced to shrug him off.

"Sorry, you're heavy."

"Haven't you enjoyed today?"

"Yes and no. Probably a lot more in retrospect. I'm glad I went."

The hotel is now in sight. People are dining by the light of the elephant orbs on the balcony over the river. The chink of glasses and the velvet hum of conversation carries on the air, a waft of frying oil and spices. Opposite the restaurant is the impenetrable black hush of the mountains, and the faint but distinct sound of wood chimes from deep within.

"You just need to toughen up a bit," he says. "Stop being so terrified of everything and then you'll enjoy life more."

She's too tired to think about that though, too focused on a hot shower, of having to walk through Reception smeared in mud and dried sweat. She only contemplates his words later, while they sit waiting for dishes of steamed rice and spiced pork.

They're on their second bottle of Tiger Beer when she says, "I wouldn't mind staying here at the hotel tomorrow, to be honest. I really don't think I can face a full day in the Jeep. I'd rather stay here by the pool. I'm shattered. Really wiped out. Do you mind?"

He narrows his eyes, then, noticing the waiter hovering, beckons him over. "Two more Tiger beers, please."

"You are joking, Louise?"

"I just thought, we've done a massive amount in four days, and I quite fancy the Lanna fire massage. It would be nice to just relax, the two of us…"

He frowns as fresh iced bottles of beer are served, waiting for the man to slip away again.

"You seriously come all the way out here to this fantastic place, just to loll about on a sun-lounger?"

She stares at him askance. "Well–"

"Seriously! We've only got one more day and I want us to make the most of this trip, don't you? I thought we wanted the same things? To really see the country? It's the most incredible road winding through the hills to Laos. And there's a spectacular mountain view I want to take you to, called the sea of mist, nearly two thousand metres above sea level."

She takes a sip of cold beer.

"Allegedly, it's the most incredible spiritual experience, very beautiful and remote – hardly anyone knows about it. It's the chance of a lifetime. Honestly, I was going to surprise you, but–"

He shakes his head and looks away. Their meals have arrived, brought ceremoniously to the sound of a gong, baskets of food held high by a train of waiters.

They each smile, thank the waiters, spread napkins on

their laps.

"It's just that I was scared today," she says, when they've gone. "We were nearly robbed twice, and the road you're proposing is five hours through the mountains, not to mention back again. A twelve-hour day at least."

He heaps rice onto his plate.

"You just need to toughen up a bit, like I said, and remember you'll feel differently after a good night's sleep. Besides, you'll really upset me if we don't go. I wanted to show you something pretty special, share a beautiful memory with you. I had it all planned. While you were in the shower I fixed everything up with the hotel – the route, all the details."

"Oh, I didn't know!"

She spoons peanut-chilli sauce onto her plate, knowing they will be going. He's right, it will be a chance in a lifetime and probably she only feels this way because she's so tired – beyond tired.

"So," he says. "We'll go then, yes?"

"Yes, okay."

"Good. So then, tell me what you know about tulpas."

The question throws her.

"What?"

"Tulpas. Honestly, Lou – you blew me away. Not many people know about things like that. I thought I knew everything about you, but it turns out you're something of a dark horse."

She hesitates.

"Well, I don't know any more than I said. I think I must have read it somewhere. Why?"

"Oh, nothing much. It's a subject that once came up before, when I was with… some friends. It was mentioned as an explanation for…"

He gazes at her thoughtfully for a moment, and she fancies she can see a drama playing out behind his eyes, as if he's about to tell her something. But then he appears to change his mind, and the moment is lost.

"Never mind. Anyway, we'd best eat up and get some sleep. Our last day is going to be a phenomenal day." He raises a glass. "Here's to you, my fellow traveller. If you can survive today, you can survive anything."

She smiles and they clink beer glasses.

"To our last day!"

Our last day…

Prophetic words she will remember. They will haunt her. Because of what is to come. Because of what she does not yet know. Because it will not only be their last day of holiday, but the last they will ever spend together.

***

Chapter Six

The road heading out of Chiang Rai is lined with mats of tobacco drying in the sun, and stalls loaded with every kind of exotic fruit, from rambutans and papaya to guava and durians. Sitting by the roadside are locals stirring clay pots over open fires, and the ubiquitous aroma of frying spices, garlic and chillies permeates the air. Some of them wave as the young couple drive past in the Jeep, and after a few minutes Louise asks Vic to stop so she can buy fruit.

The day is a hot, clear one, and already heat shimmers on the horizon, with only the distant mountains tops still swathed in mist.

"Got everything you want?" he asks, when she returns to the car.

"Yes. We needed more than we had yesterday, I was starving." She fastens her seatbelt, examining the purchases. "You did pack the Swiss army knife?"

"In the rucksack."

His profile in dark wraparound sunglasses, is handsome, serious. Yesterday now seems like a dream, all that anguish reduced to a few seconds of memory; and having slept, showered and downed a huge breakfast, part of her feels a bit silly for having been so scared. The sight of Vic, in white t-shirt and fresh jeans, with his hair swept back, catches at her heart. Like it always does. He's thirty-six, rangy rather than muscular, the kind of man who blends with confidence and ease into any situation – be it black tie or backpacking. He could have married anyone. It was, and still is, baffling that he chose her.

The wedding had been a modest, low-profile registry office affair in St John's Wood, close to where Vic lived in London, and afterwards they'd had lunch at a nearby restaurant. He'd invited two friends and so had she. No parents. No family on either side. Joanna Landry was on holiday in the Seychelles, and his father, a barrister, was in court that day. They were, Vic explained, hardly ever available, if in the country, and besides, he was something of an outcast. It wasn't clear why, except his older brother, Miles, also a barrister, was much-favoured.

"I was not the chosen one," he'd said. Yet, Vic had been educated privately and they'd put him through Eton, his career in banking pretty meteoric.

It was odd he wasn't prepared to open up about it; something must have happened, but she'd had to let it go, none the wiser with regard to what he may or may not have done to upset them all. It was clear he didn't want to talk about it and anyway, family fall-outs were private, often tangled in complex emotional webs impossible to unpick. She loved him, no matter what, and besides – the wedding had been something of a rush, with the bank sending him off to Singapore with less than a month's notice, just enough time to book the ceremony.

On her own side, her mother had died years ago, when she was just seventeen; some said the heart attack had been brought on by Len Draper, her father. And it would have been unwise to invite Len, even if there was a chance he'd make the long trip south – not only on account of his health problems, the reason she'd given to Vic, but more his legendary temper, especially after a few drinks. Len had made a career out of hypochondria since being signed off sick in 1979, his face turning puce at the slightest provocation, his illness a weapon. No one wanted to get on the wrong side of Len. No one would even drink with him in the pub.

She'd been embarrassed telling Vic, but surprisingly he hadn't seemed remotely fazed, and she loved him all the more for that.

"I'd rather just invite a couple of friends, anyway," he'd said. "A kind of runaway, spur-of-the-moment type affair? It could be rather romantic. And besides, it'll be cheaper."

Louise had done that thing of smiling and frowning at the same time. Vic had a light-filled, luxurious flat in a salubrious area near Lord's Cricket Ground, drove a Porsche 911, and his parents had a mansion in Surrey. Not only that but he was in a top job with a major bank. Why was he penny-pinching? But then he'd laughed and the smile dissolved the frown from her face. Of course, he was joking.

Before they departed for Singapore, she had hoped to meet at least one member of his busy family, but that hadn't happened. And, having been nicknamed the 'Child Bride' by Vic's best friend, Karl, she instead handed in her notice and packed for a new life.

"I think you're very brave," Ziva had said on the last day she'd seen her. "I mean, you haven't known him for long."

It was true. She hadn't.

Ziva Okoye was her closest friend, both of them staff nurses at a private clinic in London, both twenty-two, both living in the accommodation provided by the same clinic.

Marrying Vic and moving out to Singapore was not a decision that could be reversed – the room came with the job. And after her mother had died she could never go home again; not to the gloomy terrace Len sat in, day in day out, on the armchair by the fire. Close her eyes and she could still smell the place, from the grease-coated kitchen tiles to the stale bed sheets. The very thought of him made her shudder. There was no reason to go back. No aunts, uncles, siblings or cousins. Just the two friends she'd hooked up with at the private clinic, Ziva and Janice.

How quickly she's moved on, the past another world now, suspended in another time and space – a strange feeling as the Jeep heads east, the glare of sun in her eyes, lulled by the monotonous hum of the road. The roadside stalls are now few and far between, Chiang Rai smaller and smaller in the rear-view mirror. It's quiet, the highway deserted, and for a while it seems they're the only ones in the world, heading towards the mountains in the mist.

And then out of nowhere, out of the ether, comes an uncomfortable thought.

What if Vic falls out of love with me? Out here?

Immediately, yesterday comes to mind. The look of exasperation, even contempt, on his face. What would she do if he just said, "Look darling, I think we might have made a dreadful mistake…" Or if he met someone else? God knows there are millions of far more beautiful women in the world than herself. They're everywhere. In the hotel. By the pool. Everywhere. She's seen his sidelong glances, the odd smile.

Karl Lozensky, one of his friends, had fleetingly registered his surprise when he met her at the wedding. What had he seen? Someone ordinary, gauche, insignificant... poor...?

You're incredibly lucky, you know?

And then there was the quiet, almost smirking appraisal of his other friend, Nigel Scott-Renard, from Vic's Eton days, with a job-title she forgets but is, she thinks, in government, civil service or something. She'd caught him observing her over the wedding lunch, an unreadable expression in eyes that steadily met hers.

Why? Why has he chosen her?

She's never truly thought about it before, had accepted, rejoiced, been excited. Until yesterday... And now these thoughts, these doubts...

One day, she will remember the acute feeling of time standing still as they drove into the sun, further and further away from all she has ever known. She will recall the omen from the day before, and wonder if she'd stopped at the fruit stall and not got back into the Jeep, things would have been different. Or if she'd hailed a passing songthaew and gone back to the resort. Or never left the hotel in the first place, but stuck to her guns and spent the day as she'd wanted to... What if? What if?

She glances again at his profile. As they head into the mountains, with the sun in their eyes, on Route 1148.

Why, Vic? Why me?

***

Chapter Seven

The road winds through one of the most remote areas of the country, a single-track snaking higher and higher into the mountains, a sheer drop on one side. Every so often, a truck laden with produce hares down from the opposite direction, appearing suddenly on a bend, swerving only at the last horn-blasting second. It is 1992 and there are few safety barriers, subsidence and mudslides crumbling away the edges of what is a helter-skelter ride. At one point, a truck piled with melons materialises in the middle of the road, and the wheels of the Jeep teeter on the brink, as the truck careers past in a blur of screaming faces and unbelievable luck.

She cannot, she realises, be in a state of extreme fright all day. If the Jeep drops over the precipice, then that's going to happen whether she worries about it or not. Bit like being a passenger in a plane.

"Are you okay?" she asks Vic.

"Bloody fantastic, yes." He shoots her a quick glance. "Why? Don't tell me you're not enjoying this!"

"Oh! Yes, it's… quite a view."

The road levels off for a while, and a couple of motorbikes roar past on the straight, the riders leaning sideways to manoeuvre an upcoming bend.

"I'd love to have done this on the Harley. If only we'd

known about this, it's incredible!"

She's about to ask what he means but, suddenly faced with the infinite blue of pure sky, as Vic wings the Jeep around an S-bend in a squeal of tyres, the question dies on her lips.

After a while, the route finally begins to wind downwards, before levelling off again, cutting through poppy and cornfields. They pass a couple of lone roadside villages – wood and bamboo shacks – the only car on an empty road. Perhaps she's tired of being scared, or just plain tired? But almost without realising it, to the lulling drone of the road, in the warmth of the streaming sun, she slips seamlessly into daydreams.

It was around this time last year they'd first met. On the same kind of crisp, clear day, with golden leaves shimmering in the sun. She'd walked through Regents Park with Ziva and Janice in the late afternoon, from the clinic to the nurses' home on the north side, past the zoo. People had been lying on the grass, soaking up the last few days of an Indian summer, Elvis Costello on someone's radio, '*Pump it up...*'

She recalls the feeling vividly, reliving it, the prospect of going back to the nurses' home and being cooped up in her room suddenly suffocating, unbearable. It had been a matter of hours before Vic came into her life. She hadn't known, could not have done, what was going to happen, only that something would. Something monumental. And that it had to.

"Anyone fancy going for a drink?"

Janice shook her head. "No, I'm skint. And I've got an Early tomorrow."

"I'm skint, too. But it's so beautiful. I don't want to go

in."

How to explain the fizz in her stomach, the urgency to be out in the world and not, definitely not, stuck in the gloom of her bedroom overlooking the yard at the back? Could she go out on her own? With only… what had she got… about twenty pounds to last until the end of the month? They always got into clubs for free, made half a lager last all night.

"I'll come with you, Lou," Ziva said. "Just one drink, though. I'm on an Early as well."

The pub opposite their accommodation was an old-style Victorian one with frosted glass windows, a tiled tap room and a saloon bar. A pub for old men, just like the ones back home – foggy with smoke, men playing darts, middle-aged couples sitting together all evening without speaking, him with a pint, she with a port and lemon. What she really wanted to do was plunge into the electric excitement of the West End. But anything was better than staying in, feeling life ebb away.

"Thanks, Ziva. It's just the thought of shutting the bedroom door. I think I'll go mad sometimes."

"We could go to Ronnie Scott's one night, if you want?"

"Where's that?"

"Soho. It's a famous jazz club. Me and my sister went, you'd love it."

They were crossing the main road amid tooting horns and cat-calls.

"Yes, all right, then. Sounds good."

"See you in about an hour? Give me a knock, will you?"

One half of lager had turned into three halves, or four; people kept sending them over, she couldn't remember. But just before closing, while Ziva was being chatted up by a man who was slowly easing Louise out of the way with his shoulder, she'd looked over and seen him.

My God, he's perfect.

She relives it. The way she knew she was staring at him, but couldn't look away. The point at which he seemed to realise and caught her looking.

Vic had been in a group, standing near the door, pint glass in hand. White shirt, long, dark overcoat, that's all she saw – the stark white of his shirt, warm brown eyes locking with hers, and the fact he was holding an empty pint glass, ready to leave. Maybe Karl had been there, but all other details were vague. By then, the pub was packed with noisy, sweaty punters, the scrum at the bar several layers deep. Chris Isaac was on the jukebox: '*What a wicked game to play… to make me feel this way…*'

The rest of his group were draining their glasses, searching for tables to dump the empties on, but he was hanging back. She could feel it. Knew he wouldn't leave with them. As surely as if she had written the script. And the evening had ended with him taking her by the hand for a walk in the park. She can still feel the heat of his chest through his shirt when he kissed her, knows she'd fallen for him straight away, perhaps even in those first few seconds, long before, weeks before, she ever fully acknowledged it. As if his was the face, the body, the description, she'd always dreamed of. She hadn't known he was wealthy, or where he lived, or what he did for a living. Only that, without doubt, he was everything.

She tries to analyse, to feel her way through the sequence of events which led to the here and now, to this strange, liminal space in which she finds herself, suspended in a sunlit haze, winding through the mountains, further and further away from all she's ever known.

They'd met again the following evening, and the next and the next. As the weeks passed and the temperature dropped, the London trees had turned into flames of crimson and burnished bronze, the evenings smoky-cold. She'd hurried home from work each evening across the park, to the muted hum of city traffic, already anticipating the night ahead. In the flip of a heartbeat her world had become magical, although in truth it was because of him, and it was he she found magical. They would meet in various pubs around Camden and St John's Wood, but invariably end up in his flat, in his bed. He was a banker, he told her, a job that would 'bore the arse off her' should he have to explain what it entailed. One day, maybe a month or so later, she'd found a photograph on his bookcase of a woman posing naked, and they'd had a spat about it. Didn't talk for a few days. It had been torture, the separation angst-ridden and almost physically painful. No answers to her numerous calls. Until one day he'd phoned and said he missed her, explained the woman was a model and posed nude for a living, that she'd just given him the photo.

"Kind of like a calling-card?"

"You're not the only beautiful woman in the world you know, darling?"

There'd been a pause. She'd rushed to fill the silence. Yes, yes, of course. She hadn't meant anything by it.

Oh, please, she'd silently begged. *Please let it be like it was before...*

He had the power to hurt her, easily, and the insinuation still smarted, that there might, in fact, be others. But he'd called her beautiful, for the first time, and besides, it was far too late by then. Sometimes he rang her and other times he forgot. Said he'd fallen asleep, that he'd worked until two in the morning. Some weekends they would roar into the countryside in his sports car, and stay in a smart hotel somewhere. Usually, he had someone to meet and, as he said, it was a perfect excuse for a romantic weekend. Others, she'd work, coming home to the gloom of the nurses' accommodation, wondering if she should phone him or not, when several days had passed, a week, two…What was he doing? Where was he?

She murmurs in half sleep. Blanking out the flashes of pain, of walking around the tree-lined streets of Mayfair and Knightsbridge in the rain, looking up at the soft glow of elegant chandeliers behind long sash windows. Tramping past the canopied entrances of West End restaurants, hearing the chink of glasses and bursts of laughter from within. On and on she'd walked, tiring herself out, refusing to imagine where he was and who with, holding onto the dream. Christmas had been especially difficult. Not a word for nearly a month. But just when she'd given up hope, was beginning to come to terms with the fact it was probably over, that he hadn't even had the decency to tell her, he'd appeared at the clinic with a bunch of flowers, and that evening asked her to marry him. Singapore, he said, his eyes searching hers. He was being sent out to Singapore. The moment is crystallised in her memory. He couldn't bear the thought of being without her. It had taken this, he said, for him to realise.

It was a quantum leap. She hadn't even met his parents. Marriage!

He'd laughed. Why not? He loved her, couldn't she see

that?

There were no words to express her shocked delight – that he felt the same about her as she did about him, that he'd been in just as much turmoil as herself. Sorting out his feelings, he said. Thinking about her every minute of the day. She must admit, it was a big step, falling in love with someone, deciding to spend the rest of your life with them…

That evening, they couldn't stop laughing, touching each other, leaning over the restaurant table to kiss. For him, she would have gone to the far reaches of the earth without question.

She'd been so happy, so very, very happy…

A surprise then, that others had tried to defuse that happiness. Especially Ziva. Ziva's deep, dark eyes on hearing the news. She hadn't spoken when Louise told her, just put her arms around her and hugged her close. Then silently walked away. It was that last day, though, the one after the wedding lunch, when she'd come to collect her luggage, that she remembers now, seconds before she is to wake, and the feeling of Ziva's arms around her back, of bangles pressing into her spine. Ziva saying she had an interview for a job in France, for a better life. Knowing they were probably saying goodbye forever. It is Ziva's embrace she relives. Ziva's expression.

"Take care," she'd said. "Take really good care, Louise. Promise me?"

There is a brief flash of flying out to Singapore, the heavy 747 taking off oh-so-slowly from Heathrow; the bitter-sweet moment of grief on leaving England in March, when all the daffodils were out and Spring scented the air, people driving with the windows down, sitting outside cafés with sunglasses on, the heartbeat of London music and London pubs.

I'm homesick. Badly, badly homesick…

She's surfacing rapidly from sleep now, rising up through the layers. It comes to her that's what it's all been about these past two days – she's ready, more than ready, to go home. Out here she has no identity, lives in Vic's shadow, almost as if she doesn't quite exist, the real Louise having died a quiet, invisible death. But the memories of how this came to be, how the decision was made, are quickly fading now. Replaced by an uneasy lurch in her gut.

Something's wrong.

No road noise, no momentum. All is still and silent. Completely silent.

She jolts fully awake.

The Jeep is parked on the shoulder of the highway, in front a shack with a wooden table, bench and parasol. There are also two parked motorbikes, like the ones that overtook earlier that morning, and a couple of men in jeans and black t-shirts, possibly Thai, standing smoking, talking with Vic. In that easy way people do when they've known each other for a long time.

***

Chapter Eight

One of the men notices her staring, and Vic ambles over.

"Do you want a coffee? You can stay in the car and I'll bring it over."

"Yes, please."

Incredibly, this bamboo shack halfway up a mountain, hours from the nearest town, serves the richest, most aromatic coffee imaginable, and she swallows it gratefully, quickly reviving from the grogginess of sleep and the disconcerting ramble of dreams. It's left her uneasy without knowing why.

Take care, take really good care…

It doesn't look like there's anywhere to stop for the toilet. Hopefully, she'll last until they reach town, it can't be much further now. These are her thoughts as she sits sideways on the car seat, legs burning through her jeans in the midday sun, looking at the dried earth beneath her feet.

She'd watched them talking for quite a while, several minutes, before one of the men had felt her eyes on him and nudged Vic. Before that, they'd been standing quite close together, all three smoking, the other two shorter in stature, slighter in build, with only jeans, t-shirts and headbands between them and the hard surface of the road should they hit it at speed. Vic had been holding a piece of paper, clearly discussing whatever was written on it. On being alerted she was awake, he'd quickly folded up the paper and slid it in his pocket.

There's a small squeeze in her stomach again, a queasy feeling, as if she's about to fall off a tightrope. Then suddenly it makes sense. There is an explanation. Of course, he was asking them about the route to the beauty spot he wants to show her. It is isolated, well off the track, known to very few, and definitely not to tourists. He really does want to please her, to make this a trip of a lifetime.

The bikers have ridden away now, and she's waiting for him to pay for the coffees and then, in his own words, 'find somewhere to pee'.

A thought occurs to her while she waits, though. Unbidden. Unwelcome. What if those two men are robbers and they now know, because Vic has shown them precisely, that a couple of tourists are going to be in that remote location on their own? In the late afternoon, as daylight fades and dusk falls, no one else in sight, no one to call, the long road back dark and lonely? But she pushes it away, forcing herself instead to imagine the afternoon in Nan they've planned – the museum, the wat with Lanna carvings, a café in the sun for a late lunch. All with Vic. Just the two of them, in this warm, exotic, dreamy, beautiful place.

It's just that – and she kicks herself for even thinking it – she wishes they were heading straight back to the hotel afterwards.

Seconds later, Vic's running towards the Jeep and jumps back in, keys in hand.

"Ready?"

"Definitely. I'm going to need to stop somewhere, though."

"Can you hold on 'til we get to Nan?"

"I'll try."

He could change his mind, though. It was possible. What if she drags her heels in Nan, then persuades him it's too late to go up the mountain? They should set back while it's still light. It would be sensible. It's just… She tries to pinpoint what it is… intuition, a feeling? Not to go.

"Who were those blokes?" she asks, as he starts up the engine. "Were you asking for directions to… where is it?"

"Phu Hua Loan," he says, pulling back onto the highway. "Good news for us is they knew exactly where it is." He glances at his watch. "Spot of luck, eh?"

The prospect of the expedition hangs over her as they wander first around the museum, then the temple, following a lunch of steamed noodles and Tiger beer. Already it's gone three o'clock, nearly half past by the time they jump back in the Jeep.

"I really think we should go straight to the hotel, you know?" Louise says. "It'll be dark by the time we get back as it is, and there's all the packing to do."

He'd been about to turn the ignition on.

"I told you, I don't mind driving in the dark, it doesn't bother me. And besides, it's still the middle of the afternoon and we're only half an hour away. It's on the way back, too. Not even out of our way."

"Don't you think it's a bit reckless, though? What if those blokes were robbers? What if there's more of them and now they know where we'll be?"

"Reckless?" He turns to face her. "Look, are you going to do this every time, Louise? Terrified of being bitten by a snake, or getting a spider in your hair, or being robbed? They were just two regular guys who were kind enough to look at the map and show me how to get us there."

"Sorry."

He gaze softens a little, then he shakes his head like a sorely disappointed teacher.

The Jeep fires into life.

"Right, we'd better make tracks. We need to drive through a Hmong village and then we should be able to drive up the main track to a clearing where we can park. After that, it's just a twenty-minute hike from the car."

His elbow is touching hers.

"Really? We can drive most of the way and there's just a twenty-minute walk to the top?"

"Yes, exactly."

"And it's on the way back anyway?"

"Yes, for pity's sake…" He turns to look at her again. "It's supposed to be absolutely spectacular. Please tell me you're not going to spoil this? You can wait in the car if you want and I'll go up alone!"

He sees her as spoiling the holiday with her unfounded fears, and she bites back any further objections, reassuring herself. It's en-route, just a short walk, a spectacular view. And he badly wants to see it.

"No, of course not."

He kisses her, a quick jab on the lips. "Good girl. Right, let's go or it really will be dark when we set back."

The journey takes longer than anticipated, and it's almost four in the afternoon by the time the Jeep is bouncing in and out of potholes towards the Hmong village. An elderly man waves them down and a cluster of others stand behind him to watch. There's no common language, although Vic's halting Thai, together with what transpires to be a hand-drawn map, helps. A wad of baht is duly handed over, after which they're directed with much gesticulating and shouting, to a nearby area to park. It turns out the hike will be much longer than twenty minutes, as the ascending path to the clearing usually used for vehicles, is too wet for the Jeep.

"He's saying the Jeep will get stuck," Vic says. "I think he's right, by the look of it. We'll have to walk a bit further than I said."

The old man points to their hands, necks, ankles.

"Leeches," says Louise.

After locking the Jeep, they cover up and assess the climb. The steep path is thick with mud, the air humid – the kind of heavy, soupy heat that saps energy.

Vic swings the rucksack over his shoulder and grabs her hand.

"It won't take that much longer – an extra half hour, tops." He smiles. "And look, it's quite wide, no branches full of spiders snapping in your face."

"Every cloud," says Louise, holding onto him.

Once again, the noise of the cicadas is deafening. It's a tough, heart-pumping ascent in steamy launderette-type humidity. After ten minutes or so at a pace, her legs ache, and she lets go of his hand, lagging behind and panting hard. They must keep walking. There are leeches, and in the shade of the trees, mosquitoes float over puddles of recent rainfall. The light's going to start fading while they're still up here, she knows it. But he's marching up the slope like a storm trooper and there's no option but to follow. She can hardly breathe now, her lungs weighted with iron.

"Vic!"

He looks down and waits until she closes the gap a little,

then immediately sets off again.

Another fifteen minutes and the track begins to steepen to nearly vertical, the footing a crumble of scree. They scramble up the last part on hands and knees, to a ridge at the top, finally hauling themselves over the edge.

Louise bends double, hands on knees, gasping for breath. And then, like a runner preparing for a race, looks up to assess what's ahead.

On either side of the narrow ridge is a vertical drop. Walking to the end would be like going to the tip of a high-rise diving board, except instead of water on all sides, it's thin air. No safety barriers. Nothing to hold onto.

Vic turns to face her, holding out his hand.

"Are you ready? Shall we walk the plank?"

Tentatively, she takes his hand, and slowly they walk along the jutting ledge that protrudes nearly two thousand metres above sea level, with a panoramic, three-hundred-and-sixty-degree view of Thailand and Laos below, cloudless sky above and all around.

A few feet from the far end, she pulls free. If she sits down she won't sway, won't topple and fall over the edge. The sky seems to be spinning, nothing but sky, a feeling of freefalling… and she slumps to the ground, palms flat on solid earth, closing her eyes to stop the dizzy swirl.

Vic shrugs, sits next to her and pulls off the rucksack.

"I told you it was incredible, didn't I?"

"Yes," she says. "You did."

"Imagine being here at sunrise, facing east, floating in thin air above the clouds. The view's called The Sea of Mist."

The sun is behind them now, the ridge in shadow.

"I can imagine."

For a while they sit in silence.

Then he puts an arm around her. "I'm going to remember this place, this moment, forever. It must be the closest you could come to sitting on a cloud. There isn't a sound."

She nods, steadier now. It is sublime. Here, there is no busy world, with clocks, meetings, phones, jobs, noise, television sets, pavements, traffic jams, worries or chores. It's as if the world has stopped. As if they're no longer part of it. A mini-death, she thinks. And now she's here, when she hadn't wanted to come, she finds she cannot leave, that it's a piece of heaven. It's only when Vic looks at his watch and stands up, that she forces herself to snap back into the present moment.

"Come on, then. We'd better go."

And minutes later, they're heading back, retracing their steps along the ridge towards the path.

It's over.

Soon home. She pictures the return ride along the main road to Chiang Rai, having a late dinner at the hotel, then packing, showering, getting ready for the return journey to Singapore. Maybe soon they will be going home again to England?

They half-walk, half-slide down the steep slope slippery with scree, chased by the shade of late afternoon, before tramping single-file in silence down the mountain path.

"Listen!" Vic says, stopping so abruptly she crashes into him. "That was an oriental bay owl. Did you hear it?"

It comes again, an ethereal piercing, three-note, *hwee hwee hwee*.

Her eyes widen. "I wonder if there are any wild cats up here?"

"Civets, maybe. Doubt we'd be lucky enough to see one, though. Anyway, come on –we'd best keep moving."

The air's sticky, the jungle close on both sides. Sweat coats their faces.

"By the way," Louise says, as the main, wider track finally comes into view, "I meant to ask but things just go out of my head. How did you find out about this place? Where did you get the map from?"

Had he told her? She can't recall, is vague on it.

They're walking side by side now.

"Katty told me, I think."

A woman I had, I suppose...

Her heart gives a little kick. Katty again.

"The woman in Bangkok with the amulet?"

"She just said to make sure I went sometime. Only I didn't get a chance last time I was here."

"How long ago were you there exactly? In Bangkok?"

It's a minute or so before he answers, "Um... God, I don't know. Just before I met you, I think. About a year, eighteen months, maybe. Why?"

The words spiral her into confusion. He'd said it had been many, many years ago, when he first joined the bank, that Katty's brother had inked the tattoo. And before that, he'd said the tattoo had been done during a holiday. Now it seemed Katty was a more recent flame.

"No reason."

They lapse into silence again, as dusk creeps over the lea side of the mountain, throwing a dark cloak over the forest. She knows very little about his past, she realises, and it hits her again that she's never met his family. He's fourteen years older than her. Of course he's had plenty of girlfriends – it's not that which is causing unease, but there is something. And when it hits her, it's a shock. The name hadn't meant anything, hadn't fully registered yesterday. But yesterday she'd been hugely distracted and hadn't processed it, the name. Now she did. Katty.

When they'd first arrived at the hotel, he'd taken a phone call in the bedroom, said he had to pop down to Reception, and when he came back he'd told her it was about the Jeep hire. Next morning, he'd rung the hire company and had definitely, absolutely definitely, because she'd heard through the gap in the bathroom door while doing her make-up, said, "Yes, Katty gave me this number."

Katty!

They're past the halfway point now, the parked Jeep waiting in the clearing below, a carriage home. Almost there, that's all she can think. Just keep going, almost there, just keep going… The journey home plays out in her head as if she is already on it – the car seat cushioning her back, the dazzle of headlights on dark tarmac as the miles peel away. Soon at the hotel, the airport tomorrow, on the plane home…

The stifling humidity is reaching the point of unbearable though, shadows chasing along the tops of the trees. A fresh wave of sweat surfaces all over her body, her t-shirt soaked beneath the linen shirt, feet clammy inside boots. Perhaps it is panic; a different kind of panic though, from seeing a snake and one she tries to talk herself out of. It has to be coincidence! Has to be… the Katty at Reception could not possibly be the same one he'd met years ago, whether it was one year or ten. Of course not. How ridiculous. Besides, he hadn't been forced into bringing her out here if Katty was the love of his life, had he? He could have married Katty a long time ago. Done anything he wanted. It didn't make sense. She's being paranoid. But it bugs her.

"So, did Katty give you the directions as well, the ones you were showing those two men earlier today?"

He doesn't answer.

"Vic?"

Stopping abruptly, he then turns to look at her askance. "What is this? What the hell does it matter?"

"No, it doesn't, not at all. Sorry. I just wondered–"

"As a matter of fact, I just remembered the name of the place from her, and made a mental note to come here one day. So, I came with you. The directions I got at the hotel reception, and they jotted it down in Thai so I could ask the way from someone if we got lost. Okay now?"

She nods. "Yes, fine."

He takes her hand, squeezes it. "Sure?"

"Yes." She smiles. "Of course. Sorry."

But she's not sure.

Either she's going mad, or he's changed his story. First, the tattoo was done on holiday, then many years ago when he first joined the bank, then it was just before he met her. And Katty was dismissed as just a woman he knew, who he could barely recall, yet he'd kept the memory of a place she'd recommended, and the detailed map of this place had been drawn by a different Katty, one she'd never seen, at their hotel reception. Katty at Reception, who he'd gone to see when they first arrived and again while she was in the shower last night? Every time she had been to Reception it had been a man, or that little woman in the pink suit who never smiled, name badge 'Cindy'.

But any further questions along these lines and he's going to accuse her of not trusting him. He'd be right, too.

But she cannot think these thoughts. He is all of her world now. Her new husband. She adores him and he her. And yet… and yet… there's something like terror creeping up her back, spreading across her shoulders, prickling into her hair…

Something is about to happen.

When suddenly he stops dead and drops her hand.

His voice is a whisper. "Louise, don't panic."

"What?"

But she knows. Knows by the colossal horse-kick in the heart. Even before she sees the shadowy figures on the edge of the trees by the clearing. Down here, the ground is wetter, boggier, and as they stand stock-still in the shade of the forest, with the only sound that of nocturnal grass frogs, *Kraa kraa kraa…*, cicadas, and the distant screech of monkeys, all thoughts of another woman, vanish.

This is it.

What she's feared all along.

He should have listened to her. She should have been more insistent, told him her instincts weren't wrong, that she knew something ominous was coming. Just not who or when, or what form it would take.

***

Chapter Nine

She cannot breathe, her lungs taut as a drum, a suspension of life.

The cicadas have reached a deafening pitch, the jungle hissing and seething in the oven-hot dusk. From the nearby village, a dog barks, sounding a warning. And at the far end of the clearing, the Jeep glints tantalisingly. So close. A one-minute sprint.

But there are more men than at first it appeared. A shadow splits into two, then three, separating from the trees, surrounding the clearing. Are more gathering behind them, too? Creeping in from the sides? They're going to be robbed. Attacked.

Instinctively, she reaches for the clasp at the back of her neck, drops the pearl cross into her hand, and wedges it as far into the back pocket of her jeans as it will go. It's almost worthless, gold-plated, not even real pearls, nothing to the robbers but everything to her – all she has left of Marion. They can take everything else. She and Vic can hitchhike back if necessary.

"We'll have to give them our stuff," she whispers. "Everything, including the j–"

A small sound catches, one every wild animal instinctively knows, and all further thoughts are blinded. The priming of a gun.

There's a ring of them, closing in.

"We're going to have to run like hell," Vic says. "I'll be faster. Just get to the passenger door and dive in, okay?"

There's a fraction of a second when she sees another option – that of turning right and running down the track to the village instead, using their slight advantage to stay ahead of the gang, making a lot of noise. Doing it Vic's way is to run straight into a pack of wolves.

But it's too late.

"Ready? Go!"

No time. Instantly, they're both flat out. The pounding of turf slams into her ears, every step a leaden thump sending shock waves through her body. She cannot cover the distance fast enough, cannot close the gap quicker than the men darting out of the trees from every side, far more of them than imagined. Eight, nine, maybe more.

Vic is way ahead, keys in hand. The remote flashes, doors unlocking with one click. But while the distance to cover is not far now, a dozen paces may as well be a thousand, because one of the robbers is already at right angles with her, like a cheetah jumping a herd. And then there's a melee of confusion. Vic has thrown the rucksack to the ground but no one picks it up. A man dressed in combats has blocked her path, another appearing behind him. She's not going to make it. They will have to give them everything – watches, keys to the Jeep, everything. It doesn't matter. But amid all thoughts of this, she sees the rucksack lying on the ground in the dirt, in the mud, that no one is picking up.

Instead, they are circling her. Where is Vic? She swings around from left to right as the men close in. He is nowhere. But, stepping into her path is the faceless apparition of a man in a balaclava, and the smell of something sweet behind, tobacco or gum, the breath of another man breathing into her neck.

It isn't robbery…

It is as if she is waking from a very long dream. Everything is suddenly more intense, and there's a slight lull, like the second before a storm breaks when the light is surreal. The world slows down, and down and down. Her life, she thinks, really is about to pass before her eyes.

With absolute clarity, seemingly all at the same time, the heather-topped moors of home stretch out before her; cherry blossom flutters onto London streets; and her late mother's face smiles into her eyes as clear as a spring day. She is telling her not to worry about her first day at school – a primary, made of stone now weathered black, with a bell tower, and a parquet floor for morning assemblies. There is the waft of school books, chalk on the blackboard, old wooden desks carved with decades of names. There's Marion making tea in the back kitchen with her pinny on, the rumble and sway of the train on its way to London. There is Zita looking into her eyes, holding onto her forearms… *Take good care… take good care…* And there is Vic. His half-smile, eyeing her from the door of the pub – long black coat, white shirt, *Wicked Game* on the juke-box.

All this. On the foreshadow of inevitability. Swiftly followed by the engulfing of light, a cloth pressed onto her mouth, inhaling something sickly-sweet. No time to scream, to think, to fight back, to escape the iron grip rolling her over, tightening rope around her ankles and wrists, pulling a hood over her head, yanking tight a noose.

Make it quick. Don't lock me up. Just please God, don't let them lock me up!

THE GILDED CAGE

In the back of her mind, as terror rises in a black tsunami, she is vaguely aware of an engine firing up, followed by the squealing of tyres reversing in mud. A fraction of a second, before oblivion engulfs her.

***

Part Two

'For things to reveal themselves to us, we need to be ready to abandon our views about them…'
Buddha

Chapter Ten

England
October, 1992

Surely not! Is that Louise Draper?

Ingrid Houseman stares at the photograph on the front page of a national newspaper. There are dozens of similar articles in the papers, all covering the story of a missing British couple in Thailand. *Louise Landry*, the headline says, but it's definitely Louise Draper. Funny how the last time she'd seen Louise had also been on the front page of a newspaper, albeit a local one. Before that, she could have passed her on the street a hundred times and never even noticed, which she probably had.

Louise had first come to her attention three years ago, and her heart does a little flip as she catches up on the story of the couple's disappearance, can hardly believe it. This girl is from her home town. And Louise Draper of all people!

A freelance journalist, Ingrid is just back from a month's holiday. She's been commissioned to write a feature about the couple, and is scanning paper after paper, open-mouthed. They're spread across her desk in disarray, desktop computer humming in the background. This news is now considered old, already supplanted by royal exploits, celebrities and sport. The story had been on the radio, she'd been aware of it, but, distracted by the holiday of a lifetime – from Florida to Nassau – had not paid it much attention. Of course, the name had meant nothing, could not have registered. Only now does she realise who the woman is. And the jolted memory isn't altogether painless.

Three years ago, there'd been a fatal accident on the West Yorkshire moors, the same moors she now stares out of the window at. News of a hang-gliding crash had been announced on the radio. She'd been working in the advertising department of the local paper at the time, busy typing beneath flickering fluorescent lights, wanting to go home – Saturday, November 1989, the late afternoon crisp and breezy, rapidly fading to dusk. The name wasn't announced, only that a young male had been taken to hospital. But as soon as she heard about it, she knew. Had known without any doubt at all, that it was Bradley.

Bradley York had been twenty-five years old when the hang-gliding accident killed him. An exceptionally good-looking man with jet black hair, freckles and dark, sparkling eyes, he drove a racing green MG, and she'd had a huge crush on him. Bradley, however, was a lad's lad. Enjoyed pints down the pub, crude jokes, and extreme sports. He'd just landed a job with a Manchester film studio as a stuntman, and although she'd been aware their dates were becoming less and less frequent, that he'd cooled-off considerably, she hadn't known about Louise. Consequently, when the photograph appeared on the front-page next day, of the tear-stained, nineteen-year-old student nurse with both hands to her face, described as his devastated girlfriend, it had been a considerable shock.

One of her female colleagues had said, "Didn't you

know him, Ingrid? Oh, no – you weren't in love with him or anything, were you?"

"No, no… of course not."

Perhaps it was because of the painful mix of loss and humiliation, of being completely sidelined, as well as genuinely distraught, that she'd projected her ill feelings onto Louise? She must have been an easy lay, she'd thought. Thrown herself at him. The girl was plain, nothing out of the ordinary, a student barely out of school. What on earth had he seen in her? Even her clothes were dire.

For a while, she lingers over the memory, raking it up with a poison fork, reliving the empty, hollow, ultimately futile fury of having been replaced.

So, now here the woman was again. Louise Draper. Not beautiful, not exciting, not talented, not particularly intelligent, or even remotely bloody interesting. Yet on the front page again. In her face. Again.

She checks herself.

Have a heart, Ingrid – the girl could be dead.

And Bradley York was a very long time ago.

She takes a deep breath, closes her eyes for a moment. As a journalist, and one of the very few objective ones without an agenda, it was important to remove her own preconceived judgement – that Louise must have been stupid or naïve – in order to be the Excalibur sword of truth. Mind you, it wasn't going to be easy: the photograph alone had been a trigger.

She gets up to make another pot of filtered coffee. What a crazy small world! Louise Draper, who comes from Spring Bank Heights just up the road, had not only eclipsed her in Bradley York's life, but here she is a second time. What were the odds? Not only that, but she's got to write about her... find a new angle on the story of the couple who'd vanished into thin air, in the mountains of Northern Thailand. Why, though? Why did it have to be Louise bloody Draper? She can't stand her.

Ingrid is twenty-eight, and has her own flat on the top floor of what was originally a cotton mill on the edge of Huddersfield. Freelance, mostly she writes feature articles, from time to time following up on lead stories, conducting more in-depth interviews, often with a photographer in tow. She's known for her compassion, and what editors describe as, 'getting to the heart and soul of the story', but she calls intuition – being able to put herself in the head space of another person, of feeling what they might feel. But most of all she's known for producing precise, insightful copy that requires very little editing. In short, she's hard-working, consistently reliable, at the top of her game, and is paid accordingly. This particular piece, on Vic and Louise, has been commissioned by a Sunday magazine, the working title currently, *What happens when the trail goes cold?* With the subheading, *And how it affects the loved ones left behind.*

The moors are beautiful at this time of year, and even when she's away on holiday, she dreams of them. Today, as she sits at her desk gazing out of the window, rays of sunlight interplay with shadows chasing across the purple heather, and a sharp gust rattles the window. Her dark hair is piled on top of her head as she sits cupping the hot coffee, letting all the new information settle. How intriguing really, how extraordinarily coincidental, that if she were to walk out of the building and across the car park to the main gates, then onto the street, she would be able to see Louise's father's house, at Spring Bank Heights, which is nowhere near as attractive as it sounds. More like Wind Blast Heights. It's in the middle of a line of stone terraces originally built for mill workers in the nineteenth century – possibly those employed at the same mill she now lives in, recently converted into an exclusive development complete with a gym and hairdressing salon on the ground floor. The walls of the old mill are thick, solid, built to withstand strong winds and driving rain, and there's a comforting feeling of solidity about them.

Her thoughts flick back to Louise. What are the chances? Seriously? It's almost, *almost*, as if she's 'meant' to connect with her – that she's popped up again for a reason. Were she to believe in that kind of thing. Which she sometimes does. Depending if she can talk herself out of it, or not.

She picks up her notepad and pen and forces herself to read through all the published articles so far, along with press releases, background information from the office and police statements, making copious notes and underlining key points in red. Which is when a pattern begins to emerge. She reads through it all again. Is she missing something? Although Vic and Louise Landry's story has been covered by all the major media channels, especially the tabloids, there are no real answers regarding their disappearance. In fact, there's very little of substance at all. Boiled down, it's mostly official statements, oft repeated and rephrased in a multitude of ways; and speculation with varying degrees of sensationalism, depending on the clientele of the newspaper. From the sensational *Were Brits eaten by giant killer reptiles?* at one end of the scale, to the sensitive *Fears for young couple missing in Thailand* at the other.

Initially, it is the strong pull of intuition. She starts to jot down questions, the ones that hadn't been asked, let alone answered, by the press, using the truth-hunter's failsafe method of reductionism – stripping back all assumptions – followed by the trivium, that of gathering information, asking the who, what, when, where and hows, then looking for patterns. And as she works, it comes to her that there are many, far too many, unanswered questions here. No wonder her intuition is nagging and tugging. Her list goes onto a second page.

It seems the young couple vanished while exploring a particularly remote area of Northern Thailand. It happened on the last day of their holiday, hotel staff alerting local police next morning when they failed to check out and pay the bill. Their room was as they'd left it the previous day – clothes hanging in the wardrobes, toiletries in the bathroom – and the safe still contained their passports and return tickets to Singapore. The hired Jeep had also gone missing. No one at the hotel knew where they'd planned to go that day, and the only witness regarding which highway they'd taken, was a roadside fruit seller, who recalled a young woman with 'very yellow hair,' and a pearl cross around her neck.

Ingrid scrutinises each article, line by line, leaving Owen Roth's dramatic reports, in what has become known as the most comically sensational tabloid in Britain, until last. There was nothing to hang your hat on, though. Really... nothing. Yes, Owen, they could have been robbed and murdered, bodies dumped in the Mekong, Jeep driven over the border into remote mountain forests. But then again, they might not have been. Owen Roth had even been sent to Bangkok with a photographer, from where he'd invented a graphic narrative to rival any work of fiction. The couple could have become involved in drug trafficking, a subject which Owen then went on to describe, adding how many other tourists had gone missing in the notorious Golden Triangle over the years. They could have been shot, subsequently devoured by a reticulated python, or eaten by wild animals.

The couple were portrayed as innocent and naïve. There was a photograph of Vic with his arm slung around Louise's shoulders at Singapore Zoo, Louise holding a small chimp. And soon enough an impression was formed in the collective mind. They'd be dead. Had to be by now, didn't they?

Back in Britain, Vic's mother, Joanna Landry, had given a brief interview, the provided photograph that of an elegant woman at a black-tie charity dinner. Wearing an evening gown, blonde hair upswept, she had very dark brown button eyes that seemed to challenge the photographer. It was a skilled set of answers, devoid of any real information, the only give-away to relations between herself and her son, being the line, "Unfortunately, I can't comment on how Louise might be faring. We never met her."

Never met her? So, Vic wasn't close to his family, then?

Why wouldn't Joanna and Max Landry have gone to their son's wedding?

Max Landry, QC, hadn't commented, and nor had Vic's brother, Miles, also a QC. Miles' wife, Samantha, however, had been snapped dropping their two children off at a private school in Henley. Skeletally thin, wearing dark sunglasses, skinny jeans, and a shearling gilet, she had one hand on the handle of a black Range Rover, just as she turned to say, "No comment!"

Vic Landry himself, however, or at least his personal life, was covered in salacious detail, with identical photos appearing across the board – of his red Porsche 911, the apartment near Lord's Cricket Ground, an old snap of him at Eton in cricket whites, another in the beer tent at a polo match. An investment banker specialising in Futures, known for being surrounded by exceptionally attractive women, usually a different one every few weeks, is the overall portrayal, supported by a brief interview with his best friend, Karl Lozensky, a luxury brand car dealer, and various photographs taken in West End clubs.

Charmed, Ingrid thinks. *He's had a charmed life, and on top of that, he's without doubt, heart-stoppingly handsome.* 'Foxy', would be the word she'd choose. There's a deep-russet, sharp-eyed cunning about him; along with the easy loucheness of one absolutely confident of his place in the world.

She flicks her attention back to Louise's photograph, to the last one taken before the pair left England, of her and two friends at the wedding lunch in London. One is Janice Case, the other, Ziva Okoye, who'd since moved to Grenoble in France. All three girls are lifting a champagne glass in celebration, sun slanting through the windows of The Atelier restaurant in St John's Wood. What could be read into those smiles? Anything?

Louise, wearing a cream lace dress, hair in an up-do, is clearly ecstatically happy. She has a childlike aura – apple cheeks, baby teeth, and a glazed expression in the eyes, almost as if she's not quite there, not fully present.

Janice looks slightly uneasy in the opulent

surroundings, had possibly been reticent, quiet, in the company she found herself that day. Ingrid could be wrong. Could always be wrong. Ziva is different, though, looking directly into the camera lens with an almost unworldly wisdom, head held regally high. Dressed in layers of exotica, bangles and necklaces, her hair braided and coiled, she would be an astute observer, Ingrid thinks, and it's a great pity she can't be reached.

She traces a finger over the photo. *What happened to you, Louise?*

There were things that didn't add up here, doubts amassing like a bundle of rain clouds. Something didn't feel right.

Firstly, there were no bodies, so no one could definitively call this murder. Other murdered tourists had been found, left to die, bleeding into the grass, partially decomposed, partially devoured. Yet, in this case there were no bodies. No Jeep. Why had it been written off so soon? The whole thing seemed to have been whitewashed.

And why would a sophisticated, exceptionally well-travelled man like Vic Landry, go off on a remote mountain track into a gun- and opium-trafficking area in the first place? At dusk. With his young wife. Seemed a hell of a risk! Stupid, frankly.

As for being involved in drug trafficking, Ingrid shakes her head and sighs heavily. Vic was extremely wealthy, there was no way he needed the money, and just looking at Louise it was obvious she'd never even smoked weed. For goodness' sake, you have to tap into who these people are, she thinks crossly. Why they did what they did. Follow the trail. Because none of the widely accepted speculations made any sense.

And then there was the couple themselves. It just got odder...

Here, it is imperative to remove all prejudices in order to get to the core of who they are, because it seems, after looking past the superficial, to be a highly unlikely match. Vic, she feels, is like Brad York – the type of man who'd date a girl such as Louise, or indeed herself, a few times, before getting bored and not even bothering to tell her she was dumped. Yet, he'd actually married Louise. And he'd married her so quickly, it seemed there hadn't even been time for his parents to meet her. Or his brother. Just a couple of friends and Louise's colleagues from work, before they vanished from the scene.

Why Louise? She was certainly pretty, but... she flicks through the photos of Vic... hardly in the same league as the women he'd previously dated. He seemed to have had a penchant for startlingly beautiful women and in particular, sophisticated, expensive types. She examines Louise again. Her graduation day photograph. Then the terraced house she'd grown up in. Scans the interview with her father, Len Draper, a retired coalman, and the picture of him holding an oxygen mask over his face. Chronic obstructive airways disease, apparently. Couldn't get his breath. Then the photo of the couple as they'd been in Singapore before the trip to Thailand. The one of Louise holding a baby chimp, Vic's arm around her. Again, she catches a faraway look in Louise's blue lagoon eyes, a trusting, child-like essence. But Vic is so very different – a knowing, slight smile playing on his lips, a glance at someone walking past as the camera clicks...

She mustn't make assumptions.

Perhaps, he'd genuinely fallen in love with Louise? A

kind of *Pretty Woman* match, where money, glamour and status didn't matter a jot? Except it's obvious he isn't that kind of guy. There's something superior about him, smirking, a kind of hubris… Ingrid's old wound, still unhealed, smarts and weeps. He breaks hearts and he doesn't care.

"Why did Vic Landry marry you, Louise?" she asks her picture. "And why did you fall for another handsome charmer, trust him with your heart, your life? One with other women on the go? Because you must have suspected?"

She flicks back to the interview with Janice Case, where she said they hadn't known each other long, just a few months before a whirlwind marriage. Louise was besotted, very much in love with him. And 'Vic suddenly appeared after Christmas with a huge bouquet of flowers'.

Suddenly appeared after Christmas. After?

Hmmm. There's something here that's just beneath the surface, being hidden, which at the moment she cannot see. The key is in this couple's relationship, and she's as sure about that as anything. But first she must understand Louise, get into her head.

After Bradley York's death, Louise would have found out he was leaving town and hadn't told her, and quickly realised just how many other women he was seeing. They'd all surfaced once the news broke, keen to say how they knew him. Ingrid imagines young Louise's pain on learning that. So, why didn't she spot the red flags with Vic? Because after Bradley York, she sure as hell ought to have done. Bet Vic ran hot and cold, called the shots, kept Louise – she feels the pang in her own heart, remembering – waiting for a bloody phone call, sitting on the bed fully dressed, ready to go out for the evening, but he never rang. Turned up a month later as if nothing was wrong. Likely he said she'd misunderstood or misheard. Hadn't she missed him? He'd bought her something. Now he wanted her, now he didn't.

And just like that, her animosity seamlessly melts into compassion, the younger woman's essence reaching through an invisible veil.

What happened to you, Louise?

***

Chapter Eleven

Len Draper, Louise's father, would be a good place to start. Why had Louise left her home town, for example? What had her upbringing been like? Had she been happy? The readers would like to know more about Louise, she thinks, and so would she.

Clicking open a wrought iron gate, she walks up the path to Len's front door. A raw wind blasts off the moors, autumn leaves whipping round her ankles. It takes a skin of hide to do this job sometimes, something she hasn't got and, unsure what kind of reaction there'll be after weeks of intrusion into his private life, Ingrid steels herself for what is essentially a cold call. This could go either way. The magazine commission is a generous one, though, and they're prepared to pay.

From within, a radio is blasting, *Can't get enough of your love...* A Bad Company hit from decades before, and her eyebrows lift as another one plays straight after it. Not the radio then, but Len's choice of CD, or even LP. Loud. Was he dancing around in there?

The small, rectangular front garden had once been landscaped with shrubs – rhododendrons, fuchsia, buddleia, pyracantha – but is now a tangled mass of ivy and weeds, and the paint on the front door is peeling. The scene bears all the hallmarks of the depressed, chronically unwell widower depicted in the papers, one whose only daughter has gone missing. Were it not for the music. And this catches her so much by surprise that she hesitates before knocking. The music was thumping.

A thought occurs to her. Maybe he's out and this is a lodger? Now, that would make sense!

Shrugging, she raps on the door with her knuckles, hard, in order to be heard. The kid could be full head-bang, she thinks, remembering the day she once burst into her brother's room and found him with an imaginary microphone, standing in front of the mirror miming to Dire Straits.

Len Draper whips the door open on the sixth knock.

They stare at each other wide-eyed for a second, each taking stock, before Ingrid drops into auto-pilot.

"Oh, good morning. I'm so sorry to intrude. My name's Ingrid Houseman. Would you be Mr Len Draper?"

"Aye, that's me."

He's out of breath, but whether that's from exertion or chronic obstructive airways disease, it isn't clear. Older than his years, is her first impression – perhaps only early sixties, but dressed like the previous generation, in a checked woollen shirt, high-waisted trousers and a knitted waistcoat. Thinning grey hair is greased back, face ruddy, purple broken veins on his nose and cheeks, very likely wears a flat cap if he goes out.

It's an effort, a real effort, not to picture him dancing around to the now much fainter, *Feel like making love... feel like... making...* but she fails, and a smile breaks through.

"Hello, Mr. Draper. Look, I'm sorry to call on you out of the blue like this, but as I'm practically next door, I thought it might be better than phoning. I'm actually a freelance writer for a magazine, and I've just been reading about Louise's disappearance."

"Oh, aye?"

"Yes. I've been commissioned to write a feature about her friends and family, her life. So, obviously you're the first port of call, and I wondered if there's anything you wanted to talk about, or even redress. It must be extremely upsetting for you?"

"Well, aye. Course it is."

"My job is to talk to those who really knew her, let them have their say after all the furore has died down. I can't imagine how hard this must be for you. It's really nothing to—"

Len Draper grips the door handle, closes his eyes and starts to take deep, noisy, gasping breaths, as if he's having an asthma attack and about to pass out.

"Oh, my goodness, are you all right? I'm so sorry, I didn't mean to upset you."

Mid-gasp, he waves her inside. "Come in and shut the door. I'll have to sit down. I'm not well."

Closing the door behind them, she follows him through to a front room with brown curtains, brown carpet and brown furniture, where he turns off an old radiogram and slumps into an armchair. Behind it is an oxygen cylinder with a mask hanging over it.

"I'll be all right in a minute," he says. "Just need to get me breath."

"Of course, yes. It was mentioned in the papers that you weren't well."

"Take a pew. What was your name, again?"

"Ingrid. Ingrid Houseman."
"Which paper?"

"I'm freelance." She hands him a business card. "I actually remember your daughter, you know? She had a boyfriend who was killed in a hang-gliding accident on the moors. She was in the local paper, wasn't she?"

Len shakes his head.

"About three years ago?"

"That'd be when my Barbara died! Three years!" He glares at her.

"Your wife? Ah…"

"I can't remember owt about an accident. It'd be when I were in hospital. First the prostate and then it were a heart attack. Twenty year and counting I've had a bad heart. First one should have killed me. Doctor said they didn't know how I pulled through. They were fantastic in that hospital, though. They really looked after me. Angels. Said they'd never had a case like mine in all their years."

Ingrid nods.

"This doc I've got now, though, down at that health centre." He pulls a face. "I told him," he waggles a finger at her, "I'll call an ambulance next time. I'll cut the bugger out. Wouldn't be the first time I've had to be taken out of here in an ambulance."

"No." She tries to smile. "Um, would you like me to put the kettle on?"

"Aye, go on then, if you're mashing. Strong, white, three sugars."

Ingrid doesn't mind, finding the view from the kitchen into a bleak backyard a welcome respite from Len's accusing stare. There's a pebble-dashed garage with a flat, corrugated iron roof, an old shed with murky windows, and a washing line strung between the two. His energy, she thinks, is draining, and she wonders what his wife died of.

Three years ago, though – same year as Bradley York. Poor Louise!

For ten minutes he noisily slurps the tea. And she may be mistaken, but thinks not, that he's doing it deliberately. Certainly, it strains her nerves to twanging point.

"I'm so sorry to hear your wife died. She was far too young."

"Not as young as if I'd died when I 'ad me first stroke. I were forty-two, so think on that, eh? Forty-two. Delivered coal, I did. Imagine that!"

She frowns, sure he'd said a heart attack twenty years ago. "Um, yes, I can imagine. Hard work. Tough job."

"Bloody was, an' all."

Resentment is coming off him in waves, and instinctively Ingrid takes several slow, calming breaths, reminding herself his anger is not personal. Besides, she's come here to ask about Louise.

"Yes. So, Louise must still have been living at home when her mother died, then?" She pulls out a notepad and pen from her shoulder bag. "Quite a rough year for a nineteen-year-old – both her mother and her boyfriend dying. I remember the photo in the local paper. She was distraught. Now, I understand why. It was her mother, too."

"It were terrible for me after Barbara went."

"It must have been, yes. I completely understand."

"I doubt that very much," he snaps, glaring at her.

She nods. "Were you married a long time, Mr Draper?"

"Longer than you've been alive by the look of you."

"Is Louise your only child?"

"She weren't mine. I took her on when Barbara got herself into trouble. Nobody else'd have her."

Got herself into trouble?

"Quite the miracle."

"What?"

She shakes her head, "Sorry, I think my pen's run out. Supposed to be a… um… miracle pen."

His eyes are boring right through her, hard as flint.

So, Len isn't actually Louise's father, at all? She rummages in her bag for a different pen, buying some time while processing the new information. Nowhere had that been mentioned. It had always been, 'Louise's father'. My God, it certainly explained a few things, though. For one thing, the man has no love for his daughter, and secondly, his brittle moods would have had the child stuck in permanent fight or flight mode, on constant alert – seeking to please and not rile, to attend to every need or request, in case blame and shame rained down on her. In short, Louise would have existed in a state of survival from a very young age, locking down her heart. Eventually, she'd have sought love elsewhere, especially after her mother died. Finding solace in affection, any kind of affection, mistaking it for love. Grateful for the attentions of a man who said all the right things, made her feel nice.

Ingrid suddenly looks up and smiles, holding up another biro.

"Knew I'd got one. Sorry about that."

It's now perfectly clear why Louise fell for Bradley York, because it was for the same reason as herself; he'd known how to make her feel desired, wanted and special. Until he got bored. But with that understanding comes another one. Unlike herself, Louise wouldn't have seen any red flags with Vic Landry because her emotional trauma ran far too deeply. She would have latched onto any affection offered.

Done anything for it. Settled for anything. Risked anything. There's a term for it. 'Trauma bonding', that was it. She's still making assumptions about Louise, though. Her next point of call, therefore, will be to London. One of her friends, she believes, is still there.

A further hour passes in the company of Len Draper. Good God, she thinks, no wonder he's been left without any further press intrusion, or indeed any intrusion. Even his home help had apparently rung to say she couldn't come today.

She looks at her watch, unfortunately while he's mid-sentence because he catches her, and she must smile and listen politely for another few minutes until there's a gap.

"Well, let's hope you get your blood tests back soon, Mr Draper. But just before I go, could I ask what sort of child Louise was? I mean, was she happy? What sort of hobbies did she have, for example? Did she play out? Have lots of friends? How would you describe her? And is there a special memory? You know – something for our readers!"

A shadow passes over him and she suppresses her own lurking anxiety, soothing herself. What will it matter if he loses his rag with her? She has to come away from the interview with a bit more substance, so she might as well go for it.

"It were her job to help her mother in the kitchen and suchlike. Up in her room most of the time, reading. Never had much to say for herself." There's mockery behind his eyes that she can't quite fathom. What is it he suddenly finds amusing?

"Was she good at school? She passed all her nursing exams, anyway."

"That were Barbara's department, all that."

She pretends to make notes. "Okay, and one more thing – would you happen to have any old school photos, or maybe some taken with her friends, or grandparents?"

He passes her a bottle-green leather photo album from the bottom shelf of the bookcase.

"You can take what you want. They're no use to me. There's one of her with Barbara and Marion you can have."

"Marion?"

"Barbara's mother."

She leafs through.

"Oh, is it this one? Two women with a toddler? So, this would be all three generations?"

Around the older lady's neck is a cross made from pearls, and it stirs a flicker of memory. Oh, yes – the roadside seller in Thailand had remembered yellow hair and a pearl cross. So, Louise had her grandma's keepsake, wore it all the time, probably. She was close to her maternal grandma, then? A lonely child who read alone upstairs, keeping out of the way, while her mother pandered to this man. Waiting, counting the days, until she was old enough to escape. Which she did, first chance she got.

Well, Louise. Now, I'm in your head, next stop London!

***

Chapter Twelve

Ingrid's initial impression of Janice Case hadn't been far off the mark. She was most definitely the quietest of the three – the one who didn't go on wild nights out, but usually stayed in her room, saving her salary for a place of her own one day, and regularly going home to her parents in Hull.

The two women walk across Regents Park from the private clinic to the nurses' accommodation, on what is a gloriously golden October day. At five o'clock, the light is beginning to fade, the air crisp, trees shimmering with copper penny leaves.

Janice wears her nurse's uniform under a grey overcoat, her shoes flat, black and sensible. She's very short, perhaps only five foot two, and plump. Even her face is pillowy, with round cheeks that squash clear, observant blue eyes. Perfect complexion, Ingrid notes – as pure as a toddler's. And a mop of short, glossy dark hair cut flatteringly around the jaw, with lots of layers and outward flicks. Modern, pretty.

The introduction had been easy. And Janice, it turns out, wanted to talk.

"I'm still really shocked," she says, several times.

Ingrid believes her. This is a young woman who only recently left the sheltered safety of home, to live in the equivalent of a student hall, with a communal dining room and lounge, her own bedroom (Ingrid pictures a bed piled with soft toys), and goes back to Hull on the coach every other weekend. At the clinic, she works on a ward where there's a daily routine, fussing over wealthy patients like a personal maid – homely, comforting, capable and thorough. Most days, she'd walked to and from work across the park, with either Louise or Ziva, sometimes both. They'd sat across from each other at breakfast like college girls, often meeting up at lunchtime, too. Occasionally, she'd been out for a drink with them.

It really is a resounding shock to her that Louise could possibly be dead.

Ingrid lets her talk. No one had asked Janice anything except how long she'd known Louise, what kind of girl she was, if she'd taken drugs, had lots of boyfriends. Tried to find the dirt. The gossip.

"But she wasn't like that," she says, frowning. "Louise was… I don't know how to put it, but really innocent and kind. She liked to go out a lot, especially with Ziva and her sister. They went to nightclubs and sometimes to the West End. It's all she wanted to do… just go dancing. She was so lovely, a really lovely friend…"

She pulls out a large, white cotton handkerchief, the kind Ingrid's dad uses, and blots away the tears. "I still can't believe it."

"I know. I'm so sorry."

After a while, Janice says, "I can't dance like that, but they loved it. We had a lot of fun. We used to sunbathe on the roof last summer. Climb out of the top window and down the fire escape. There was a flat bit and we'd all be on there with the radio on–"

"At the nurses' residence?"

"Yes, you can't see it from the outside – it's hidden by all the chimneys and attic rooms. We were really close, almost like sisters. You should have seen them when they went out! Ziva went out this one time in a full-length white crochet dress. I think Louise idolised her a bit. It's a shame you can't meet Ziva, she'd be better than me at explaining things."

"What things?"

Janice hesitates. "Well, this might sound funny, but I always thought Louise was kind of rushing at life, if that makes sense? Like she'd been trapped in a cage and had only just burst out of it. The cafeteria at the clinic's in the basement and there are bars on the window. You had to look up to see the sky. It really bothered her being stuck inside all day, not being able to see outside. Her room at the nurses' home upset her a bit, as well. Hers was at the back overlooking the yard, north-facing. She couldn't stand being cooped up."

"I spoke to her step-dad the other day. The family house overlooks the moors. Maybe she was homesick for the wide-open spaces?"

"Hmmm. You could be right. But she never went back, did she? After her mother died, she left first chance she got, and as far as I know she didn't go home again, not once."

"But she was happy here, you think? In London? With her job?"

"I think so. To be honest, though, it's difficult to say. I mean, I'm not sure who the real Louise was. With Ziva, you knew exactly what you were getting, and if you didn't, she told you." Janice laughs. "But Louise sort of changed depending on who she was with – out all night dancing, but if there was only me here having hot chocolate and an early night, so would she. She'd say she didn't really drink, then go out drinking; that she didn't smoke and then she'd be in the lounge smoking with the Irish girls. They were really wild, by the way." Janice laughs again. "Then at work she'd be very quiet and dutiful. She wouldn't go against anyone, either. If she was asked to take sides on something, asked what she thought, she'd say she didn't know. So, who was she really? Do you know what I mean? I sometimes think about that. Sorry, bit deep…"

"No! God, no. Good observation."

A survivor, Ingrid thinks. Like most kids from emotionally abusive backgrounds, she'd learned to read the energies, watching for the slightest change of mood, saying and doing whatever gave her safe passage. She hadn't had the freedom to safely explore her own personality, let alone be confident in it. That goes on for too long and it becomes impossible to remember the good, only the trauma. No wonder Louise never went back home.

"How about Vic? Was the wedding the first time you met him?"

"No, he came over two or three times to pick her up. That was at the beginning, about this time last year. I remember because I came downstairs in my dressing gown and slippers at the same time she was going out all dolled up." She laughs and Ingrid can picture it. Imagines Janice's dressing gown to be pink and fluffy. "He was really good-looking. Bit of a bobby dazzler."

Ingrid smiles at the term, hasn't heard, 'bobby dazzler' for years.

"Yes, I've seen the photos."

"But in person, though! He's ever so…what's the word? Arresting! Really bright brown eyes, broad shoulders, very tall, very…" She laughs again. "He was wearing a tan leather jacket and a white shirt and he just seemed to sort of fill the room. You wouldn't not notice him."

"Did you speak to him?"

"Louise introduced us, but he wasn't very interested."

"Did you like him? I mean, when you got to talk at the wedding lunch, for example?"

"Yes, he was all right."

"But did you like him? Did you think he was in love with Louise?"

They've reached the main road and traffic is fizzing both ways.

"What will you print, though? I mean, the press twist things, don't they? I don't mean to be rude, but so far, the things I've read don't sound like the friend I knew at all, and they've hardly printed anything I told them."

Once out of the park, it's noisier, and they hurry across the main road, after which they head towards the end of the block. Just around the corner, almost on the corner in fact, is the nurses' home, a large, regency-style property now housing staff from all over the world.

Ingrid reiterates the kind of article she intends to write, that it will be compassionate; that it's about people like Janice having their say, and quite different from the sensationalism in the tabloids.

"Well, to be honest then, Ziva and I both had bad vibes about him."

"In what way?"

"Just a feeling. She'd have probably been all right if she hadn't, you know, gone and married him." Janice sighs heavily. "One of his friends at the wedding was really creepy, just watching her, hardly saying anything, smirking at her. You can tell what people are like by the company they keep. And I wouldn't have trusted any of them. Not wide-boy Karl and certainly not that Nigel."

Ingrid makes a mental note. Ah yes, Karl Lozensky, the luxury car dealer, and Nigel Scott-Renard. Nothing known about the latter yet. Certainly, there'd been no pictures of either.

"Could be his friends were jealous. That can happen. Maybe, they felt she'd hijacked him from the gang, leaving them behind?"

"He was thirty-six!"

"Even so–"

"I wasn't getting that... I'm beginning to sound like Ziva. She was psychic, by the way. It's such a pity you can't talk to her. She knew about energies and auras. She said Nigel, the sly one, was dark. A dark energy. She felt tired, drained and uncomfortable in his company. Do you think you'll be able to find out what happened to Louise?"

Ingrid shrugs. "Me? I don't know. What do you think happened to them, Janice? Best guess?"

"Well, I don't think it should have been written off so quickly, with it already decided they're dead. It's rather indecent haste, for one thing."

"I agree."

They've reached the corner of the street, and turn down the quieter, tree-lined residential avenue, the traffic gradually becoming more muted.

"I really liked Louise. She'd been through a lot, you know? Her first boyfriend was killed in an accident, then her mum died. And her dad, well step-dad, used to hit her. That was another thing, the press kept saying he was her father and he wasn't. I told them, as well. Anyway, he'd lock her up in a shed in the back yard. Her mother never said a word, used to tell her not to make a fuss, not to upset him, that it'd just make it worse. Louise only told me that once, and never said anything about it again. She just wanted to leave it all behind and have a life, that's what she told me. She had nothing, not a bean to her name, and unlike me, no home to go back to. But you couldn't have met anyone who wanted to live life to the full more than Louise. She was so in love with Vic, as well."

"I think they did print that."

"Yes. She really was, though. She wouldn't hear a word against him, not from me or Ziva. And that's why I think she made such a mistake."

They are standing outside the front door of the nurses' home, at the bottom of the steps, both shivering in the shade of the late afternoon, backs to the sharp wind.

"What do you mean? What mistake?"

"Well, she never really checked him out, did she? She never met his parents, or his brother, or even his friends until the wedding day. Never went to his place of work. He'd stand her up loads of times. Didn't contact her for weeks, then out of the blue he turned up and asked her to marry him. It just didn't feel right."

Ingrid checks her notes. "They got married at the beginning of March this year, then flew out to Singapore. So, what happened last Christmas? I mean, you say she never met his parents or his friends, but if he was planning to ask her to marry him, you'd have thought that was the perfect time. What did she do last Christmas, can you recall?"

Janice shivers in her big coat, shakes her head, trying to remember.

"I went home for the whole fortnight, I was lucky. Oh yes, that's right. I came back on the second of January and it was freezing, frost on the ground. I remember walking into the hall with my suitcase and she was sitting in the lounge on her own. The only one there. She wasn't very happy. I made us some tea and she said she hadn't heard from Vic in weeks, didn't know where he was. She could hardly bring herself to talk about it. I'd never seen her like that, just really deflated."

"Well, I suppose they hadn't known each other that long? If it was a family holiday overseas–"

"Yes, but she hadn't heard from him at all. I think it was about three weeks. And it was quite a while before he contacted her again. Then suddenly, middle of January, he turned up with a huge bouquet of flowers at the clinic, and left them at Reception. I think he took her out to a West End restaurant shortly after that, told her he'd been skiing on a family holiday. and then he popped the question."

"Wow! So, was she shocked?"

"God, yes. Me and Ziva were, too. She barely knew him, but she went from being down in her boots to dancing around, massively happy. Completely transformed. Like a rag doll brought to life. He told her he couldn't imagine life without her, apparently."

Janice raises both eyebrows.

"We didn't want to bring her down, but we wouldn't have been very good friends if we didn't at least try to get her to think about it properly, would we? In the end though, you can't stop people doing what they want to do. They've got to follow their own path. And she did get upset when Ziva started to ask her a few things."

"Do you think that maybe he didn't take care of her out

there? That he's somehow put her in harms' way?"

"I can't think of anything else. I'll be honest, I didn't really like him that much. I thought he was out for himself, so I can believe that if there was a robbery, then he would have scarpered and left her. That's my best guess. That he got away and she was taken."

Ingrid nods. "So, you don't think he really loved her?"

Shivering, Janice huddles more into her coat. "I think he loved himself more. Maybe he just wanted a little wife, someone to make him feel good? Will you be going out there, to Thailand?"

"No plans to, no. Anyway, it's getting cold. I'll let you go in. Just one more thing – do you happen to know anything about Karl Lozensky? Or the other friend, Nigel?"

"Karl sells motorbikes and sports cars like it said in the papers. Nigel's at the Foreign Office. Apparently, he and Vic were at Eton together. Neither of them had much in common with me and Ziva, so we just talked about music and stuff."

"Either of them married?"

"Nigel is. They live in Chelsea. And Karl's got a place near Clapham Common. His uncle runs that pub, by the way." She indicates the one directly opposite. "That's where Louise and Vic met, would you believe?"

Ingrid glances across the road at The Queen's Head, taking in the frosted glass of the saloon bar, the bottle-green tiles above the door, and the proprietor's name carved above it. Such is the phenomenon of London, she thinks; an eclectic mix of multi-million-pound residences, run-down hovels, on-trend restaurants, historic landmarks and time-warp relics like The Queen's Head, often all on the same street.

"Lovely."

They both laugh.

"But thanks for that. Anyway, look, I'll let you go in. Thank you ever so much, Janice. I didn't mean to keep you so long."

"I don't feel like I've helped very much."

"Oh, you have. For one thing, I now understand why Louise acted so impulsively. I'm kind of more in her shoes. And I know where to go next now I've spoken to you. Sometimes it's like that – one bit of information leads to another."

Janice nods, smiles.

"Actually, I feel more hopeful now I've met you. Before today, I thought it was all going to die a death and I didn't know what to do about it. You know, I watch all these old detective series, where they have a strong hunch but everyone else thinks they're crazy?"

Ingrid nods. "I do, too."

"And they're the only one with that hunch. No one else believes them and they get blocked at every turn, but they stick with it and dig around into relationships, personalities, backgrounds, family psychology, and so on. Everyone gets angry, upset, even their boss. Then suddenly there's a breakthrough and they're proved right. All on a hunch. So, I think you might hit on something no one else has, is what I'm trying to say."

She's turned a bit red in the face, as if suddenly aware she might sound a bit off-the-wall herself, as if Ingrid might think her boring or silly.

"Anyway–" She holds out her hand. "Good to meet you, Ingrid. Please keep in touch."

Ingrid shakes her hand. "Not silly, at all – intuition

never lies to you. And thank you, I will. Good to meet you, too."

"Oh, I just thought. Would you like a photo of them? Karl and Nigel? I've got one from the wedding if you can wait a couple of minutes?"

"You have one? Ooh, definitely! Yes, please. That's brilliant."

Only now does that glaring omission truly hit home. There hadn't been any photos of Vic's friends in the papers. There were several of Janice and Ziva, none of Karl or Nigel, despite the wedding lunch being mentioned, and Karl being interviewed.

After the big oak doors click shut, leaving her alone on the steps, Ingrid turns to look at The Queen's Head public house, picturing the Victorian tap room, with its worn tiled floor, tar-stained walls, rows of tankards on hooks above the bar, and fancies she can hear the roar of drunken conversation in the hot swell of the crowd, time being called… and can almost see Vic and his friends swilling down the last of the evening's pints.

Karl Lozenky's uncle owned the pub. So, Karl had brought Vic to Louise's door.

I think you might hit on something no one else has…

***

Chapter Thirteen

Karl Lozensky. She's had to pay him because he didn't want anything more to do with the press, but now he's talking, he's firing on full throttle.

"They just print whatever the bloody hell they want," he tells her. "I mean, why interview me in the first bleedin' place if they're just going to make it all up?"

She shakes her head, remembering Janice had pretty much said the same thing.

"What did you say that wasn't printed?"

He lights a cigarette, leans back, and eyes her through the exhaled smoke.

Early thirties, Karl is a fast-talking cockney, making good money selling sports cars and motorbikes to men like Vic Landry. Parked outside the café window is a Vincent Black Shadow, behind it the River Thames. She waits for him to answer the question, disciplining herself not to fill the silence, as first his glance flicks to the Black Shadow, then back to her again. Sizing her up. Of course, he doesn't trust her: in his eyes she's just another hack without a moral code. Anything for a story, a piece of someone else's trauma to sensationalise for a pay cheque. So, why is he talking to her at all? Took the money because he could? A chance of righting a wrong, having his truth heard? Or because he'll find something out? Right now, she thinks, he doesn't know, and is working out how to play the game.

He takes another drag of his cigarette, and a smile flickers around the corners of his mouth. She returns the smile, faintly. Oh, the irony. A car salesman not trusting a journalist. But then from out of the quantum entanglement of their unspoken exchange, a tiny shock breaks free, an unwanted one – the effect he has on her. There's a disarming boyish charm about him, a crinkling around the eyes, narrow and green; long slim lips, and dirty blond hair cut short. He's wearing jeans and a slim-fitting white shirt, biker boots, a brown leather jacket thrown over the back of the seat.

"This article you're doing, yeah?" he says, completely ignoring her question. "Who did you say it's for, again?"

She repeats her spiel, that it's about the couple's friends and family, to give them a platform, a voice, while also finding new angles. "'What more can they tell us?' That kind of thing. My remit is very different from that of the newspaper journalists. It's more about Vic and Louise's lives, about who they really were."

His eyes bore into hers. He and Vic must have made quite a killing on the night-life scene. She pictures them in city-sharp dark suits, white shirts worn with narrow ties. Tries not to think of how many women they casually picked up, lied to, seduced, forgot about.

"So," she says, feeling she's done more than enough explaining. He has, after all, contracted to talk, been paid. "You said the press didn't print what you told them? Maybe I can right that for you? What should they have said?"

Another moment passes, then he nods, appears to make a decision, stubs out the cigarette and leans forward.

"Well, for a kick-off, darlin', they made a massive fuckin' deal about Vic being a rich investment banker – photos of his Porsche and the luxury flat in St John's Wood, pictures of him at expensive clubs knocking back champagne, whole fucking table's full of it, like, three hundred quid a bottle."

She nods, takes a sip of cappuccino, dabs the froth from her lips with one finger.

"But what I told them, right? And this is all of them, yeah? Is that in actuality, he hadn't got nothing. Worse than nothing. Fucked up in a major way, did Victor."

'Fucked' sounded like 'facked' and 'nothing' like 'naffink'.

"Sorry?" Ingrid stares at him for a moment, eyes wide. "Are you kidding me?"

"D' you know how trading in Futures works?"

"A bit. New companies hire an investment banker to present on their behalf to potential underwriters. They either buy in at the start, or not."

He nods. "The investment banker will have a portfolio of clients, and his job is to make them money in the medium to long term, have an eye for the superstars of tomorrow."

"So, for varying degrees of risk they're in at the beginning, buy shares when they're low, then cash in later down the line when the company's worth squillions?"

"That's the idea. Except Vic lost them quite a bit."

"Quite a bit?"

"Tens of millions."

"Really?"

"Really. Tens and tens of millions."

"Sheesh! So, would the bank cover the clients' losses?"

He nodded. "Yeah, except, and this is the extra-special juicy bit – those clients of Vic's were powerful family connections who poured money into companies going nowhere because they trusted the private investment bank, that only employed Vic as a favour to his dad. But basically Victor, their mate's son, got greedy, didn't do his research, took backhanders, talked the talk and hyped the hype. So, there he was creating error accounts, siphoning off investment funds and living the life royal, ducking and diving like a market geezer with a suitcase full of knock-offs. Only a matter of time before it all caught up with him, wasn't it?"

"But, I don't understand, the bank still sent him out to Singapore. Promoted him, the papers said. Why didn't they sack him?"

"Maybe because of whose son he was–"

"But hang on, his dad's only a barrister."

He laughed and shook his head.

"Obviously, you 'aven't heard of insider clubs? Of which there are many. But the one his dad's in, is pretty near the top of the pyramid. Look at the mother's side if you want to find out who's who and how he got there, though. So, I'm guessing, and I really do mean I'm guessing, the old boys at the bank paid off the investors, fucked Vic off to the other side of the world, and brushed the entire unfortunate episode under the proverbial carpet, rather than have the market, should we say, lose confidence."

"But then the couple disappeared in Thailand and Vic hit the headlines."

"Bit awkward, innit?"

"So, here's my next question: if Vic didn't have a bean to his name, what did he do with all the filthy lucre he siphoned off? Where did the money go? If he was broke, as you say, why did he do it?"

"Well, starting around the summer last year, he told me he was in a 'spot of bother'. That's how he used to talk – 'a spot of bother.' I think it must have started to catch up with him round about then, I can see it now. He was sort of nervous and agitated, said 'they' were following him… bit paranoid if the truth be known – definitely in trouble but he wouldn't tell me no more. Not 'til he turned up in the early hours just before Christmas, saying there was no money, that it'd all gone, and 'they' were onto him. He had a bad gambling habit, snorted coke, and very expensive tastes. There were a lot of people on his back, to be honest. But, and this is where I'm a tad confused, Ingrid, neither the press nor the police were interested when I told them that quite a few people wanted him dead. Now, you would have thought that was pretty fuckin' important, would you not?"

"And they printed the opposite… So, hang on. Back up a minute – how do you mean, he had nothing? Even if he'd used investors' money to service gambling debts and a high-end lifestyle, he still had–"

"His assets weren't his."

"You mean the flat? Was it rented?"

Karl stubs out his cigarette. "No, mother dearest owns it. It's part of *The* Joanna Landry portfolio – charity figurehead, always travelling and networking, patron of this and chairwoman of that. Joanna has a great deal of what you might call, passive income." He grins. "You seen her, by the way?"

"Only a society photo in the papers."

"Fucking terrifying. Dead eyes like a shark's. I met her

and Max once, up near Temple Bar when me and Vic were going up the West End one night. Well anyway, it's her what owns the flat, not Vic. So, he can fuck up and that flat can never be repossessed. As far as I know, the only thing he had in his own name was the Porsche, and I only know that because I sold it to him for cash. Oh, and the Harley. That's his."

"Why didn't he sell them to pay off his debtors?"

"He did sell the Porsche. But we're talking debts with lots of noughts on the end, darlin'."

She frowns. "Not sure I understand. I thought the bank settled the debts. And why send him overseas with another position in Futures trading? So, he can do it all again? Doesn't make sense."

"Odd, innit? Although, I don't think he's doing any kind of trading, probably in charge of dusting the filing cabinet. You've got to remember the optics – family name, bank's name, investor confidence."

"Yes. Right, I see that. Seriously though, it's down as an official statement, that he'd been promoted and transferred to Singapore to run an entire department." She reads out the quote. "Here he is, described as a rising star. All that hope, all that dazzling brilliance, lost in a tragic accident."

Karl leans back, reaching in his pocket for another cigarette.

"Like I said, though – they'd already lost tens of millions, so they wouldn't want the whole bleedin' bank going down due to lack of confidence, would they? Best just cover up the unfortunate details and make out all was fine and dandy, wouldn't you say? Who's going to know any different? Only to me, he was a good mate, we had a lot of laughs, and I'd like to know what happened to him."

He lights the cigarette.

"So, how long have you known him, Karl? Since he bought the car from you?"

"Before that. He had the Harley, that's how we met, through mutual acquaintances, a biker gang if you want to call it that. We even had a biker trip in Thailand, of all places. I'll tell you a story about that if you like. We met this girl called Katty. Bit weird, bit creepy, but Vic was besotted. Anyway, one night we went to her brother's tattoo parlour in the arse end of Bangkok, sandwiched between a derelict warehouse and a brothel. I waited for him outside because I had this really bad feeling about it. Anyway, there wasn't another soul in that alley, not even a rat in a dustbin. It was like one of those scenes in *The Twilight Zone* where there's just nobody there at all, no one living, different dimension. Then when he came out, right? He was shaking, shivering, and muttering to himself like he'd got a fever or something.

"I'm like, 'You all right, mate?' Anyway, we go back to the hotel and he had black coffee after black coffee. But he was like just staring at the wall and jumping out of his skin every few minutes. I said, 'What happened? I thought you was just having a tattoo?' And he says, 'I've got a spirit with me now'."

"Pardon?"

Karl stubs out his cigarette.

"Yeah. That's what I said. Like, 'What the fuck?' So, it turns out they conjured up a dark spirit, and he made a contract. It would get him whatever he wanted and in return he would pay the price. Got to be honest with you, I don't think it's a good idea to mess with that kind of stuff, what you don't understand and all that. But that girl,

Katty, had some kind of hold over him, see? And he did seem to change after that."

"In what way? Psychologically? Emotionally? It seems more like mind games to me, than dark magic or whatever. And what was in it for her?"

"Good question, I don't know. But it's strange, because it was right after we got back that he started to take more risks, spend more money, go to casinos and the kind of clubs you need a password to get in. Bought the Porsche off me, like I said, six months old, hardly any mileage, for cash."

"A sort of Faustian pact…?"

He regards her thoughtfully for a minute. "I don't know about that, but now I come to think of it, he really did change. We hired a boat on the Thames for this massive party last summer, and he started going out with the most gorgeous women – vacant but beautiful, if you know what I mean? That's when the high life really started to crank up a gear. It did all happen after he met that girl, now I come to think of it. Almost as soon as we got back."

"How long ago was the holiday to Thailand?"

He shrugs. "Be early last year."

"So six months or so before he met Louise?"

He stares at her, pulls a face, shrugs. "Guess so."

"Did this Katty ever visit him here in London?"

"Few times, yeah."

He drains his espresso, and shoots another glance at the Black Shadow.

"Interesting."

"Probably completely irrelevant, though."

"I'm just wondering why his parents didn't help him financially? Obviously they're very wealthy. I mean, if he was in so much trouble he was scared?"

"They were the last people he'd go to. Never talked about them. He'd just be told to attend certain events and make sure he went. Mostly he'd be in a casino trying to win enough to keep the wolves off his back. Best way to describe the situation Victor was in, would be a black hole that kept getting bigger."

"But this is really key information. Really important. If he was in such financial peril, the kind he couldn't get out of, then there's a screaming motive for someone to have been threatening him. It throws a whole new light on the case."

Karl shrugs, shakes his head, shoots another quick glance at the Black Shadow.

Ingrid starts to smile at the obvious infatuation, when she realises he's still staring out of the window. Not at the bike, though. But across the street.

"Fuck!"

"What?"

"See that white van over there with blacked-out windows? He used to tell me but I never believed him. I thought he was going off his rocker…"

She follows his gaze to an unmarked white van parked a few spaces down the road, with what looks like an aerial on the roof.

"See the number plate? Be my witness and jot it down, will you? That's been parked outside my garage all fuckin' week. Wherever I go, so does it, like Mary's bleedin' little lamb."

"But why?"

They're both staring at it, when he says, "Don't suppose you'd mind holding both my hands in yours and gazing at me lovingly for a few minutes, would you?"

She does as he asks.

"Got to say I think you're making this up, though. Why on earth would anyone be spying on you? You only told the police and the press that he was in financial difficulties. And I can completely understand the decision not to publish anything to do with the bank. The legal ramifications to do with loss of confidence, or whatever, makes sense. But if Vic was indebted to someone threatening him, had colossal gambling or drug debts – well, that would shift the focus from a random tourist robbery to a targeted abduction or murder, and that's a criminal mat…"

She stops mid-sentence as the full implication hits her.

"Exactly," he says. "See, I think he was in major shit, don't you?"

She stares into his eyes for several seconds.

Someone has the power to silence the entire media, ensuring that the story be abandoned early with a topline summary, that the young couple were naïve, unlucky, and the police had no further information. When that really wasn't true. And that same person, or persons, could just as easily silence anyone asking questions or contradicting the narrative.

Outside of the main press corps, which has clearly moved on, here are the two of them working things out. Why would a possible murder be covered up?

She's still staring into his eyes, when a frisson of alarm catches in her stomach.

***

Chapter Fourteen

Karl suddenly leans forward and darts a kiss on her lips. With all the audacity of a cocky teenager.

For a second, she's too astonished to react. But, aware of the van parked outside that could have a zoom-lens trained on them, she hesitates only briefly before returning the kiss with a feather-light brush of her own. This charade, she thinks, should at least be convincing or what's the point? Besides, it's not unpleasant.

What would it be like to fall for a man like this? She imagines he doesn't like to answer questions, comes and goes as he pleases, roars off on a highly polished motorbike, his house little more than a place to sleep now and again. Yet intrinsically, deep-down, he is a soul with conscience, the warm, rhythmic pulse of his heartbeat a sonar wave resonating with hers.

"So, what was Vic like when he was with Louise? Were they in love, do you think?"

"I think we should hold hands for a bit longer, do you mind?"

She smiles slightly. "How long has the van been there?"

"Not long. I was checking the street every few minutes, you must have noticed?"

"Yes."

"Don't worry, I doubt they saw you scribbling."

"Hope not. Anyway, I'll have to believe they didn't or I'll be paranoid for the rest of the day. So, Louise then…?"

"Yeah, well to be honest with you, it was a shock seeing her at the wedding. I only knew about it a couple of days before. I remember calling him a sly old bastard. Barely remembered what she looked like."

"Hang on, so you never saw her in the entire time he'd been going out with her? Not once?"

"Not since the night he met her, no. That'd be in The Queen's Head, my uncle's gaffe, opposite where she lived."

"Yes. I'm just surprised if she was going out with him, your best mate, that you never saw her. So, what do you remember about the night they met?"

"Just that we was about to leave. Jan, that'd be my uncle, had called time, the bar was packed about four or five deep, and we was ready for off. Then Vic notices this blonde bird staring at him. Open invitation, basically, so we drank up and left him to it. I never saw her no more, although I knew her name – that'd he'd seen her a couple of times. I think one time I rang and she was in bed with him at the flat."

"But you never saw the two of them out together? At clubs or bars or parties? Not over Christmas? Nothing?"

He shook his head. "No, in fact he was seeing this other bird. Gawd, what was her name? Christina, that was it. And then there was Marsha whatserface, the one that went out with one of the royals, was in all the papers – legs thinner than what you'd see in your average bird's nest, sniffed a lot." He mimics snorting coke. "Anyway, he went skiing with her in Klosters last Christmas. So, you can imagine the shock when he first of all says he's getting a ball and chain, 'cause he was a man somewhat set in his philandering ways, and second, when I walked in and saw it was her. I mean, bleedin' hell! To be fair, I don't think I kept the smacked arse expression off my boat race for a good five minutes."

She squeezes his hands slightly before letting go to root around in her bag for a tissue, or a lip salve, or anything. Just a second or two to think. Blimey! Sheesh, this just got worse and worse for Louise, while at the same time it was highly intriguing.

"Oh, blimey! I don't think Louise knew about any of this."

He laughs. "Course she fuckin' didn't."

"So, what was it like at the wedding lunch? Wasn't it a bit awkward?"

"You could say that. But in the end, it's none of our business, is it? There was one of her mates, Ziva, I know she thought something was off. She just didn't know what. And nor did I. To be fair, Ingrid, I really didn't know what the fuck he was playing at. Do you want another coffee, darlin'?"

"Yes, please. Straight, no milk."

Every time the door opened, cold air breezes onto her back. The morning is grey, drizzly, and the strangest feeling of having stepped out of the known, sane world precedes her next question.

On returning to the booth, Karl puts down the two coffees and, taking full advantage of their watched situation, kisses her on the cheek before resuming his position opposite.

She laughs and shakes her head, then takes a sip, relishing the hot liquid burning down her throat.

"Is the van still there?"

"Yup."

"I hope it doesn't follow me."

"Not in a hotel all on your own, are you?"

"Few hundred others in there, as well," she says, a bit more sharply than intended. "So, what's your take on it, Karl? Why do you think Vic married Louise? I mean, that's the second thing doesn't make any sense."

"What's the first?"

"That the press didn't mention that someone with a grudge against him could have followed him to Thailand, and it could have been a targeted attack. You know that yourself. See, there's nothing about Vic's financial situation from the police, either, and I chased it up only yesterday. No further news. And nothing from the Embassy. Not even a whiff of speculation."

He doesn't take his eyes off her. "Cover-up. Obvious, innit?"

"Yes, as we said – probably to protect the bank or the family, or both. No digging allowed. Except, Louise got caught up in it."

"I feel sorry for the poor mare, to be honest. Don't you?"

"Yes. Very. And that brings me back to my question, Karl, because there just isn't a single credible explanation for that marriage. Nothing about it makes any sense to me, at all. First, he was seeing someone else. Secondly, he'd pretty much dumped Louise already. And finally, you'd think if he was being threatened by the kind of people who'd have him killed, he wouldn't have taken on the added responsibility of a wife. He knew they were watching him, that he drove a Porsche and went home to an expensive flat. Louise was a liability, really…"

Karl sighed heavily.

"What?"

"I sold the Porsche for him. Like I said, the proceeds barely scraped the surface of what he owed. He was just getting by from day to day."

"All right, so his pursuers didn't know that. But Vic did. Which begs the question, if he was about to abscond, why take on a wife? And why Louise? If she'd been the daughter of an oil baron or something, I could understand it, that it was for money. But Louise was almost penniless."

"I don't know, Ingrid. Like I said, I was so shocked when I saw the girl, it knocked the breath out of me. I mean, she's just a kid. If he was going to use someone, to say, I dunno, provide the optics, be part of some charade, why not pick any number of women who'd not be so… What's the word?"

"Innocent? Trusting?"

Something flickers behind his eyes. Possibly a glimmer of enlightenment, but it flares and dies.

"What?"

He shakes his head, sits back, and again glances out of the window.

"White van's pissing off. Looks like you're off the hook."

"Maybe they believed we're a loving couple. Blimey, my acting skills must be better than I thought."

He puts a hand over his heart. "Now, that's very hurtful, that is. Ingrid. I must say I feel very used, very hurt."

She laughs. "So, come on then – what's your best theory? Why did Vic marry Louise? Because I'm guessing he lost interest in her after a couple of weeks. I know that by Christmas, she thought it was over. Her friend at the clinic told me she worked the whole holiday, had taken to wandering around central London on her own, and was quite depressed about it all. Then out of the blue, he rings, sends her a huge bouquet of flowers at the clinic, takes her out to dinner, and proposes. He's going to Singapore and can't live without her!"

"Wanted to believe it, didn't she? Cinderella and her prince."

"Maybe, he really did love her?"

"No fuckin' way, mate. Sorry, but I've known Victor a very long time, and Nigel's known him since Eton–"

"Nigel! That would be…" She scrabbles for her notebook and flicks back to the conversation with Janice.

One of his friends at the wedding was really creepy… I wouldn't have trusted any of them… wide-boy Karl… and certainly not that Nigel.

"Nigel Scott-Renard?"

"Wily tart in the Foreign Office, Vic's best mate since they were about thirteen. You definitely wouldn't buy a used car from him, let's put it like that. I'm an angel, Ingrid, compared to Nigella."

Ingrid splutters and puts the cup down with a clatter. "We're talking about the same guy, are we? Married, lives in Chelsea with wife and children?"

"How many more Nigels do you know with the surname Scott-Renard who work in the Foreign Office and went to Eton with Vic Landry?"

She shrugs. Pulls a face.

"I call him Nigella because I happened to find out what he does to other people."

"How do you mean?"

"Collecting information on them, videos and photos. Concerning what they do for pleasure. Using said photographs later when they're in a position of authority. Making them do nasty things to innocent people. The little shit thought it was funny – I caught him bragging about it. Oh, gawd, you're looking at me like a little wide-eyed woodland creature. I don't have to start telling you about fetishes, orgies and rent boys, do I?"

"No. No, thanks."

"Good, 'cause whatever you can imagine, it's a helluva lot worse than that. I really don't want to be the one red-pilling you, Ingrid. But the world ain't what you think it is. There's ours, and then there's another one manipulating it. Like scriptwriters behind the theatre curtain."

Deep inside her stomach, there's another tug of unease.

"You mean blackmail?"

"People with dirty little secrets do what they want them to do later, don't they? By which time they've got very nice houses, titles, public office, and kids at private school. Their fall from grace would be a hard one. It's a long way down. Public disgrace, whole lot in the papers."

"And that's Nigel's job? To find the dirty secrets?"

"Enjoys it, too." Karl drains his coffee in one. "Nasty little fucker. Started crying when I gave him a slap, though. Said he'd close my business down. I told him, 'You try that and you won't be able to leave your house, mate!' Sort of called a truce after that."

"Hang on… 'Do what *they* want them to do later?' Who are 'They'?"

Karl reaches for his jacket.

"Look, I'm gonna have to shoot off. Got a meeting, could be lucrative. But if you want some advice, I'd say do yourself a favour and do not go sniffing round Nigel Scott-Renard. I might have given him a slap but I very much doubt I'd get the chance to do it again. He's what's known as a fixer. Deep inside the club. He crossed the line a long time ago, Ingrid. Seriously, take my advice and don't go anywhere near him."

She frowns.

"That girl, Ziva," he says. "She saw him for what he really was, like a laser beam. First time I've ever seen him squirm, to be honest. Pity you can't talk to her. Gone to Switzerland, I think she said?"

"Grenoble. French Alps."

He stands up, puts both hands on the table, and peers down into her face.

"My opinion, for what it's worth, is this – if anyone knows why Vic married that young girl or what happened out there in Thailand, it would be Nigel. Yet, he hasn't lifted so much as one tiny pinky to help find his old mucker. Not been interviewed, no boat race in the papers. So, you've got to ask yourself why, haven't you, Ingrid? Why didn't the press even knock on his door?"

***

Chapter Fifteen

It was a good question, and after he's left it's one that lingers. In fact, the whole conversation lingers.

It would be interesting to talk to Nigel Scott-Renard, though.

Should she try? Why not? The request could only be turned down. But while the mind is willing, intuition twists her stomach into a tight coil.

The world isn't what you think it is… He crossed the line a long time ago, Ingrid. Seriously, don't go anywhere near him…

She reaches for her bag, smiles at the waiter on her way out, and steps onto the now-crowded street.

Louise's dreamy smile floats into her mind as she walks, and the newspaper photograph of her at nineteen with both hands over her face. She'd told Janice about the abuse from Len Draper, but never mentioned it again, had instead yearned for life, for love, for escape. But what had she escaped to?

No, she can't just leave this. Vic could have been tracked down for any number of reasons, but Louise had been innocently caught up in something murky. Karl sensed it. Janice had sensed it. A girl from her hometown. A girl with no one to look out for her. She could still be alive.

Nigel Scott-Renard, though…?

She checks up and down the street for the white van with blacked-out windows, but it isn't there. Imagined or not? She bites her lip. If she approaches Nigel, it might flag her up as a trouble-maker, end up with the project being shut down, and achieve nothing. But there were other ways. What about Vic's colleagues at the investment bank, then? There'd been precious little about Vic's personality in any of the published articles, come to think of it. All the focus had been on The Golden Triangle, the supposed robbery, and how dangerous the area could be for tourists. *The Tourist Trap!*, had been the headline for Owen's sensational final piece, and to most people not looking beneath the surface, that was where the story ended.

She picks up pace, on what is a raw day with a stiff breeze coming off the River Thames. The story has, in fact, only just begun. In no way has Louise been given justice. This is not about a missing couple of tourists, it is not tabloid fodder, it is about Louise, and more than ever she has an inexplicable conviction she must find her. That if she lets Louise go, she somehow lets herself go, and every other innocent caught in the cogwheels of someone else's agenda – discarded as collateral damage, expendable, not important. But she was important, *is* important – she is a human soul.

So, why did Vic marry her? He hadn't even introduced her to his friends, let alone his family. Why the sudden turnaround? Something about the whole thing just doesn't feel right.

She cuts away from the wharf, heading towards Trafalgar Square and Soho, towards the hotel, deep in thought. The office intern is supposed to have been setting up an interview with Joanna Landry's PA, and she ought to ring in. But the conversation with Karl has opened up whole new set of channels. What about that girl he mentioned, Marsha Seabrook, the one Vic spent Christmas with at Klosters, while Louise was hanging around waiting for him to call?

Shit! She's missed a trick. Should have asked Karl for her details. She scrambles for her mobile and calls him straight back.

"Karl! Sorry, it's Ingrid again." There was a smile in his voice. "Ingrid! Bit forward, innit – chasin' me so soon?"

She laughs. "Very funny! Listen, I forgot to ask and I hope you don't mind. I think it was the white van thing that threw me off. But I don't suppose you'd know how I could get in touch with Marsha Seabrook, would you?"

He sounds out of breath, there's the click of a car unlocking, then, "Yeah, just a minute. Got a pen?"

"Yup."

She jots the number down, phone tucked under her chin while people walk around her in a parting of the waves

"That's the one I got, anyway. If she hasn't changed it. Today's Thursday, innit? You might be in luck – we used to meet her in The Phoenix just off the King's Road. About ten. Just offer to pay her and she'll talk to you, probably gibberish but bung her a pony and there won't be a problem, guaranteed. Bit of a habit to finance." There's the roar of an engine starting up. "Got to put you on hands-free now, darlin'."

"No problem. Look, the other thing is, do you know if any of Vic's former colleagues at the bank would be willing to have a chat?"

"Not off the top of me 'ead. Oh, hang about, come to

think of it you could try Fraser Dawlish."

"Fraser Dawlish? Why him?"

"On the edge of burnout, one of the eighty percent who don't make it on the trading floor. Fucked. He might talk. Look, take my advice and don't ring the bank, all right?"

"Sure."

He shouts above the road noise.

"He likes The Viaduct Tavern, if not tonight then tomorrow night. Early twenties, sharp suit, probably a blue striped shirt and a red tie to match his face. Looks like a chain-smoking, alcoholic choir boy. Curly golden hair, like a fat cherub. Anyhow, you get him well-oiled and I think he'll talk."

She can see Fraser very clearly.

"My half-crown's worth – he shouldn't be in banking, the poor little sod. So yeah, he'll be bladdered by eight. He's your best bet, anyhow. Yeah, I'd go for him if I was you!"

"Okay, I might try that, thanks. So, how do you know him?"

"Me and Vic had a few with him one night, had to throw him into the back of a cab. Poor geezer couldn't stand up no more. Dropped him off at Canary Wharf. And here's the long-abiding image I've got of him, Ingrid – of him sort of merging with the river fog, stumbling down the road. Got a flat down the Whitechapel end. Shame, innit, in a way? Poor sod."

She holds the phone away from her ear while he issues a stream of expletives, presumably to a driver who just cut him up.

"Yeah, and up yours as well, mate! Sorry, not you, darlin'! So, where was we?"

"No, I think that's it. Thank you."

"No problem. So, listen – call me when you're ready to commit properly, yeah? I'm not into one-night stands nor nothing."

She laughs. They both know she won't be taking up the offer, but on some level they've connected. He's helping her, seems genuine, a fellow truth-traveller, if only for part of the journey.

Dropping her mobile into her pocket, she weaves now through the burgeoning throng of tourists and shoppers, hurrying back to the hotel. And fifteen minutes later, she pushes through the revolving black-glass door, and takes the lift up to her room. The hotel is quiet, the bed has been made, bathroom cleaned, the hum of traffic beyond white net curtains, muted. It's a blessed relief to kick off her shoes and lock the door.

The room is a double with a small adjacent lounge, and after dropping her bag on the table, she orders room service before noticing the message light flashing. Holly, the office intern, has asked her to call back as soon as possible.

"Hi, Holly!"

"Hi, Ingrid. So, Joanna Landry is still in Los Angeles?"

Ingrid nods into the silence. There's more silence. "Yes?" she prompts.

"But we've just had a call, and her PA will meet you tomorrow?"

"Okay."

"Do you want me to give you the details for that?"

Obviously...

Ingrid bites her tongue. "Please."

Holly begins to talk about photographs being sent to the office and Vic's schooldays, and Ingrid stifles a yawn, can hardly wait to put the phone down. Itching to get on with the day. Because what's far more interesting is going way off-piste to talk to Marsha Seabrook, and find out what really happened with Vic last Christmas.

Bung her a pony and there won't be a problem. Guaranteed. Expensive little habit.

A pony. Was that five hundred quid?

"So, I'll give you a call tomorrow morning just to confirm? But it's eleven-thirty at the Bloomsbury, and Claudia will meet you in Reception."

"What? Oh yes, thank you. That's great."

Ingrid lies back on the sofa. Psyches herself up, takes a few deep breaths, then, deciding to seize the moment, rings Marsha. Who, incredibly, picks up on the first ring.

Sure, Ingrid can come to The Phoenix in Chelsea tonight if she wants, about nine.

Marsha's voice is a kirsch-dipped, chocolate truffle in biscuits kind of voice, gravelly, seductive and rich. "Get there a tad early, darling. And then we can talk before the girlies arrive. Bring the filthy lucre. And wear something delicious."

Ingrid's still smiling long after the call is over. And after Room Service arrives – a tray of chicken sandwiches, salad-garnished, chips, and a pot of coffee – she lies on the bed and considers what to wear to such a sophisticated place. The failsafe option? A sleeveless, short black tube dress, with black heels and a long black jacket over the top? Probably. She'll tie her long, dark hair into a high ponytail, and paint on cat-flick eyeliner, the overall impression professional, sophisticated, but kind of invisible, too. A uniform of sorts. Marsha, on the other hand, is a model – skinny, messy-haired and pouty – wears miniature slip dresses over bare legs, the just-got-out-of-bed look being her trademark. Let Marsha be the star of the show. Let Marsha relax in her company. And then just wait for the secrets to escape.

Bung her a pony and there won't be a problem, guaranteed...

Outside, there is a constant drone of road noise, almost hypnotic, and she closes her eyes. How will this go? What possibilities? Potentials? She tries to foresee the evening, to walk herself through it. The Viaduct Tavern in the City for about seven-thirty; after that, a cab to The Phoenix. Early, so she can talk to Marsha before her friends arrive. She smiles, quelling the fizzing inside. Something is going to happen tonight. Another revelation, more light on the path ahead. The one that leads to a secret, the thing being hidden that she knows is there. But what? First things first, though. She will need to look good, will have a long soak in the bath, take her time getting ready...

But just as her eyes close the idea comes: a visit to The Queen's Head and Karl's uncle, Jan Lozensky. He would have known Louise. And he certainly knew Vic.

What about fitting in a trip there first?

Something is going to change, possibly very quickly, and this chance may not come again. So what if she arrives as soon as it opens? When it's quiet, about six, before heading into the City?

Decision made, her eyes snap open and she jumps awake, momentarily disorientated. What had felt like a couple of seconds had actually been a couple of hours, and it's already four o'clock.

***

Chapter Sixteen

The scent of the trail is exciting. She could have spent the afternoon in the hotel spa, had dinner, then prepared for the trip home tomorrow. But she will not be taking the easy get-out clause, and deep down has always known it would be this way. Just as she also knows clarity will come. Currently, there is something obscured – like a shadowy figure distorted by a veil of fog and city lights, merging with the swell of the crowds. So far, there has only been a fleeting glimpse, the flicker of a ghost. But it's definitely there. A secret.

At just gone six, the cab drops her off at the north end of Regent's Park, opposite the corner to the nurses' home. Early evening is darkening with the gloom of impending rain, and her footsteps echo on the pavement. It seems eerily quiet, and briefly she's reminded of the character, 'Deep Throat', in the X-Files – a middle-aged man in a dark coat stepping out of a doorway, a black sedan drawing up behind.

Ingrid hurries across the road. Of course she isn't being followed. How stupid, how dramatic! She's really not that important. Even so, the street does seem strangely deserted. Oh, for heaven's sake, why is she doing this? She could have had an aromatherapy massage, then, after seeing the PA tomorrow, spent a couple of days writing the whole thing up from the comfort of her apartment. Invoice the features editor. On to the next job. She slows down, level with the oak door to the nurses' home. It's not too late to go back to the hotel. To change her mind.

The moment is a decision point. A second chance. Glancing up at the dark windows of the once grand regency building, she pictures how it might look inside – high ceilings, cast iron radiators painted brown, bare floorboards, and a communal dining room downstairs. The echoing clatter of a boarding school. No wonder, after the cloistered misery of her childhood, Louise had felt trapped, had grasped at whatever glittery threads of a better life she could find outside.

Oh God, Louise!

She draws in a long, deep breath. No, there can be no turning back – she has to try and find the truth. At least try.

On the other side of the street, she spots the inviting glow of a lamp inside The Queen's Head, and she crosses over.

The pub is empty apart from a young woman polishing glasses behind the bar.

"Is Mister Lozensky in today, please?"

"Who's asking?"

She introduces herself and goes to wait at a table by the window, sipping what is surprisingly good coffee while going through her notes, recapping, rereading.

"Ingrid, is it?"

She almost jumps. That keeps happening. Off she goes, squirrelling out of time and space into her own thoughts.

First impression – Karl Lozensky's eyes. Quite startling. Jan has the same narrow, green, watchful expression, same dusty blond hair, same pale skin and long, wiry limbs, although he's at least twenty years older than his nephew. Flipping round the wooden chair opposite, he sits with his legs astride it, arms resting on the back. Pellets of rain spatter against the frosted window panes, hard and cold, the lamps behind the bar casting a buttery glow across the wooden floor. Time stands still in this old pub, with its sepia photographs lining the walls, and bottle-green tiles around the fireplace. From out of the past, comes the boozy roar of a packed Saturday night, a rolling wave of tobacco, beer, and damp coats; the rapid draining of pint glasses, the bell calling Time.

"Yes. Thank you ever so much for agreeing to talk to me."

She gives her well-rehearsed spiel, and after a moment or two, he nods and asks if she'd like another coffee.

Ingrid prefers not to drink alcohol, largely because of what it did to her father. Every Friday night, wage night, he'd go straight to The Rose and Crown and spend most of what he'd earned, staggering home a different man to the one he'd been that morning. Her father didn't just get merry, a bit rowdy, or throw up, he changed character completely. He didn't know his own family; became irrational, dangerously angry and strange. They dreaded the thud of his body against the back door as he lurched in long after they'd gone to bed, shouting up the stairs. Maurice Houseman would drink until he had no more change left, until there was nothing left in the last beer barrel, until he was hurled out onto the street. She used to think it was just what being an alcoholic meant, but by the time she hit her teens, that view changed. There'd be a dark shape around him. 'Dad's shadow man', she called it.

"No, I'm fine thanks. You and Karl look very alike, by

the way."

"He's a very handsome boy, wouldn't you say?"

He roars with laughter at his own joke.

She can neither agree nor disagree. "You got me there."

"He said you were a bit of a looker, too. On your own here in London, are you? Need someone to show you round?"

She laughs again. They really are alike! And Karl had obviously rung ahead. Must have guessed she'd do a thorough job and check out his uncle.

"I'm going home tomorrow, but thank you anyway. Actually, I've been to London loads of times, just not to this neck of the woods. I really just wanted to ask, if you don't mind, if you ever met Louise Landry? I mean, with her living just over the road, she must have come in here with her friends? Ziva and Janice? You saw their photos in the papers, I guess?"

His eyes are glinting like those of a mischievous sprite. There's going to be some game playing, isn't there?

She shakes her head, smiles. "I believe it was around this time last year when she and Vic met. Do you remember anything? She'd have been with Ziva. Vic was with Karl and a few others."

"What's the accent, then? Yorkshire?"

"I didn't think I had an accent. Really? Is it noticeable?"

He roars with laughter again. "Come on, have a drink, Yorkie. What's your tipple? What do they drink up there?"

She raises her eyes to the ceiling. "Well, along with my copy of *Whippets Weekly* I usually sup pints of Tetley, but I'll settle for another coffee."

He signals to the girl behind the bar. "Bring a couple of coffees over would ya, Stella darlin'?"

"Thank you."

"It's just that you say *lasst*, and down here we say *larst*. Obvious you're not from London, innit?"

She laughs, thanking the barmaid for the coffee. "Fair cop! So, Jan… do you remember Louise, at all? Or anything about the night she met Vic?"

"Yeah, I do remember, as a matter of fact. She came in here a few times with that other gel – Ziva. Now, Ziva was a beaut! Glamorous like her sister. They used to go down Camden to the clubs. Can't say I noticed Louise, back then. I was just, you know, aware she was with the other two. But the night she met Vic – now, I do remember that. Him and Karl was with two geezers they was going down the West End with. Karl raises his hand above the crowd - they're going, right? I didn't much notice, mind, too busy, until we're calling Time and trying to kick everyone out. That's when I spot Vic sitting with Ziva's mate in the corner by the jukebox. I was surprised, to be fair, that Vic hadn't left with Karl, as the only reason Vic ever comes in here is because he's with Karl. Drops into see his dear old uncle Jan now and again, see? Anyhow, Vic and this little blonde gel seemed to be getting on pretty well. First time I looked at her proper, to be honest. Then after that she'd come in on her own a few times. Sit where you are now, waiting for ages sometimes, looking at her watch. Sometimes, he'd join her and sometimes not."

"Maybe this became their meeting place?"

"I'll tell you what I do remember. This one time she came in last Christmas – a couple of weeks or so before, anyhow, decorations strung up everywhere. Place was packed out, and she was just on her own by the window, not talking to no one, getting crushed by the crowd. I remember thinking she must be waiting for Vic again, but thing was, I knew for a fact he wasn't coming, because Karl had been in a couple of nights previous and said he'd gone skiing. I said, 'Oy, where's young Victor tonight?' And he goes, 'Had the summons. Gone to the family shindig in Klosters.' So, that poor gel didn't know, see? Just sat there waiting. Never saw her no more after that."

Ingrid frowned. "How well did you know Vic?"

He shrugged. "Just a bit of banter at the bar now and again. Him and Karl rode bikes, and I've got a Harley out the back, so it was a point of conversation. They had a laugh, pulled the birds. Vic went out with some right corkers. Both of them did. But that Christmas it must've been that one what's always in the papers – Marsha somebody?"

"Marsha Seabrook."

"That's her, gawd love her. Daughter of an earl or something, ain't she?"

Ingrid stares at him for a minute. So, the Klosters trip was actually a family party. Marsha must have known the Landrys pretty well? And he hadn't even bothered to tell Louise. This was more and more bizarre. He'd definitely dumped her, no question.

The pub is beginning to fill up, and Jan's attention flicks to the line of customers waiting at the bar.

"Okay, just one last thing, Jan. I won't keep you." She rummages in her bag for the photograph of Karl and Nigel Scott-Renard, that Janice gave her yesterday. "Do you know the guy on the left next to Karl?"

Jan takes it from her, scrutinises it.

"Can't say I do, and I'm very good with faces, Ingrid. Very good. No, never seen him before. Our Karl looks very handsome though, don't he? Don't he look handsome? Very good-looking our family is. A cut above, don't you think? Blessed with good Polish genes."

She laughs, agrees they're all very good-looking.

"No worries. Just thought I'd ask."

"Anything else I can help you with?"

She smiles and stands up. "No, but thank you ever so much. I really appreciate it. I've got to go anyway. Got another appointment."

"What, now? Where you off to, then?"

"Square mile. Meeting one of Vic's friends, hopefully."

"Well, mind how you go, won't you? From what I heard, he pissed off a lot of people. You want my opinion, someone followed him out there and did him in. I know Karl thinks so, too. Anyhow, you be careful, a slip of a girl on her own asking questions."

There is genuine concern in his eyes. Thanking him, she quells another flicker of unease, and moments later steps out into the London rain, pulls up her jacket collar and hurries towards the main road to hail a cab.

It seems increasingly likely that Vic was deliberately hunted down and killed, and Louise was just in the way. But that still did not explain why Vic married her in the first place. She wasn't in Vic's crowd and never had been, and she'd been dumped after a few weeks just like she thought. And Karl had been telling the truth – he didn't even know her.

Was that significant, though? Maybe what Karl and Jan suggested was enough? She's probably running blind up a dark alley with all this. Even so, it would be interesting to talk to Marsha. Was Marsha a family friend, or was she closer to Vic than the current-girlfriend status Karl and Jan had implied? It would be good to have a chat with her, anyway. Take it from there... She'd have done her best. And tomorrow, this whole thing could be wrapped up, and she'd be on the train home.

A black cab catches her in its headlights, is pulling into the kerb. Squinting into the rain, she flags it down and clambers in.

"The Viaduct Tavern on Newgate Street, please!"

"You from Yorkshire?"

"How on earth did you get my accent from that?"

Pulling out into traffic, the cabbie briefly eyes her in the rear-view mirror.

"Little hobby of mine – guessing where people came from in the first sentence."

"Like *Name that Tune*!"

"That's it, yeah. Got a Texan on the first two words tonight. Personal record."

Smoothing back her damp hair, she smiles. The rain is coming down in needles, forming a grey screen across Regent's Park, slashing at the windows. She wonders if anything Fraser Dawlish says will bring clarity to this story. Sometimes a breakthrough can be as simple as an impression, a throwaway remark that transforms the picture entirely, a single brushstroke of light on a dark landscape.

Or will it be Marsha?

So, I think you might hit on something no one else has.

You can learn something from everyone, she thinks. Nothing is ever wasted. Everyone plays a part, has a piece of the jigsaw, a perspective, and it only takes one of them to suddenly turn the entire thing on its head. And then everything will come together.

***

Chapter Seventeen

Fraser Dawlish is easy to spot. Karl's description was spot on – choirboy looks with curly fair hair and flushed cheeks, a pink cherub in a crowd of grey faces.

It has not been an unpleasant hour, people-watching in The Viaduct Tavern, soaking up the décor, the atmosphere. Reputedly haunted, the pub was built in the late 1800s on the site of what had once been a debtors' gaol, the old Giltspurt Street Compter, on the corner opposite Newgate Prison. From every window it had been possible to view the public executions, that graphic choice of entertainment the reason people drank there. It is, however, a strangely beautiful place, for all its macabre history. A former gin palace with an opium den on the first floor, it is all etched glass, polished wood, wall frescoes and chandeliers, with an embossed ceiling and an original ticket booth behind the bar. The atmosphere transports her swiftly through the ether, to a time when an openly debauched underworld seeped through the cracked veneer of upper-class respectability, in a purple haze of intoxication, bawdiness and lust.

What a fitting juxtaposition this place is, she'd thought, as more and more of Vic's life is being peeled away. Had he crossed the same invisible line as his Victorian forefathers, straying from the confines of sheltered comfort into a hard drinking and gambling world, infinitely more brutal, thinking he could still strut around safely?

Just before Fraser arrived, customer numbers had begun to swell and it crossed her mind he might not show up. After all, there was no guarantee. She'd been nursing a slimline tonic for a good hour, and one or two men at the bar had pointedly glanced her way. That's central London for you though, she thought: the difference between the City and everywhere else. It carries an electric charge, as if anything could happen in a heartbeat. It houses some of the most powerful people on earth, is a hub for the obscenely wealthy, and a magnet for the most talented, the most beautiful, the hopefuls and hopeless alike. Evil prowls with salacious glee. Into an eclectic hotchpotch of dreams and nightmares, side by side, the poison and the passion. The air buzzes. Fizzes. In the darkness, the hum of conversation, the clink of glasses.

But then, much to her relief, he had appeared.

Fraser heads straight to the bar, to its intricately carved gleaming wood, to all the glinting multi-coloured bottles and gilt-edged mirrors, to the smile of the blonde girl in a tight black dress pulling pints.

Ingrid takes another sip of tepid tonic water. Observing.

He sinks the first pint, before reaching for his wallet. He'll have another. Pulls out a packet of cigarettes. Hasn't even begun to calm down from his day yet. It's definitely him. Karl had described him perfectly. He's still a boy, really – flaxen hair, cut short but now curling around his ears as the evening drizzle evaporates; mid-twenties and already overweight, not looking after himself, drinking to sedate. She gives herself a mental ticking-off for assuming anything, for encapsulating his character before he's even had a chance to speak. He's onto a third pint already though, another cigarette in his mouth, packet of crisps in hand. Still wired, his shoulders are, however, finally slumping a bit and soon he's looking around the crowded bar for somewhere to sit.

Now, she thinks – now!

Instinctively, she pulls her mac onto her knee, the movement catching his eye. There's space for him to sit here, she's tacitly saying, while also conveying she could shortly be vacating, perhaps waiting for someone who hasn't turned up yet. A professional woman, polite, not looking for a pick-up. It's safe.

"Anyone sitting here?"

"No, not at all. I'm just waiting."

Fraser sits, eats the crisps, tips the packet of remaining crumbs into his mouth, then drains his pint and nods towards the bar.

"Can I get you anything?"

"Um, no thanks." She holds up the quarter of a glass she still has left. "I'm good, but thank you."

He comes back with another pint and a whisky chaser.

Patiently, she waits, occasionally peering round at the door. The cacophony of the crowd is near deafening, quite hypnotic.

"Your friend not coming?"

"Doesn't look like it, does it? It's okay, not a problem." She drains the tonic. "I'll probably head off home in a minute. I don't suppose you can recommend a good takeaway, can you? Only I'm not from London, just here for the day."

They chat easily, comfortably. He fetches another pint

from the bar, another chaser, plus an orange juice for her. And it isn't long before he's telling her how he hates his job. How he wanted to be a musician but his parents told him there was no money in it, that he had to make something of himself; and for a while she's drawn into his story, can feel the eternal struggle between the logical mind and the passionate soul. He has never been allowed to be himself, she can see the built-up pain. One day it will rush back into his heart and it will hit him that he must find a way back, or... A brief, unbidden image appears before her eyes, of a body floating face down in the river, splayed-out raincoat, sodden flaxen hair, and immediately she dissipates it.

Their eyes lock, and for a moment there is a connection.

"So, what about you?"

She's working on a back story, she tells him, about a missing couple, Vic and Louise Landry. He's probably read about it in the papers?

There! She's said it.

Fraser doesn't flinch. Knocks back the chaser.

"Back in a bit. Just getting another."

When he returns, she tells him she's interviewed Louise's stepfather, plus a few friends, and that there's just one more she needs to talk to, a girlfriend of Vic's before he was posted to Singapore.

"It's the family and friends angle," she explains. "Not investigative, although in a way I wish it was, because then I could go to Thailand." She laughs. "It's such a shame for them though, isn't it? I mean they're just married, living out in Singapore, him given a new job at the bank. They'd only just begun."

Fraser nods. A deep raspberry-stained flush is creeping

up his neck. He swills the whisky round and round in the glass, staring into it.

"He wasn't given a new job," he says quietly.

Her eyebrows shoot up.

Really?

"Wasn't he? Oh, sorry. I must have got that wrong, then."

"Like everyone else. I don't know why all that was in the press. He was actually sacked. Ages ago. Before last Christmas. I work at the same bank he did, so I know."

Sacked?

For a second, she's stunned.

"For real? But–"

"I know, it said in the papers, blah-blah-blah! I probably shouldn't have told you, but to be honest, who gives a fuck? You don't know who I am, don't know my name, and I'd deny it anyway."

She laughs and answers truthfully.

"No, don't worry. It's not in my remit to interview anyone from his work."

"I'm not surprised. No one was allowed to speak to the press or the police. We were told it was being handled officially and anyone caught… well, you get the gist. Anyway, when the story came out, everyone sort of just looked at everyone else. Like, you know, what the fuck?"

"So why was he sacked, if you don't mind me asking? Don't worry, it's completely off-record. I can't write any of this up and the magazine wouldn't print it, anyway. Guess I'm nosy, that's all."

Fraser stares into his whisky, seems unsure. But there's something else he's battling, and she's just trying to work out what it is, when he knocks back the chaser and turns to face her.

"Oh, what the hell? Unauthorised trading. He used to do fuck-all every day, if you want the truth. Lazy, smirking twat who did loads of illegal shit. I knew him and a mate of his for a while, and I could be wrong but I don't think so. He got that job on account of his dad, a favour to Sir Max Landry, and in the end they had to bail him out to the tune of millions. What a mistake, eh? Can't imagine that going down very well in the Gentleman's private club, can you?"

Fraser's anger is palpable, a release of pent-up rage and injustice burning into her eyes.

She looks away.

Rain is blurring the windows, the bar steamy with wet coats, wet hair.

Vic, she has a strong feeling, had begun to think of himself as invincible. She can picture the self-satisfied smirk, the swaggering image he'd projected; and yet the reality was so very different, the hole he'd dug a deep one, an abyss without light. He could not get out. And the rats down there were big. Not angry, disgruntled youngsters, but big, fat old ones with thick, leathery hides and yellow teeth. Suddenly, Karl and Jan's theory begins to fall away. Why would an angry creditor have Karl watched?

Fraser continues to talk, a stream of consciousness, while she listens, half numb.

He was actually sacked. Ages ago. Before last Christmas...

Oy, where's young Victor tonight? Had the summons. Gone to the family shindig in Klosters...

At half eight she makes her excuses, gives Fraser's arm a squeeze and kisses his cheek, before wending through the crowd to the door, and stepping back onto Newgate Street. Through a wash of drizzle, there is a surreal moment, a brief, heart-lurching trick of the eye, when the old prison appears before her, and on the gallows is a face-covered executioner poised with a raised axe. Holding it high. There's a roar from the jostling, jeering crowd, a woman in a white mop cap elbows her way to the front, eyes gleaming. And then the image is gone, the baying mob merging into clear rain-lashed tarmac.

Nothing there.

Still partly numb, the enormity of what Fraser has just disclosed hasn't yet settled. And it's only when she's inside another black cab heading downriver, that it truly hits home. Not only had Vic been sacked and the papers not reported that, but Karl hadn't known, either, which meant Vic had lied to his best friend. Why? Either that, or Karl had lied to her? No, that didn't make sense. Or why would he have thrown her a line with Fraser? Fraser didn't like Vic, that was obvious, and Karl would have sniffed that out, had probably witnessed Vic putting him down, laughing at him. An inferior. A loser. There really was only one answer. Karl hadn't been his closest friend, at all.

Take my advice and do not go sniffing round Nigel Scott-Renard…

Fine sheets of rain are blowing across the windscreen from the Thames, as the cab heads towards Chelsea.

Too Much Too Young, by The Specials is on the radio, and the cabbie turns it up, singing loudly, "You've done too much… much too young…"

Poor Fraser. For a while she worries about him. She does this, she realises; soaks up other people's emotions, problems, struggles. His parents had pushed him into the most unsuitable career imaginable for his kind of personality. Seriously though, she thinks, will people ever stop pushing others into lives they cannot live? Trying to mould them to suit themselves and their own ideas of what other people should be? Her reflection stares back at her, a ghostly face in the amber glow of city lights.

She ought to know.

"There's no money in the arts," her dad had said.

Oh, how badly she'd wanted to go to art college, to work in fashion and textiles. It was in the blood, both her great grandmother and late grandma talented seamstresses. But the mills were closing and that's all her dad could see. And so, she'd stopped painting, and taken the first suitable job that came up, on the local paper, in the advertising department, age eighteen. He wasn't going to keep her. She'd to find work. Shortly after that, he'd said since she was now earning, she could find a place of her own, and the mouse-trap sprang shut. It had been a struggle for a while, with going to night school as well, but in the end it didn't matter. She enjoyed what she did and had done well, although sometimes she could see herself living that other life, the one she'd really wanted to create. Certainly, she could understand how Fraser had got into such a mess.

Not that Fraser's mess was in the same league as Vic Landry's. Effectively, what he'd done was siphon off vast amounts of money and lost it. Had gambled it away, spent it, squandered it. And what of all the other people he owed money to? No job. Reputation ruined. No income. He really couldn't come back, could he? Had his family disowned him? Yet, he'd spent Christmas with them, and that was after he'd been sacked. After! Were the investor names among family friends, as well as the owners of the bank? No wonder none of them were at the wedding.

She begins to spiral down into the complexity of the

mind, into the fog of confusion. When Simply Red comes onto the radio with *Money's Too Tight to Mention*, she almost laughs at the synchronicity. He was a lad in trouble, that's for sure.

The rain is coming down hard now, pelting on the roof, bouncing off the pavements, the cab standing in nose-to-tail traffic.

"Phoenix off the King's Road, you said, didn't you, darlin'?" the cabbie shouts above the noise of the rain, the music, and the hum of the heater.

"Please, yes! No rush."

He laughs. "No kidding."

A biker whooshes past, weaving in and out between buses and cars, jumping up the kerb, riding the pavement.

"Bladdy lunatic! Total madman!"

Bubbles of rainwater chase across the side window. The list of questions planned for Marsha is going to have to change. She pulls out her notebook, squinting at it in the half light, crossing out a few questions, adding new ones. A little fizz bomb is beginning to spark and pop inside her stomach. Marsha is the daughter of an earl, had been invited to spend Christmas with the Landrys. She drinks, parties, and snorts cocaine. And if Fraser is correct and Vic was sacked, then Marsha will know. She'll also know he'd been bailed out by the bank, people who were his father's friends. Tens of millions. So, what had his family's reaction been? Did she know he was treading water, robbing Peter to pay Paul, selling his possessions, had to leave the country? Did she know about Louise?

And what about Nigel Scott-Renard? Does she know him?

She underlines his name.

The answers existed. A crucial connection. It was just a matter of finding them.

***

Chapter Eighteen

"Darling, he was only there for a couple of days. Persona non grata as usual. I don't know what you people want to know, really."

Shock number one. Vic was only at Klosters for a couple of days! Really? Ingrid makes a mental note: quite definitely, all the newspaper reports said he'd 'spent the annual Christmas holiday with family and friends at a private gathering in Switzerland'. She's read them enough times, gleaned every extract of information, and cross-referenced for contradictions between each media group, finding none.

Marsha Seabrook is a work of art, a wayward child with mussed-up hair, pouty lips and baby-perfect skin. She is also wispy-thin, the silk blouse she's wearing with velvet boot-legs, undone to the breastbone, no curves. Lean and lithe. Straight up and down. Kind of like a teenage boy, Ingrid thinks, if it wasn't for the baby girl face with long, fluttery lashes. She is also not remotely grounded. Marsha's pupils are hugely dilated, and the frequent sniff, together with erratic movements – she jumps up mid-sentence and gesticulates wildly to elaborate on some story or other, without inhibition, without awareness – suggests she's already high on cocaine. Ingrid can see the young child in her, the performances put on for adults, dancing, singing, making up plays in the family drawing room; and can't help but like her. She's the best friend at school with juicy secrets and inside information, the one who leads others into terrible, terrible trouble; enchanting, exciting, yet completely without substance. Confetti in the wind. Whisked away in a black Bentley, leaving those who followed her with wrecked grades and shattered futures.

They're drinking mojito cocktails in an exclusive bar, one that requires a password at the door. Ingrid has virtually no idea where she is. After less than half an hour at The Phoenix, Marsha had said she was bored, and there'd been little choice but to run after her onto the street and follow her into the back of a cab. This bar, plush, with dark red velvet seats and black glass tables, is a softly lit cavern, each floor connected by a spiral staircase. There are marble pillars, crystal chandeliers, squishy sofas, and private, curtained booths. There's even a swimming pool in the basement. And in the darkly opulent bathrooms, the tiles glint with quartz, the taps are gold, the surrounding mirrors a hall of reflected lights.

Her hair is now down, jacket cast off. Nirvana blasts *Smells like Teen Spirit* through the bar, and she resolves to stay sober, to not, absolutely not, follow Marsha down the dizzy corridor of temptation. She hadn't meant to stay out this long, much less succumb to alcohol, and should have made her exit long ago. But something about Marsha is mesmeric, an irresistible mixture of elfin-wicked and completely disarming.

On the table between them is a bottle of Moet and two champagne flutes. The night, it seems, is young.

"I spent a lot of time in Northern Thailand, by the way! You know – the place where our two lovers went missing?

Do you want me to tell you about it?" Marsha's voice is surprisingly loud, booming and molasses-thick. "It's quite all right, it's not like anything I say will ever be printed. Everyone thinks I'm totally mad. Oh God, do you think there are actually any waiters in here?" She waves her hands around in the air. "Hey! Hi! Anyone! We need someone to come and open our champagne!"

Ingrid laughs, grabs the bottle and pops open the cork. "When were you out there?" she asks, pouring froth into the glasses.

Northern Thailand had been shock number two.

"Oh gosh, it was aeons ago. I must have been about eleven or twelve or something. Had a holiday with the uncle. You must remember, it was in all the papers – he was gunned down?"

"Yes, vaguely. Local bandits, wasn't it? Would that have been Nathan?"

Marsha grabs her Chanel bag, a cerise padded-leather clutch, and pulls out a packet of cigarettes.

"Smokies?"

"No, thanks."

She lights up, blows a plume of smoke at the starlit ceiling, before replying. "Uncle Nathan, yah! It was an inside job, of course. The local bandits thing was just a cover story, but you must know that, right? I can remember swimming in his amazing turquoise pool, in a palace with giant Buddhas everywhere, gold pillars, marble sunken baths and a view of the mountains. There were these tiny little geckos on the wall, with beady black eyes and miniature fingers and toes. It was just me and him, you know? That was odd, don't you think? Just me and him on holiday together? Miles from anywhere?"

She narrows her eyes while taking another drag of the cigarette, regarding Ingrid through a haze of smoke.

"Apart from the staff, of course. You know, the masseurs…"

She pauses, watching Ingrid's reaction. Which is when shock number three begins to sink in. Is Marsha telling her she was abused?

"Anyway, yah, he was shot. After that, the firm, the family that is, had the special services drafted in, you know – to protect what was ours?"

The question does not require an answer and Ingrid nods again, pretending she understands, but doesn't, not really. Just let Marsha talk, she thinks, while she's on a roll. That she's part of a much more powerful, affluent family than her official bio suggests – daughter of a wealthy Swiss financier – is becoming clearer by the minute. Marsha refers to heads of state, royals, and various dukes and lords as, 'Uncle Frosty,' or 'Piggy Trotters'.

Shock number four would be, 'They had special services brought in'.

They!

And what was it that was theirs in that part of the world? She presumes Marsha means land. But wasn't that part of Thailand wild and mountainous, notorious for opium trading? She vaguely recalls reading about Khum Sa, a drug baron and gun-runner.

"I wonder if Vic and Louise got caught up in something like that? I mean, your uncle was shot in the same area they went missing. Well, that was the assumption in the media. Owen Roth did a huge thing on it. I suppose it's possible," she posits, hoping Marsha will dispute it and run with another thread. But she's floundering. "Maybe they were caught in the middle of something? Like your uncle?"

Marsha continues to observe her as if she couldn't possibly be that stupid, downs half a glass of champagne and refills it. "Come on, Ingrid, you're not drinking enough, darling. We can hardly have you remembering what I've said now, can we?"

Ingrid laughs.

"Not that it would get printed, like I said. I can say whatever I like."

Ingrid laughs again and takes a tiny sip of champagne. "To be honest, I'm just speculating. Like everyone else, that's all it is – hot air."

Marsha nods and Ingrid is seized with a moment of panic. Marsha's about to switch into bored mode. She could up and vanish in a flash.

Leaning forwards, she ups the energy in her voice. "I'll tell you what I really do find puzzling though, and I would like to get this right for my article if you don't mind, and it's why Vic would only stop over at the ski resort for a couple of days? Why two days and not the full holiday like the rest of you? And also, you've been cited as his girlfriend, yet a few weeks later he proposed to Louise." She takes another tiny sip of champagne. "Just seems odd."

"Oh, Lord! No one had even heard of the woman."

Ian Curtis is singing *Transmission*. It feels incongruous in the opulent surroundings, and automatically Ingrid is transported to her hometown, to the smoky, grimy, heart-pumping backstreet pubs and clubs. She can almost see him on stage, with his eyes closed, his whole body shaking, and her soul aches a little. What the hell happened to Ian Curtis? There was a double life going on there, too… wasn't there?

"No one? Not even his family? So, Vic just turned up in Klosters for a couple of days, then vanished back to London, and no one asked why? He didn't even mention it was to go back to Louise?"

She's blagging, but Marsha has gone suddenly gone quiet and, if anything, seems mildly, faintly, amused. But not hugely interested.

"Give me a minute will you, sweetie?"

Before she leaves for the bathroom, however, she leans over and kisses Ingrid full on the lips.

The shocks keep coming.

And when Marsha returns, it is to dive onto the sofa opposite, once again colourful and dramatic, a leading lady revived and restored, back in costume and ready for centre stage. The bar is filling up now, though. If she doesn't ask about Nigel Scott-Renard soon, she might not get another chance. How to phrase it? What to say?

But Marsha hits the floor running and there's no time to think.

"So, you wanted to know why Vic flew in and out for just a couple of days, yah? Well, he was summoned, darling! Summoned! He didn't *want* to be there. But when you've sort of pissed off your parents, I mean they arranged for him to be at that investment bank, you do know that, because he was completely hopeless, absolutely hopeless? And there he was, siphoning off people's money from all sides, even making up company portfolios. Terribly clever and tremendous fun while it lasted. Vic knew how to throw an amazing party. We once had this jaunt on a yacht moored off the coast of Corsica, for a week, and he paid." She shrieks with laughter. "There were seventy of us. Seventy, darling! Can you imagine a yacht that size? Full staff and plenty of ice…"

Ingrid smiles a frozen smile, now realising just how Vic had got through so much money. Perhaps he was insane? Wasn't there a condition where people thought they were hugely rich, hugely lucky, that there was no limit to what they could get away with? Not delusions of grandeur but something else, well documented… She'd have to look it up. So, that was how he got himself into such a mess, anyway.

"I think Joanna had to be bloody quick off the mark with transferring all his assets and setting up trusts, so he didn't squander the entire family fortune. He was far naughtier than me. On the naughty step for months… and months… Properly spanked, and spanked jolly, jolly hard." She laughed, snorting champagne down her nose. "Sorry, but that's actually incredibly funny."

It's a while before she stops giggling.

"Anyway, anyway, listen… so, they summoned him. Summoned."

She seems to find the word, 'summoned' hilarious, can hardly speak for mirth spurting out in bubbles.

"So, there he was. *Summoned*. Told what's going to happen by the frightful overlords. It was all worked out. I think they'd come to some sort of arrangement between them. The old reptiles making him pay the price. There's always a price, don't you think?"

"So, he wasn't sacked, then? Someone said he was."

"Of course he was sacked – the silly tart lost them squillions and they hate that, made them look like complete fools. Not only that, but he had half of the rough arse of London looking for him, as well! It was bedlam, darling." Marsha was talking in rapid-fire, without prior thought, animated, excited. "I think the old guard had a lot of clearing up to do, paying people off just to stop them from killing him. Everyone wanted to murder him. Anyway, you mustn't ask me anymore."

She lifts her hand to wave at a clique of people who've just arrived.

"Listen, darling. Marsha's friends are here now." She leans over, her nose almost touching Ingrid's. And then kisses her again, on the lips.

Shock number five. Or was it six? Or seven? Ingrid doesn't know what to do or how to react, except to keep perfectly calm and still. She would soon slip out of here like a cat burglar into the night. But there's just one more burning question before Marsha's friends come over. Well, two things…

"Marsha? I just wondered–"

Marsha kisses her again.

"You taste delish."

"Um, thanks, um… Look, Vic was pictured at Klosters with a woman described as his girlfriend who they said was you. There's a photograph on the slopes where he's got his arm around a woman in a fur coat and hat, but she has her back to the camera and I remember thinking how short she was, tiny, whereas now I've met you, I can see you're very tall. Taller than me. I've only just realised."

"Poor darling Ingrid. No, I've never been his girlfriend, I'm not that way inclined, as you must surely have guessed?" She pouts. "No, he brought his Thai girlfriend again. Kitty or Katty or something."

Katty! Shock number seven or eight, or was it nine?

Ingrid doesn't flinch. Takes one tiny last sip of champagne. It does little to quench her thirst, sugary and sweet, cloying and heady.

"Ah! I see, thank you. Okay, well the very, very last thing, I promise. Do you know his other friend, Nigel? The one who was at his wedding?"

Marsha draws back sharply. "Oh, you mean Nigella?"

"Um…"

"That's what they called him, you know?" She glances over to the crowd at the bar, waves with both arms over her head. "Over here!" Then looks back at Ingrid, as if she's forgotten who she is. "Oh, yes. Yes, he used to lurk around the… Oh, never mind. Hey, come over to the party on Saturday if you like? I'll give you the address. Hang on a mo, let me find something to scribble on."

A woman approaches, bounces onto the sofa next to Marsha, then pushes her back against the seat, hugging and kissing, play-fighting.

Good grief, Ingrid thinks, are all of them high?

"For pity's sake," Marsha says, "stop it, I've got to give this woman an address."

This woman…

"Here you go!" Marsha says, handing her a scribbled-on bit of paper. "About nine or so, and bring a friend if you like."

"Thanks. That's really kind of you. So, do you know where I could find Nigel?"

There, it's out. Blunt as you like in the end.

"No idea. I can't stand the man. Something slimy in the corridors of power – what you might call a fixer. He was certainly close to Vic, though."

"What you might call his handler, more like," says the woman with her arm around Marsha.

"Shush!" says Marsha. "We're sure we don't know what

you mean, do we, Ingrid?"

Ingrid shrugs, smiles, and truthfully says, "Positive. Anyway, thank you ever so much for the drinks, Marsha. It's been a pleasure."

"See you Saturday and don't you dare not show up!"

By the time Ingrid steps out of the club's dark womb, into the sobering reality of a deserted rain-lashed street, it's gone eleven. Time has vanished and her head's spinning from one mojito and a few sips of champagne. How Marsha can function is beyond comprehension.

Thankfully, the rain has now stopped and a brisk wind has whipped up, blowing cold and wet off the Thames. Deep in thought, she automatically sets off in the direction of what she hopes is a main road, from where there should be a few cabs sailing by. Hers are lone footsteps, her mind busy stitching together information – trying to make sense of it all, to get a picture of what it is to be in the wild, wild wood of Marsha Seabrook's world. But her head is a dizzy swirl and all she can see is Vic's arm around a tiny figure in the Swiss Alps. A tiny woman in a full-length fur coat and hat. Katty. Marsha had been invited anyway, she wasn't with Vic and never had been, she was a family friend. Vic had actually been summoned to attend. Gone after two days. After he'd been dealt with.

Told what's going to happen by the frightful overlords...

Of course, he was sacked...

Nigel... oh, you mean Nigella... what you might call his handler...

Oh, Lord! No one had even heard of the woman.

By the time she realises she's lost, it's to find herself in a residential square. Here, the houses are white and regal, several storeys high with iron railings enclosing steps to the basements, steps up to imposing front doors, and long sash windows. Some are lamp-lit, chandeliers glimmer from upper rooms where curtains are open, and there's an air of hushed, established wealth, a discreet purr of luxury. It isn't clear where this is but she assumes Kensington and Chelsea, and heads north accordingly, towards Kensington Gardens. It will all become clear soon – the taxi ride with Marsha hadn't been far, so her bearings can't be too far out. It is, however, extremely quiet, with no sound of distant traffic.

Her footsteps click-click on the tarmac as she turns corner after corner, until eventually a road appears ahead, which should lead to Sloane Square, but doesn't. This is Mayfair, east of Kensington Gardens, and the road is a minor one. For a minute or two, she's completely thrown. Well, at least now she knows where she is. Besides, walking all the way back to the hotel wouldn't be such a bad idea. It will clear her head.

At that exact moment, however, a voice carries on the night air. With a name that stops her dead.

Upcoming, on the right, is the sort of establishment that previously only existed on the periphery of her imagination; something she had thought barely real, belonging to another time, another world. The building spans three Georgian town houses, is several floors high, and a discreet green canopy shelters a central door, with wrought iron railings running the entire length on either side. And it is on drawing level with a darkened garden area, that she hears the conversation. At the sound of the name, her heart bangs wildly, the breath paralysed in her chest.

Through the gaps in the trees, two men are standing together in the shadows of the lawn, behind them a lamplit room, French doors closed behind them.

Vic Landry!

The first voice is an ice-cold blade, the kind that slices into the heart with sickening precision.

"He has done it, though?"

The second is weighted with squirming terror. This man, she knows instantly, is subservient. Weak with fear.

"Well, bit of a glitch…"

There's a pause then, a holding of breath. She can almost see their eyes search each other's, as each realises at the exact same moment, they've been overheard.

***

Chapter Nineteen

There's no option. It's instinctive.

Quietly, swiftly, Ingrid resumes walking, quickly picking up speed. Alas, the chop of her heels resounds like gunfire, at least to her own ears, ricocheting around the empty square. There are other people here, behind the lamp-lit windows. This is a sane, modern world, she has only to call out and they will see her.

Local bandits was just a story, darling.
He's what you might call a fixer.
I can say anything I want and it won't get printed…
Oh, dear God – what really happened to Louise?

Level now with the green canopy, a movement catches her eye and she glances up the steps, just as the door to the club opens – into a gilt-edged, dark interior of polished oak panelling, Tiffany lamps and oil paintings. An old-style gentleman's club, with discreet personal service and the hush of privacy.

Hurrying past, she repeatedly reassures herself. There's nothing to worry about. To them, she was just an unknown woman walking past. No threat to anyone. Even so, her breath lodges like a small stone in her chest, unease creeping up her spine.

At the end of the building, there's a continuation of wrought iron railings between the club's private lawns and the street. In between the branches of the yew trees, she glances into the shadows, convinced someone's there, keeping abreast. Her footsteps click-click-click smartly towards the street corner, where briefly she pauses to glance at the road name. This isn't quite where she thought it would be, there should be a main road here. So, which way? To the left, there's another long, dimly-lit residential street that must head north. Ahead lies another tree-lined square. Best to go straight over, still heading west.

It is only the most fleeting hesitation, however, no longer than a second, when out of a side entrance, from under the arch of an iron gate, a man suddenly rushes from out of the garden, swings her around and pins her to the railings, both of them spreadeagled in star-shapes. It happens so fast, the breath is knocked clean out of her.

Instantly, he slams a hand over her mouth, the hard bones of his kneecaps pinion hers, a steel grip clamping both wrists in one movement. Malt whisky and a musky, aromatic aftershave waft into her face. But he's not looking at her, his face isn't scanning hers at all. And it is only then, on the periphery of her vision, that she sees the other man. The one with his hands in his pockets, standing in the umbra of the shadow.

The man ramming her into the railings is waiting for approval, jeering and triumphant. She is his prey, a sport, a joke. Look what I caught! Maybe, it's some kind of loyalty test? Either way, she is nothing. Collateral damage. To them, not even human. And all these possibilities run through her mind in the split second it takes to recognise who the other man is. There is no mistake. It is absolute.

The horror is a gut punch, her reaction a blur. She throws her whole body weight forwards and chops down on his forearms. And in the split second of surprise, the man's grip is broken, the smirk still half on his face as he staggers backwards. He is, it seems, pretty drunk, or his reflexes would have been faster, and seizing the momentary advantage, she turns and runs flat out.

She does not look back but sprints towards the residential square opposite, pauses briefly to kick off her shoes, then continues running, over the next road, over the next, the thud of the pavement pounding into her joints, not stopping until a stitch tears at her muscles, and finally, thank God, the amber wash of a main arterial road appears ahead.

And only then, by the side of the wet tarmac road, does she double over for a couple of seconds, gasping for breath, before continuing on, still gripping her side. How crazy must she look, in the heart of sophisticated London, sprinting in her stockinged feet as if the devil himself is on her tail. It's lucky, really lucky, there are no passing onlookers to stare or laugh, no horde of drunken men to leer and catcall. Couples to turn away in disgust. She checks her overactive imagination, calming herself enough to notice the street name on the corner. Grosvenor Street. Nowhere near where she thought, then. But there's a black cab heading south, and she dashes into its lane, waving urgently, not even noticing the vacancy light is off.

But he stops.

Thank God, thank God, thank God…

She wrenches open the door, slams it shut behind her, and slumps onto the back seat, her voice broken and tearful, not her own. Not her own, at all. This can't be her.

"Malmaison, please. Charterhouse Square."

As the driver swings the cab around in a U-turn, the

dimly lit street she's just run down flashes past. The street is empty, quiet, and dark. But just for a moment she fancies there are shadows shifting among the trees, separating from doorways, creeping along the walls of the houses.

The other man was Nigel Scott-Renard.

But it's only fleeting and she turns to face the front, staring into oncoming headlights, the sound no longer her own panting, her own heart thudding, but the comforting hum of an engine, and tyres swishing through puddles. Unable to stop herself though, she peers over her shoulder once more. Nothing. Only darkness. Closing in around them as if what had just happened, never had.

It was Scott-Renard. The one with his hands in his pockets, the one with the voice like a lethal shard of ice.

"You all right, Miss?"

"Yes, sorry." She's not. She wants to cry, but blinks away the tears, wanting only to get back to the hotel, to concentrates on that, to feel the safety of its lights and warmth and normality. "Sorry. I got lost and took a wrong turn, it spooked me out a bit, that's all."

"You ought to be careful."

"I know. I didn't realise. Thought I was south of Kensington Gardens but I wasn't."

"You don't know London, then?"

"Not well, no."

"You from Yorkshire?"

She sighs, almost laughs. "Yes."

And just like that the raw terror dissipates, like a bad-tempered storm rolling over the moors, nothing more now than a distant grumble, retreating from whence it came.

Ingrid leans back against the seat, only now aware of her damp, wild-looking hair, smudged mascara, ripped tights, and the shiver spreading across the back of her shoulders in a cold sweat. It ripples in a freezing breeze, she's shaking all over, hugging herself, must close her eyes for a few minutes.

It was Nigel Scott-Renard.

And there's no doubt they were discussing Vic Landry. But the man's voice! Even before the flash of his eyes had lasered into hers – intelligent, knowing, cruel – there had been that utterly chilling voice. She replays the scene, questioning herself, doubting the clarity of her memory, but she is not mistaken. It was him. Those were his eyes.

After Janice had handed over the photograph of him and Karl, she'd examined both of them for a while, realising in retrospect how difficult it had been to look at Nigel for long. He hadn't photographed well, she'd thought originally, seemed slightly out of focus. He had a receding hairline with a distinctive widow's peak, straggly dark hair brushed back from a long, bony face, the skull brutally angular. Those features alone would have set him apart, but it was his eyes that burned onto the mind. There was something oddly inhuman about them, deep-set in shadowed orbits, glinting and coal black. They were very, very hard to look into. Gaze too long into the darkness, she thinks, and eventually it gazes back. It sees you, recognises you. Will find you. And join you on your journey.

Cold has set in, she's shivering uncontrollably, the cabbie chatting away, when all at once, tears fill her eyes in a scalding burn. Maybe, it's his kindness? Whatever it is, it's unblocked a dam, and there's nothing for it but to let it stream over. He can't see her in the half-light, but asks if she needs the heater turning up, chit-chatting away. Here he is, out working at this hour, stopping for her when he could have cruised on by. Heading home at the end of a shift, he'd said, when he saw her rush into the road in stockinged feet; and now he's going the opposite way.

Sade is on the radio. *Diamond Life*... And she knows she will never forget this moment, this song, this feeling. The kindness of a stranger.

It takes a long time to calm down, their conversation already a forgotten jumble of words, but outside the hotel, she pays the fare and then doubles it, thanking him profusely, wiping the tears from her face before hurrying into the bright lights of the hotel and up to her room.

Still shivering uncontrollably, soaked to the bone, she kicks the door shut and flicks the lock, orders room service – soup and a toasted sandwich from the twenty-four-hour menu, with a pot of tea – then runs a bath, hot and steamy, full of bubbles, screwing up the clothes she will never wear again and lobbing them into the bin. Her mind is numb save for the driving need for home comforts, to sink into warmth, wash the night off her skin, feed herself, pull the covers over her head. But how to wash the mind?

Eventually, she drops into fitful dreams, wandering through red-painted rooms echoing with laughter in a haze of drug-induced delirium, pulling back curtain after curtain, unable to find a way out, running up and down black-lacquered stairs, searching for a door. She half-wakes in an attempt to stop the dream, but slips straight back in. Now, she's outside on an empty dark pavement, and two men in suits are chasing her, hard on her heels, as she sprints flat-out down streets that never end, turning corner after corner, only to find more streets, and at the end of each is a white van with blacked-out windows. Down another street, then another. A clatter of footsteps echo around the walls, hers and her pursuers, when suddenly a man leaps out of a side gate.

She wakes with a slam to the heart.

The room is velvety dark, the hotel quiet. The digital clock shows four-fifteen in the morning. No traffic. Nothing at all.

Not real, she reassures herself. It wasn't real, just a nightmare. The room is safe, the lock is on, plus a chain. No one is here. Still, her heart pounds in leaden thuds, and it takes a while to stop her mind churning over the night's events, accepting that yes, she has been assaulted. *Assaulted...* Before oblivion, sweet oblivion, blanks it all out.

For a while.

At six-thirty she wakes again. Early traffic is fizzling past in the darkness of early morning. A bath is being run in an adjacent room, toilets flushing, people talking in the corridor outside. A television set is on loudly upstairs, canned laughter and tinkling music. The lift pings in the hallway. Another day has begun.

"Shit, I'm wrecked!"

The room is gloomy grey, lit periodically by the flash of headlights through the gap at the far end of the curtains. And only now does it hit her. What a coincidence it had been! Seriously, she thinks, what kind of bloody coincidence was that? To lose her bearings, walk past a private club, and hear Vic Landry being discussed. And the man discussing him was the one she wasn't supposed to go anywhere near. His best mate. 'Something slimy in the corridors of power.' What were the odds? Almost, as if it was meant to be.

There's no need to get up before eight, even eight-thirty; she could go back to sleep for another couple of hours. But her thoughts have taken flight and will not rest. Because there's something else, too. What is it? On the periphery of her mind, teasing, flickering, like trying to recapture a rapidly fading dream. It's to do with Vic.

Suddenly it's there. The overheard conversation.

"He has done it, though?"

Done what?

Hang on, hadn't Marsha said something about… what…? She throws back the covers and grabs her bag, scrabbles for her notebook and flicks the pages. What, what, what?

He was summoned… all worked out… an arrangement… making him pay the price.

So, what had Vic agreed to do to pay the price?

"Bit of a glitch."

And not done?

In Thailand!

***

Chapter Twenty

At nine, Holly, the office intern, phones to confirm the interview booked with Joanna Landry's PA at The Bloomsbury Hotel.

Ingrid, showered and back in bed with a continental breakfast on a tray, jots everything down.

"So, you won't need the photographer because everything's been sent through already?"

"Yup."

"She's just going to have a bit of a chat with you about Vic as a boy, his achievements and hobbies, and so on? It should be really nice, actually. So, you know her name's Claudia?"

"Yes, thanks."

"And then…" There's the sound of keys tapping and a rustle of paper. "So, yah, and I've actually spoken to Samantha Landry's secretary this morning?"

"Oh? She has a secretary?"

"I think it's Miles' secretary, actually? She works for both Miles and Samantha Landry?"

Ingrid checks herself for irritation. She's tired and tetchy, but why does this girl have to use an upwards inflection at the end of every sentence, so the listener has to keep saying, 'Okay' or 'Yes'? God, she's ratty this morning, and no wonder. It would have been better to have had more sleep, but that was impossible now. Would probably be impossible for a long time.

"Okay."

"So, I'll just read out the message to you? 'Samantha wishes to pass on her regrets, but unfortunately her schedule is currently too busy to fit in an appointment. However, if there is a window in the foreseeable future, we will be in touch'."

"Samantha was in Klosters last Christmas with the family, wasn't she?"

"Um…" There's more tapping. "Ah, perfect! Yes, we've got some photographs of Sam and Miles at the Swiss chalet. And another of her outside the gym in Oxford? And a gorgeous close-up of her when–"

"Hang on a minute – the gym in Oxford. It's called, The Hazel Grove, isn't it?"

"Yes, my sister goes there. Actually, I shouldn't say this but Tabby's in the same yoga class – there's one this afternoon. Apparently, she's rather obsessive. Goes every day. Very beautiful, though."

"She's not that busy after all, then?"

Holly laughs. "Probably not."

"Okay, no worries. I've almost got enough for the article, anyway. Thank you. So, I'll see Claudia at…"

"Eleven-thirty?"

"Yes, eleven-thirty. And then…" She leans back and closes her eyes for a moment, mind suddenly racing. "No, actually, hang fire. I think I'll stay here for another night."

It would be a fairly quick train journey to Oxford, wouldn't it? She could head out there by lunchtime, and go home tomorrow instead?

"Perfect! I'll just pop that into your schedule." Tap-tap-

tap.

"Thanks, Holly."

"And your copy will be ready when?" Tap-tap-tap. "I think they wanted it by next Tuesday or Wednesday?"

"Monday, all being well. Monday evening. I'll work over the weekend."

What's to stop her going down there? There's just enough time to book a return fare to Oxford before getting dressed, and nothing to lose. A few hours at the most. She puts the breakfast tray on the next bed and reaches for the phone. Engaging Samantha in easy chat shouldn't be too difficult, sharing a coffee after yoga class, describing herself as a friend of Marsha's. And that would be true. Well, it would! She's been kissed. And Marsha's scribbled party invite is in her bag.

Busy in thought, she opts to wear jeans with a white shirt, tan ankle boots and a matching leather jacket; slings her gym kit, originally intended for use in the hotel, into her messenger bag, and throws in a clip to tie up her hair later on. Finally, she zips the suitcase, ready to leave either tonight or first thing in the morning, both options being open. And an hour later, sets off for the Bloomsbury Hotel.

She's close now, to a breakthrough. There are really two main questions: if Vic is not employed in Singapore, then what has he been sent to do, and why take Louise? There's a slight hint of danger in the air, and it hovers around her shoulders, tracing up her neck and into her hair like a fine prickly net, as she enters the hotel foyer and asks for Joanna Landry's PA.

It must feel like this to be a spy, she thinks. There is self-revelation in this – deceit doesn't come easily to her – and Claudia's eyes, when she shakes her hand, seem to burn knowingly into hers. In fact, from time to time, while chatting in the lounge over a pot of coffee, Claudia appears to scrutinise her intensely. It occurs to her then – what if this meeting was agreed to, in order to size her up? She could be wrong. But a few days ago, nothing had been forthcoming from the Landry side. Now, suddenly, after seeing Karl – after... oh God, after the white van – here is Joanna Landry's personal assistant just inches from her face.

This has become something else, hasn't it?

On the surface, it's an interview with the remit of shedding light on the missing couple. Underneath though, deep, deep currents obscure a buried truth. Someone or something is being protected. She does not know what she does not know. Really ought to leave it. What on earth does she hope to find? It's crazy, and yet the urgency inside her is increasing by the hour.

Her eyes meet Claudia's. And it's as if the River Hades runs between them, thick and dark. A catch in her stomach reminds her of the voice laced with malevolence last night, and the dull pits of the man's eyes.

Fear or truth? Fear or truth...

But there is Louise. Does she let her go?

For a few loaded seconds, she bows her head, busying herself writing. It's possible this woman knows exactly where Vic is, and what he was really sent out to Singapore to do. Maybe she even knows what happened to the couple. Is she a trusted, paid confidante, or has she heard Joanna and Max talking? She must have. The question is, what side has she chosen? Truth or lies? Light or dark?

There's a lull in the hushed silkiness of the lounge, as if the space-time continuum has slowed, voices slurring thick as molasses, a top-note of crockery clattering, a door closing, a lift pinging. While she considers how to play this.

Finally, she looks up, smiles, can't help pushing just that little bit more. "Vic must have done really well at the bank to have been promoted?"

Claudia raises an eyebrow.

Ingrid stirs her coffee. "So, I'm wondering if there's anyone they knew out there who'd be willing to have a chat, you know, on the phone? Maybe a friend at an ex-pat club, for example, or a bank colleague? Just for, you know… background. Do you know which club they belonged to?"

Claudia stares at her without blinking.

"I really wouldn't know, Ms Houseman."

The other woman's eyes are as inscrutable as flint, no reflection.

"Okay, no worries. Just thought, you know, it would be lovely to include a bit about being an ex-pat, if the couple had joined any of the clubs there. It doesn't matter."

"I think it's best we stick to what Joanna instructed, don't you?"

"Oh, for sure. It was just another angle. I'm very thorough." She laughs. "But I think I've got enough, thank you."

She does not have enough. Nowhere near enough. This is a cover-up and she's never been more sure of anything in her life. Where did they hire these soulless individuals from? Were they even human? They were talking here about a young woman's life, and if Claudia knew something that would help, she ought to say. As did all the others in the Landry family who'd closed ranks. Maybe the payroll was a fat one?

A polite smile is stuck on her face, as she closes her

notebook and drops it into her bag, dismayed to see her hands are shaking slightly. It's time to go. She's done her job here. But Sam Landry is Louise's sister-in-law and she'll definitely know what happened. It's her best bet. Perhaps her only bet, unless Karl finds anything out.

She checks her watch. Twelve-fifteen.

But Ingrid never even catches the train.

On leaving The Bloomsbury Hotel, a little nauseous from lack of sleep and too many black coffees, she steps onto the pavement intending to head to the nearby tube station, when her heart jackhammers in her chest. Blood rushes to her face.

A white van with blacked-out windows is parked directly opposite.

The façade of the street ripples like the surface of a pond. Jammed with traffic and people, it's a blur. There's a second of hesitation. A rush of thoughts. She can vanish into the throng and be at the tube station in minutes. They'll never know where she's heading. Quickly, she turns and walks smartly in the direction of the tube station. They will be photographing her. Zoom lens. Click, click, click, click…

Why, though? Why are they following her today? No one followed her yesterday after she left Karl. Or in the afternoon, or the evening. Why now? And why the sudden agreement to an interview with Claudia? Because whoever's in the white van knew where she'd be? How? One thing's for sure – she must be over target. They do have something big to hide.

But they will not follow her to Oxford. They cannot know her plans. She hadn't known them herself until a few hours ago. They won't even know what train she catches.

She'll reach Sam Landry long before they even know she's done it. And she will find the answer she's looking for. All roads have now converged and led to this. It has, she realises, become... an obsession.

Weaving in and out of the crowds of locals, shoppers, tourists and day-trippers, she heads towards the archway above the entrance to the tube. Only she never makes it there, either. Because halfway down the steps to the tube station, a neat, dark-haired woman in a grey suit bumps into her, and in a confusion of apologies, presses a piece of paper into her hand.

Stunned, Ingrid briefly looks down, unfurls her palm. The note has her name on the top: Ingrid Houseman. Together with her phone number. And home address. Her mouth is still open as she stares up into the myriad of oncoming faces, bodies, all piling down the steps, some knocking into her, as she makes a swift about-turn and tries to climb back up again after the woman, against the tide, eliciting curses of annoyance.

Breaking back out onto the busy street seconds later, Ingrid scans the horde of people in both directions, but the grey-suited woman has gone. Less than ten seconds and it was as if she never was. The beat of her heart still pulses heavily in her ears as she looks in all directions, examining every face, each person in turn.

There is no white van on the opposite side of the road now, either.

Nothing.

Only the note, which, once her back is against the solidity of the wall, she now reads with a thudding heart.

If you persist in asking questions about Vic Landry, you will be removed. Do not go to the police or you will hasten your own departure. Dearest Ingrid, what a meteoric international career you could have. Your choice. By the way, we love the ballerina watercolour in your bedroom. Do you paint?

***

Part Three

'Once on a time, the ancient legends tell,
Truth, rising from the bottom of her well,
Looked on the world, but, hearing how it lied,
Returned to her seclusion horrified…
'

'A Legend of Truth' by Rudyard Kipling

Chapter Twenty-One

Laos, South East Asia
October 1992

Louise wakes to a cool grey mist, beneath her a greasy makeshift bed of straw filled with darting, scuttling creatures – beetles, mice, and spiders. She shuts out the images. The jungle is rarely quiet, but now, in the pre-dawn hours, there is a lull, a pause, a hush; the only sound that of hollow wind chimes, faint on the lightest of breezes. For a while, she lies half-awake, half-dreaming, until a wave of remembrance washes over her, and anxiety grips her insides once more.

Every day she wakes here. Every day the screaming of macaques in the trees, the rising cacophony of cicadas, the heat and humidity. Her stomach growls with hunger, but she lies rigid, almost too afraid to breathe. What are they waiting for? Why is she here? They could kill her but they don't.

How many days has it been? She thinks this is the third but cannot be sure. Fragments of memory are gradually returning, if she could only stay awake long enough. Sometimes she wakes up with another piece of the puzzle, but her head thumps so hard on the crown, the pressure of concussion intermittently knocks her back into oblivion, sweat coating her skin, oily, clammy and hot.

There had been a chase. Running for a Jeep through the forest, its metal glinting in a clearing. She hadn't made it. That's right. She and Vic had been to the top of a mountain, to see a vertigo-inducing view of Thailand and Laos. He'd so badly wanted to see it, hadn't he?

Shall we walk the plank?

His voice. Vic's. Loud and clear in her head as if it was yesterday. Dear God, where is he? Come to think of it, where is she? He might even be in the same village, both of them held captive? Her head pulses with great throbs and her scalp itches in the straw. There are quick pattering and slithering sounds on the dirt floor and she squeezes her eyes tightly shut, trying not to picture rodents with long, gelatinous, pink tails, lizards, or the slither of rat snakes. But she must think! Formulate thoughts

Why would she and Vic have been separated?

'Think, Louise! Think! Try…'

It's all a blur and periodically she passes out, coming-to repeatedly, asking herself the same questions again and again. The Jeep, yes. Running to the Jeep. But then what happened? A cloth or sheet thrown over her head, the sound of frantic acceleration, a screaming engine, tyres rutting in the mud, petrol fumes. So, she'd been on the ground, had already fallen when the Jeep took off. Had the robbers killed Vic, thrown him in the Jeep and taken him somewhere? But why not kill her, too? They could have done that easily. Yet, here she is. Alone. They've been separated. Why? If it was a robbery, why take one and leave the other? Where is Vic? Is he dead? Alive?

Her eyes burn with tears, a collision of pain from the heart, an unstoppable storm. They stream down her face, choking in her throat. There is no pain like it, that of love for another when that other has gone. The warmth of his hand enfolding hers, the beauty of him, the reassurance of his presence, his powerful presence, replays like a favourite film watched over and over and over. Now there is a gaping, yawning hole in the fabric of her life, which he'd once filled. And there is nothing of herself to replace it.

After a while, the now-familiar sounds of morning filter in, and she jump-starts awake again. The people here shout to each other, chickens cluck and squawk outside the bamboo walls of the house, inches away, alongside the rhythmic pounding of grain. She is not permitted to leave the village or even the longhouse, and soon the girl named Noy will arrive with a bowl of water to wash in, and some food. She reaches for her small cross-body satchel, relieved it's still there. Inside, there's a small purse containing Thai baht, her pearl cross, a brush and hair band, a small purse of cosmetics, and the hotel room key. Everything else of value is in the hotel safe or back in the condo in Singapore. This is all she has then, and the clothes she stands up in. Did she put the cross in the bag? Wasn't it in the back pocket of her jeans?

She frowns. Something afresh doesn't make sense, but her addled brain cannot yet separate logic from preconceived conclusion. They were robbed. Yet she has her bag and everything in it?

Noy is standing before her with a small bowl and Louise opens her eyes. The water bowl is placed on the floor. Noy then puts her palms together and smiles. The water is from a mountain stream, cool, clear and fresh. Later, the day will be sticky with humidity and the sheen of sweat will rise and glisten on her skin. Grateful, she presses her palms together in thanks.

Noy is beautiful, Louise thinks, after the girl leaves and she begins to wash herself. Perhaps early teens, she is small and slight, with jet hair wound into a tight coil at the back of her neck, and soft, golden eyes that dance with flecks of light.

Maybe today is her last day here? Maybe today she will be found? Perhaps Vic is looking for her?

She has this part of a longhouse built on stilts, to herself. Sectioned off with bamboo partitions, the rest is full of women and small children. Some of the children are fractious in the night, and one of the women sings, a melodious, ethereal song, haunting and soothing at the same time. From deeper in the village, as soon as nightfall comes, there is the sound of fire crackling, of low talk and occasionally music and laughter; and later, as the breeze picks up, sweeping through the trees, the ever-present melody of wind chimes, carrying over the mountains.

As she washes, the women pummel grain outside, calling to each other as they work. Louise picks up her tiny hand mirror and scans her face. Pale and drawn, she ties her hair up, moistens her lips with a strawberry balm she originally bought in Camden Market so very long ago, and smudges her eyes with the blue eye pencil she packed the day they left the hotel, just in case. Just in case… of what? A robbery and abduction? It is too much effort though, and after a few minutes she flops back on the straw, exhausted. Wood smoke drifts through the walls, fires lit for cooking. The heat is beginning to rise. Cicadas screaming, building up in a frenzy of outbidding each other. A sawmill, she used to say to Vic.

Is anyone out looking for her? Will she ever go home?

But how will they find her out here? How long does this go on for? She looks through the gaps in the bamboo walls, to a bird's eye view of a mountain range covered in jungle. Tens and tens of miles of densely packed forest. The vast terrain stretches into a misty horizon, and it comes to her that she is as lost as if in outer space. This is no tourist area. These people are not selling things. This is as raw and remote as it is possible to get. She might never be found. This might not end!

A huge lurch of panic threatens to engulf her in its darkness, its madness, and she struggles to hold onto the threads of what she has, what she can see, what she knows. To steady herself. To breathe regularly.

This will end. All things end. Therefore it has to.

I am safe and all is well. I am safe and all is well...

Hours pass, and although it's still morning, it's steamy hot by the time Noy returns to take her outside. After using the toilet, a shack in the forest, she goes with the other women to the mountain stream, to bathe and wash her hair. Each time, there is a small ritual beforehand, an honouring of the water spirit, a dish of libations left on the rocks. Afterwards, the women chat and relax, and she tries to latch onto oft-used words, occasionally catching a slight sly smile sent her way. Wherever this is, she thinks, and whatever happens, it is sublimely beautiful. Both beautiful and deadly.

While sitting in the shade, drying herself, one of the elderly women, with a face as deeply grooved as a walnut, her teeth stained red from betel nut, suddenly shoos her away from the nearby tree, screeching and flapping her hands as if scaring away a giant crow.

She jumps up.

"What? What have I done?"

The old woman glares at her, pointing at the tree trunk to a large black and white spotted butterfly.

"A butterfly. Yes."

How can that be dangerous? She frowns, shakes her head. But the old lady is adamant. And some of the other women now chime in, using sign language to depict an imminent death.

"It's poisonous? Really?"

She mimes slicing her own throat.

The others nod.

Cautiously, she moves away, watching in wonder as the exotic, dazzling butterfly flutters and dances into the gloom of the forest. She does not know how to say thank you, instead pressing her palms together, bowing slightly. But the old woman has already moved on, muttering to herself. There is an undercurrent here, ancient, timeless beliefs and knowledge passed on, carried down the centuries. If only she could work out what they're saying.

Back in the confines of the longhouse, Noy brings breakfast and sets it before her.

"*Nue phueng tzue ze,*" she says, pointing to the plate.

Louise tries to smile. It looks like peanut sauce with chillies and spices.

"*Guchi chae!*"

Noy shouts louder, as if Louise is extremely retarded. As if by shouting she can get her to comprehend.

The sauce and root meal are tiny portions, served with rice wrapped in a leaf. And it strikes her they are sharing with her all they have – nuts, fruits, onion roots, wild greens, and grains.

"Thank you."

Noy nods, bows slightly, hesitates. Then points to her own heart. Then to Louise's. And smiles. They are the same, she seems to be telling her. All human souls. What's mine is yours. And for the first time since she's been here, Louise feels her deep unease lift. Her heart swells with gratitude at the connection. These people don't mean to hurt her.

It is therefore a huge shock when, just after dusk, a terrible, raucous scream pierces the air. She jumps straight out of a deep pit of sleep. How long has she been unconscious? It's going dark. All day? All darned day? Her head is heavy and fuzzy, as if drugged.

Outside, there's a big commotion – the rhythmic pounding of drums and chanting. Staggering to the door, she peers through the gap. The atmosphere has changed, it's raining, a deluge pitting the dirt, splashing into puddles, dripping off the eaves. She looks through a veil of rain and smoke, to a fire in the centre of the village, which crackles and spits, its flames leaping in tongues. A man with a painted face and an elaborate headdress of fur and feathers and silver, is holding a long staff, chanting with his arms and face held out to the sky. The village shaman?

An electric excitement is building up, pulsing. The whole village is outside, dressed in costume. She is the only one left inside. She thinks quickly. A ritual. A sacrifice? Could this be the build-up to a sacrifice, like the Wicker Man? They were quite nice to him. Smiling. Hospitable. Believed it perfectly sane, to kill a man for better crops.

Oh God, they're going to sacrifice her, aren't they?

Is it possible? Really?

Who would know?

Her stomach contracts. That she's been abandoned, she

has no doubt. No one is coming to save her. No one. They aren't coming. And this is real. This shit is real…

She slides off the bed and slinks down into the furthest corner of the room, blending into the shadows, putting her hands over her face, pulling her knees up, locked into the darkness of her deepest fears… instantly transported all the way back to Spring Bank Heights. Even the rain was the same, pummelling onto the roof.

***

Chapter Twenty-Two

Perhaps it is the monotonous, rhythmic beat of the drums, the chanting, the heady smoke filtering through the bamboo walls, or the empty churning of her stomach, but when she next comes to, it is dark. And it's with a deepening realisation.

The men who attacked her weren't robbers. If it was a robbery, they'd have probably shot them both and left them to die. And besides, why take one and leave the other? The most likely explanation, and it pains her to the core, is that it was kidnap –Vic is from a wealthy family – and that he took off and saved himself. He would have been just that little bit quicker to reach the Jeep, had jumped in and reversed out at speed. Leaving her to her fate. Which means there is only herself to hold to ransom. And no one has paid. No one is coming. The tribe, therefore, has one too many mouths to feed, and they are going to sacrifice her to their gods.

She takes her hands from her face and stares into the gloom. Outside, the smoke and heat now mingle with the smell of roasting meat – pig crackling on a spit. The scream must have been when it had its throat cut. At the back of the house, on the other side of a flimsy wall of protection behind her head, is dense jungle. The domain of animals and spirits. Whereas here in the village it is carnal. And she is going to die like the Wicker Man, while the people laugh and sing and dance to music. Perhaps they will get a better harvest? Be more prosperous? The horror within her is cold, profound, but ultimately quite still. Because the worst thing, by far the worst, is the new knowledge, that Vic abandoned her.

She rolls the information around and around, getting used to it. But the more she does, the more other things begin to surface, too. The bikers he'd been talking to that day, laughing like they knew each other. And there'd been his insistence they go to Phu Hua Loan, irritation when she'd said she'd rather not, the map already drafted, the name of the place inscribed on his memory by a woman called Katty. Another woman called Katty at the hotel reception, who he'd seen the night before they set off on the trip, while she was in the shower…

But why? It's a swirling carousel of nonsense. He would hardly plan his own kidnap, would he? Of course not. He'd escaped and she'd been left behind. Maybe the kidnappers thought they could get some money for her, the one they'd caught? And now they know they won't.

It's a horse kick to the stomach.

Why hasn't Vic paid the ransom? If he escaped, then why hasn't he, his family, the police, done a deal with the kidnappers? Or… or as it went wrong, perhaps the police are now looking for her, and there's a search party out right now, at this very moment? But then, they're going to be too late…

A sharp noise snaps her from the reverie. Noy is here with an evening meal. Finding her huddled on the floor in the shadows, she looks puzzled.

Perhaps, Louise thinks, she has this all wrong and

they're not going to kill her? Her heart leaps with hope. Or why would they feed her? There is a chance… is there not… that there is some other explanation? She points to the outside, making a Gallic shrug of incomprehension, raising both hands in question.

"What is happening?"

Noy nods, puts the tray down, then holds up one hand with three fingers showing.

"Three days?"

Noy smiles. And then to Louise's horror mimics someone dying, using the same cut-throat gesture she herself had used yesterday at the waterfall, before dropping to the floor and playing dead. After which she bounces back up with a smile, eyes as bright as a blackbird's. Three fingers held up again.

Louise uses sign language as best she can.

"So, three days and then someone will die?"

Noy smiles, nods. Then bows, a small inflection at the neck, before gesturing to the dish on the floor.

"*Mochue-cha-lum.*"

Louise stares at her, still in shock. But hunger and good manners preside. She places her palms together, thanking her. And after Noy departs, the aroma of the stew wafts over, hitting her square in the stomach. It is pork and potatoes, spicy and hot. And despite everything, she wolfs it down. Besides, if she's going to make a run for it she's going to need strength and stamina. The people here are small and wiry, thin, have little food, but she's much bigger, used to a lot more, and her stomach growls constantly, her head light and dizzy. The water is boiled and swims with herbs, the rice wrapped in a leaf. She devours the food but leaves the water – that's probably how they're drugging her. Because they are, she decides, drugging her. A bump on the head would explain the headache for a few days, but she wakes in the morning, then, after breakfast, she is knocked out again. All day. It would be wise, then, to pour the water away.

The kidnap theory is beginning to gain traction. Would make sense. A mild sedative of some sort would be just enough to keep her calm and stop her from screaming, or running away. Perhaps Vic escaped and has organised a search party? Except they might not reach her in time. She must escape. There is no Marion to come and let her out of the shed. No mother waiting for Len to go to the pub or the bookies before she rescues her. She has to save herself. And never give up hope.

Outside, the chanting, drumming and clash of cymbals has become a fervour of excitement. And in the darkness, with firelight flickering across the floor, for some reason, the story Vic told her about the tattoo ritual comes to mind.

So, after I'd consumed the sacrifice, he said to keep repeating the particular words I'd been given, and then he left me in the dark to keep chanting them, over and over, and not to resist whatever came.

She had thought it nonsense. Yet now, out here in this remote mountain village, with the fire and the ceremony outside, it seems all too real. They believe in their rituals and they believe in blood sacrifice and binding. And if she is murdered, then no one would ever know. No one knows she's here. How on earth would anybody find her among miles and miles and miles of forest-covered mountains, with the few tracks there are deeply rutted in mud, the whole area dense with jungle and wild animals?

She peers through the gap in the bamboo, into the tar-black interior of the forest behind. There's no one back home to kick up a fuss, either. No one to pressure the press or the British Embassy. Len Draper wasn't going to put himself out. Another cold stone drops into the emptiness of her stomach. It hadn't mattered before, back home. All that mattered was freedom. Finding a new life. But in truth, she has no one. No blood family at all. And the only person who knew that, the only person in the world she'd ever told, was Vic. It had been just before last Christmas at his flat, they'd shared a bottle of wine, been in bed, in the silence of the night beneath the covers, his breath on her hair.

Again the thought breezes in… Had he planned it?

But it didn't make sense. And why? What on earth was in it for him?

Yet he'd insisted they go to that beauty spot. Had really meant them to go. Pushed on, even though twilight was approaching.

For the first time since last Christmas, doubts begin to creep in about Vic. Does he love her? Really? Enough to try to find her?

There was a time, back in London, when she'd been dressed and ready to go out, waiting in the lounge downstairs with Janice, who was in her pink dressing gown and fluffy slippers. He was supposed to pick her up but never showed. An hour had passed. She went to ring from the main phone in the hall, worried something had happened to him, phoned several times. But he never returned the call, and hadn't contacted her again until long after Christmas. A huge chasm of loneliness opens up inside her – memories surging – of tramping around the West

End that winter, ending up in the leafy squares of Mayfair and Chelsea, standing in the drizzle looking up at warmly-lit, elegant townhouses twinkling with Christmas lights, passing canopied restaurants and pubs heaving with people merry with cheer. The aroma of garlic, wine and beer wafting from doorways. All those people who knew each other, belonged somewhere, were loved by someone…

She'd spent Christmas day working at the clinic, changing drips, dressing wounds, emptying catheters. Spent most of January that way. He never asked. She never said. The smell of colostomies and blood had still clung to her hair and uniform as he stood in the hallway of the nurses' accommodation one day, unannounced, smiling, tanned, holding a bouquet.

And then the wedding itself. Not a single member of his family had been there. And that man, Nigel. The way he'd looked at her. Knowing, amused, contemptuous. On her wedding day.

Ziva: *Take really good care, Louise. Promise me?*

And Singapore. Now she comes to think of it, every day Vic went to the bank. Six days a week. Sometimes seven. Often in the evening, not coming home at all sometimes. He'd fallen asleep at his desk. Had to be one hundred percent committed if she wanted the luxuries of life. Yet, she had never asked for the luxuries of life. And she'd never met a single colleague. In truth, she'd spent most days alone in the air-conditioned flat or by the pool. Why had she never met anyone? Instead, she'd been confined to a high-rise, gated condo. Why had she never asked? It hits her now. And her pulse suddenly picks up alarmingly.

It's as if she's been in a coma all her life and is only now waking up. A spell has broken. What if Vic was not who he said he was? What if Vic is now dead? What if there is no search party? She cannot know the reason for any of this except nothing makes any sense, at all. But she does have to get out of here.

Outside the longhouse, the pitch darkness of the jungle seethes, a living, pulsing, breathing mass. The *kweek, kweek* of a Savanna nightjar rends the air, the blanket blackness at the back of the longhouse a stark contrast to the fiery party on other side, and the orange glow inside. They are singing now, as one, in harmony. But deluded, she thinks. Utterly deluded. To believe that killing her will bring them luck! Tears spring into her eyes. And for the first time ever, she tells herself she deserves better. She is just as worthy as anyone else.

Perhaps it is anger. Perhaps it is pain. Perhaps it is love for her own God-given soul.

But tomorrow night, just before dawn, while the others are sleeping, exhausted, she will escape. And she will be going home.

***

Chapter Twenty-Three

Sometime around midnight, the drumming ceases.

Louise surfaces from a hot, fitful sleep. In recent days, she hasn't woken before dawn, so it seems the herbs in the boiled water were indeed the sedatives. There is still, however, a lingering effect – dizziness, brain fog, and a sickly thump in her head. It will take a while to fully leave her system. Smiling assassins. But she should have thought of this before, instead of assuming it was concussion. At least there will be no more now, and by this time tomorrow her head will be clearer.

For a few minutes she lies motionless, only gradually becoming aware of a presence nearby, a stealthy padding around the back of the hut. She lies motionless, eyes wide open in the dark. Man or animal? The footfalls are so careful, so skilful, she has to shut her eyes again to focus on it. There! A slight movement, light as air, a matter of feet away from her head. The breath is paralysed in her lungs. She holds it for as long as possible, but there are no further sounds, and eventually, slowly, she exhales again.

Now fully awake, cautiously, she sits up. The night is underground-black, the air muggy. More rustling outside, but further away. A wild cat? The jungle is full of nocturnal hunters and there's nothing to defend herself with when she leaves the safety of the bamboo house. No torch, no lantern, either. But what's the alternative? She has to try. If she can just make it to a main road, there will be someone who can help.

The camp is quiet, the sound of soft snoring coming from the quarters beyond her own. Why not go now?

Quietly, she reaches for the clothes the women gave her to wear each day – a hand-woven, long blue skirt to fasten over the cotton shirt she sleeps in, and a cropped cotton jacket – and slips her cross-body bag of belongings over her head. Her hair she ties back before wrapping it in a cloth headscarf, and tying it under the chin to protect it from insects or whatever lurks in the trees. Later, the cloth will serve as a flannel or a tourniquet if needed. She looks around the smoky darkness. There's no food, no bottle of water; and nothing to light her way but an infinity of stars.

This is it, then.

Best to head downstream.

Every movement is slow and soundless, as careful and stealthy as the padding paws of the wild cat prowling around the periphery. The women and children beyond the divide are breathing deeply, rhythmically, the air thick with sleep. There's no other exit apart from the door at the front, and no choice but to creep past the flimsy walls, inching towards the door. On levelling with the door, a small child suddenly wakes and stares at her directly, eyes clear and bright. Louise pauses, puts her fingers to her lips and smiles. Waits. The child takes a while but eventually goes back to sleep, while Louise stands with her hand on the door, praying they don't whimper. Then pushes it open with a soft, low creak of bamboo against bamboo.

No one stirs. No one watches. To them, she is safely drugged, miles and miles from anywhere, and could not survive out here on her own, especially stumbling around in a stupor in the dark of night. They wouldn't be worried.

Outside, high up in the mountains under a clear sky studded with stars, the air is fresher and brighter. On the horizon, a crescent moon is suspended over the forest, casting a ghostly sheen across the village, and Louise steps back into the shadow of the eaves. To date, she's only ever been taken around the back of the huts to the waterfall, and must quickly get her bearings.

The village is very well designed, with a ring of long houses on stilts positioned around a huge swing. To the side is the remains of a bonfire, and a spit above a pyre of rocks, where the squealing pig must have had its throat cut. At the bottom, it's just possible to make out the spirit gates, and beyond those, a faint grey ribbon leading down the mountain, a forest track.

Her pulse picks up. She looks over her shoulder at the impenetrable jungle, then in the direction of the waterfall, knowing there's a steep climb from there to the top of the mountain; then down to the spirit gates again. And the track. Down there. It's the only way.

As she is about to step out of the shadows, however, there's a sudden movement behind, and she whips around with an audible intake of breath. It takes a second or two to realise what it is – a pangolin shuffling out of the foliage. The primeval-looking creature is working its way along the periphery, minding its own business; and eventually her heartbeat steadies again, her eyes becoming accustomed, and the cool breath of night breezes on her skin.

She'll walk smartly down to the spirit gates and onto the track, travel as far as possible under the cover of darkness. The track will lead somewhere, it has to, and as long as it's downhill, then sooner or later it will join a main road to a town, or at least to the river below, a market, anything. There could be an early morning farmer hurtling down the mountain road, truck loaded with produce? She pictures it, agrees with herself that it would be likely. And she is just preparing to step out of the shadows again, when the silhouette of a man, the grey, ghostly outline of what she'd thought was a bundle of rags and sticks propped up against the next longhouse, shifts and sighs.

Shit!

A lookout.

She should have realised.

She stares at his profile. He appears to be facing forwards, hasn't turned around to peer in her direction. Undoubtedly, he'll have highly acute hearing, be alert to the slightest sound. It would be foolhardy to try and walk past him. From there, he can see the whole vista, too and would easily spot a figure moving past on a moonlit night like this. Instinctively, she backs closer to the wall of the longhouse that's been home for goodness knows how long, and makes herself very, very small, folding into the darkest part of the shadows, creeping around the side inch by inch, before turning, and walking into the forest.

Immediately, its velvet cloak closes around her.

There must be a thousand eyes on her, she thinks, standing stock still. The midnight jungle breathes, rustles and hisses with hidden creatures, camouflaged on branches, clutching to bark, slithering through the undergrowth. But going the other way is far too risky. And besides, it's only necessary to go in a short way, before veering down to join the forest track a bit further along. She can do this. Has to. Cannot even think about anything other than making it down to the main track. To think that only a few days ago, she'd been terrified of doing this in broad daylight with two men in front hacking the path clear.

She puts out her hands in front, as if blind, instantly jumping at a creeper that is stroking her face. Beneath her feet, a twig cracks and she hesitates. The creatures, it seems, hesitate with her, for the longest breath-holding moment. But it's vital to keep going and she forces herself on, her only option being to focus on the outcome, to reach the path that will take her to a road, to freedom and out of here. The blackness is total, the foliage so dense it's a wall of fronds and creepers. At every step, it feels as if something is crawling out of the trees onto her arms and back, or out of the mud to climb her legs. Constantly batting away invisible critters, she stumbles over roots, forging through a barrage of branches, fronds and leaves. Time has no concept, there is only the present moment, each tiny step a milestone.

Just keep going, keep going, keep going…

After maybe twenty steps, she turns left and heads downhill, to the track that should be running parallel. It's slippery and steep, a sharp descent, and she grabs at the branches to stop herself from falling, previous fears no longer paramount, the need to exit the forest, to get out of the thick, pulsing, smothering blanket of the jungle, overriding everything else. It seems, however, to be an interminable trek. And the forest path does not appear below as expected. Her heart catches on a beat. Something's gone wrong. The descent is endless.

On and on it goes.

After a while, it becomes confusing, disorientating. The track ran level with the village. So, where is it? And then it occurs to her – what if it coils around in hairpin bends and the bend had looped around before the point she thought she'd emerge from? In which case, she would have been well wide of the mark, and is now somewhere in the middle of hundreds of miles of mountainous jungle. With no way out.

Her spirits drop like a stone into a deep, dark well.

"Oh God, please help me!"

The forest seems to be getting thicker with every step, too. Slashing at branches with her bare hands, she slips and slides downhill. She cannot, must not, give up. If she does, she will die. But there are no tears anymore, no anger, no despair, just determination. This cannot be the end. Deep inside, she knows it cannot be. She has to fight, to find strength from somewhere, from within, to take care of herself, to love herself enough.

In the bag around her neck is Marion's pearl cross. It gives her comfort that it's there, and now she thinks of it and, remembering the love she was once shown, she taps into how that felt, how it was to love someone with the soul. And the strongest feeling then begins to fill her heart from the inside, in this, her darkest hour; a swelling that ripples out and spreads until the whole of her being is filled with it. This is not her time. Not yet. She has been given life, like anyone else, and will not give in. Will not give up.

Hours pass, and a dusting of stars becomes visible through the canopy, a veil of silvery mist curling in the trees. Perhaps it is two or three in the morning? When all at once the slope levels off and there's a clearing ahead.

At first, it is almost impossible to believe. She stands on the edge, still under cover of the trees. It's the site of an abandoned slash and burn village, now overgrown with shoots of grass and saplings springing through the dirt, the bamboo houses empty. But it is not the remains of the village that cause her to stare aghast. And it is strange, so strange, because there's the strongest feeling of having been here before.

Only it is so difficult to process. Because, on the far edge of the clearing, is a corpse, spread-eagled in the branches of a tree, with fragments of white cloth still hanging from the bones.

***

Chapter Twenty-Four

The mountainside is swathed in mist, and from across the clearing the corpse appears to be levitating, suspended in thin air, a macabre spectacle of bones and rags, ethereal in the silvery pre-dawn light. Cautiously, she crosses the clearing, gravitating towards it as if beckoned by an invisible hand. Only to reel back at the close-up horror of eye sockets not fully pecked clean, tendons ripped from joints, and a chest cavity emptied of its contents. Rope still ties the bones of one ankle, and one wrist, to the branches, the rest of the skeleton splayed precariously in the tree, creepers already closing around it like a Venus fly trap. There is still some flesh, some fragments of skin, of hair, cloth, and she clamps her hand over her mouth. It is horrible, terrible… And recent.

From the valley below, a long, loud, wailing scream pierces the air, followed by a melancholy *bop-bop-bop*. An owl. Just a fish owl. It sounded close, in the vicinity of the river, judging by the proximity of its cry. She must be further down the mountain than she thought. And it is then, in the stillness and the mist, as she stands staring at the corpse in the tree, that the feeling of being watched creeps up her back. And she turns around.

The bird is large, possibly a foot long, raven black, with ruby-red beads for eyes. A black drongo. Vic had pointed those out before, he'd told her lots of things, and she wishes now she'd paid more attention, done more research of her own. It stares straight at her, insolently and fearlessly. On the periphery of her vision, something darts from its hiding place and momentarily she takes her eyes off the bird. A large brown rat is scurrying from out of one of the dilapidated huts. And in that split second the drongo moves towards her.

It stops again, head tilted to one side, assessing the situation, then suddenly advances, jumping closer, hop-hop-hop, opening its shiny beak wide. It's going to shriek, make a horrible raucous caw that would ricochet across the valley. It was probably the same one that pecked out the man's eyes. She retreats a step, then another, and another. The bird keeps hopping towards her, closing the gap, until eventually her back is level with one of the longhouses. She glances over her shoulder. Its roof has long since caved in the middle, creepers entwining the bamboo walls, and on the floor are bundles of rags – old bedding and belongings. Another rat scuttles across the dirt, and in the corner is a brown coil. It takes a moment to process what it is, a coil with a head, and a tapered tail.

"Oh, God!"

Flapping her hands at the drongo, she hisses, "Shoo! Shoo!" Then she walks quickly away, heading downhill out of the village, and doesn't look back.

Behind her, a cacophony breaks out in the treetops, an alarm call in shrill staccato from dozens and dozens of unseen creatures and birds. It echoes around the mountains, a ripple effect, transmitted to more and more inhabitants, the forest breaking into a frenzy of screeches and squeals.

Picking up pace, she passes through what had once been a grand entrance to the long-gone village and hurries down the slope to what will hopefully be the forest track she'd missed higher up. It is only when she comes to it, however, that she sees how tightly it zig-zags down the slope, looping back and forth in horseshoe bends. It's also deeply rutted and muddy, narrow and very overgrown in parts. But it is, at long last, and thank God and all the angels, a definite track.

Deeply rutted. Recent tyre tracks. Her spirits lift at the sight of them. A vehicle has been this way fairly recently, which meant this track came out at a main road. Rainwater has filled the ruts, the mist thick all around, but the going is a lot easier and it's so good to be out in the open with the night sky overhead.

Had whoever driven the Jeep out here, been responsible for murdering the man in the trees, though? Brought him all the way out here, tied him by the wrists and ankles to the canopy, splayed him out in a sacrifice, then left him to die? There wasn't a soul around. It could even have been yesterday. Or the day before. There'd been flesh still on the bones.

On and on she walks on a journey that doesn't seem to end. How many hours now? The faint light of sunrise is beginning to penetrate the misty whiteness shrouding the jungle. Every few minutes, she scrutinises the dark, hazy interior, before checking over her shoulder, then fixing on the way ahead once more. Keep going. Keep going. At one point, half-hypnotised by the monotony of the white mist and her steady, plodding walk, she is brought up short, and stands for a moment, paralysed. There is something traversing the path, from left to right, a long, fat, dark brown muscular tube.

She cannot breathe or even blink. The python seems to be without an end, on and on, perhaps twenty feet, maybe more, in length. She is sick with revulsion. But eventually the body thins to a pointed tail, the crossing complete. Where it has gone, she dares not imagine – up a tree, or lying in wait… It would sense her body heat, wouldn't it?

Without allowing another thought, she breaks into a run. If that thing had been in the forest a few hours ago, when she was blindly stumbling through it, stumbling and sliding to the ground… and if she'd been as drugged as she'd been for the last few days, and fallen asleep, just lost consciousness… It doesn't bear thinking about.

The lane hooks around sharply again, suddenly tipping down more steeply. This has to come out somewhere soon. It's important to get to a main road before anyone notices she's gone, because there's a very real chance of escape. Someone in a nearby market town, or village, will surely be able to help? There will be police. And they would know about a couple of missing tourists in the area. After that it will be a call to the British Embassy. And home.

Home?

Home… where would that be…? Vic's flat?

Exhausted, Louise slows to walking pace again. The track hooks back around once more, and facing east, with the rising sun in her eyes, another hour passes. It's getting warmer too, mist beginning to lift from the path in a wet cloud, and there's a clear view of the mountain range ahead. It doesn't, however, look like Thailand. There's a different feel to it that's hard to explain. She stops for a while, hands on hips, still panting. Wild, mountainous jungle terrain spreads out in every direction – no terraced slopes, fields or temples, just miles and miles of pointed, triangular-shaped hills, densely forested with no visible roads or houses. The air is quite still and soundless, broken only by the *keek-keek-keek* of a bird and far away, a drilling woodpecker.

A singular thought comes into the silence. After she and Vic were attacked, after the Jeep had reversed away at speed, and the cloth had gone over her head, there'd been a blackout, a void of amnesia, before waking up in the long house. So how did she get there? And did these tyre tracks belong to the same vehicle that had delivered her to the tribe? To the same people who'd hanged the man in the trees?

The track is leading towards another hairpin bend, a ski slalom of a passage downhill, and the flow of a river is not far away, its fresh rush cooling the air. Not far now. Soon, there will be a main road. She pushes on, aware now of throbbing heels and the rub of sore skin inside her trainers. It can't be much further. Rounding the bend, the lane still a narrow cut through the jungle, she picks up pace.

Then stops.

It's in the middle of the road. A Siamese fireback, a pheasant-like bird that stares at her astonished, but without comprehension or decision.

Later, she will thank the bird with all her heart, because its presence causes her to stand absolutely still, to wait, and to listen. Otherwise, she would undoubtedly have been seen. Without the drum of footsteps, inner mind chatter, and the breath pulsing in her ears though, there is silence. Blessed silence.

The bird and the woman stare at each other for a while, as they both become aware, at the same time, of voices. Men's voices. Followed by what sounds like a heavy-duty vehicle revving and lurching in and out of ruts and potholes.

Louise's eyes widen. There's a slam in her chest. And the bird snaps out of its paralysis, darting into the jungle with barely a rustle, instantly vanishing despite its brilliant plumage.

Slowly, quietly, she advances, keeping close to the trees. Just in case. Just in case these are the same men who abducted her, or these men had something to do with the corpse in the trees. They could be drug or arms dealers. Merging with the shade of the forest, she slips into the cool, dark interior, coming face to face with a small, vivid green tree frog, its fingers and toes splayed on the bark of a nearby tree. Gasping in surprise, she steps back with a crack of twigs, and curses.

Despite being unable to see anything yet, she knows the vehicle is close – revving, wheels spinning – and a man is shouting instructions to another.

In English!

The excitement, the joy, the relief, is overwhelming. They're not far away. They could be the search party, could be out here looking for her. Shaking all over, it is all she can do not to tear into the lane, to run up the middle waving her arms, calling out. But something holds her back, some deep inner instinct. Maybe, it's the tone of the men's voices? And so instead, she continues to stealthily creep parallel with the track, camouflaged by the trees, each footfall soft and careful. Until finally, the entrance to a tribal village comes into view.

Parked in front of it, by the gates, is a four-by-four. And after scanning the immediate area for snakes or critters, she warily crouches down low to watch.

Two men, broad-shouldered, dressed in jeans, polo shirts and baseball caps, are now outside the vehicle, talking loudly. On the side of the four-by-four is an internationally recognisable symbol for White Clover International, a religious charity well-known for dispensing aid, with thousands of charity shops and regular TV appeals. She has given money to it in the past, and her pulse now quickens. It's going to be okay. They're bona-fide. But, and maybe it's the swagger or possibly the sheer size of them as they shout to each other, instinct keeps her watching for that little bit longer, as they walk through the spirit gates into the village, like they've been here before and know it well. One is wearing wraparound black sunglasses, has his hands in his pockets, the other carries a sports holdall.

For a few minutes, they stand in the centre of the driveway. The one in sunglasses looks at his watch. And then the one with the holdall calls out.

"Hello? Anybody home? Hello!"

Eventually, a much smaller man comes down the driveway, dressed very differently from the village she's just left, in a black tracksuit and trainers. And trailing after him are three young girls, each wearing full tribal costume. With only the most cursory of nods, the man with the holdall hands it over, the village man unzips it and checks the contents, and then the three girls mutely follow the men to the vehicle. One is quietly crying, the other two are poker-faced, as all three then climb into the back, and the doors are slammed shut behind them. It doesn't feel right, not at all. Are they taking the girls for money? Her stomach tightens into a knot. Oh, dear God. What was going on? The man in sunglasses, the driver, jumps in and proceeds to reverse up to the gates, winging the steering wheel hard right, while the other one, in the passenger seat, looks up the lane. The car is rocking in and out of a deep rut, the windows are down, and for a heart-splicing second, his gaze is a heat-seeking missile.

He's seen her.

A hard stab of fear plunges into her stomach.

She holds her breath, closes her eyes.

Please God, no!

No, he can't have, that's ridiculous. He can't possibly see a thing in the gloom of the forest, especially with the sun in his eyes. But for a second it feels as if he can. A minute stretches into all eternity. And horribly, indescribably, there's a neon green pit viper hanging in one of the branches close by. It had been perfectly concealed by the leaves. Their eyes meet. Its tongue flicks. She breaks a sweat while doing everything she can to calm her nervous system, to control her breathing, and slow her heart. If her eyes are closed and she barely breathes, they won't know she's here. If her eyes are open, they'll know.

Please go away, she silently pleads to the men. *Go, go, go... just go!*

And then a voice says, "Come on, mate, give it some welly!"

The engine revs to screeching pitch, more dirt flies, there's a sudden lurch, and then the vehicle bounces out of the rut and accelerates away.

English. They were definitely English.

With a hammering heart, shaking from head to foot, she gently steps back, away from the viper, foot by foot, until a safe distance is between them and she's back on the track at last. The man in the tracksuit has gone, the drive to the village now deserted. She doesn't need to guess. It's obvious. They've sold those girls.

Keeping well out of sight, she quietly slips past the gates. The village exudes an air of despondency, a feeling of emptiness. No children's voices, no women singing as there were in the tribe she left, just a monotonous song coming from a radio, a warbling voice and repetitive melody. She hurries by as quickly as possible, past a rubbish tip piled with aluminium cans, tyres and bottles, and a washing line pegged with brightly coloured nylon shorts and t-shirts. A deeply worrying thought now burrows into her mind. If those two men are using the charity as a smokescreen for taking young girls, then what if the local police are turning a blind eye, too? Being paid off? And if they're all corrupt, then she can't trust them, either. Which means, who *can* she trust? Where can she go to get help?

Her stomach contracts again, the knot tightening.

Then again, what choice is there? Except to keep on walking and find out.

***

Chapter Twenty-Five

She follows the fresh tyre prints. One thing's for sure, they'll lead to a main road. But what if they come back? If the one in the passenger seat saw her and raises the alarm? He couldn't have, though. A quick glance into the darkness of the gilt-edged jungle, reassures her – it's impossible to see a thing. Within it are millions of creatures, on the forest floor, in the branches, camouflaged against bark and leaves, all veiled by the slant of weak morning sun shimmering through a haze of mist. He saw absolutely nothing. It is all her own fear, and it's important not to let that overwhelm her. Her thoughts could easily spiral downwards and she must remain positive, believe there are good people in the world and they will help her get home. There's a long way to go yet, and this is a vulnerable situation. Got to be mentally strong, keep optimistic, be vigilant, keep going. Think about nothing else but going home. On the plane. Going home…

The sun is beginning to rise above the horizon now, burning away the highest layers of fine mist to reveal a clear blue sky. Soon, it will be blisteringly hot and she hasn't any means of basic survival, no water, no food, her head light and dizzy. At times, it feels as if she floats, her conscious mind cutting out for minutes at a time.

Once, when she was a little girl, Marion took her for a

picnic on the moors. She'd been collected at the school gates and they'd taken the bus to a well-known beauty spot, with a shallow brook and a stone bridge. They'd had roast chicken sandwiches, and afterwards she'd paddled in the fresh shock of cool water, and Marion had dried her feet in a towel and had only packed up when the sun dipped behind the purple heather hills, the day still balmy and warm.

Ah, those moors. Another memory surfaces then, a blissful moment, when a boy she'd loved had taken her to the same spot, rolled her onto her back and kissed her. He was beautiful, with dark brown eyes and a long, slow smile. It had been the first time she'd been held. And then in a flash, Vic is there before her. A moment relived. Looking at her from the doorway of the pub, so similar… so similar… It has not occurred to her before. But yes, the same lazy, self-assured smile, same kind of looks… Same kind of power… Like a cat with a mouse.

'*What a wicked game to play… to make me feel this way…*'

The song lyric springs into her head and her chest suddenly contracts. Tears erupt and at first she brushes them away with a harsh swipe of the hand. No. She doesn't cry. Never cries. Will not cry. Whether he drove off and left her or whether he refused to pay a ransom, he didn't love her, did he? The tears erupt more strongly, she can't stop them, and then the pain bursts out so violently, there's no option but to let them come. Sobbing openly, loudly, she keeps on walking, until her eyes are red and swollen, her body slumps, and there are no more tears left. Until his face begins to fade in the hot glare of the sun.

And when she looks up again, there's a road ahead – a

mirage, a floating, shimmering, silver river.

By now, she's been walking for many hours, swollen feet blistered and bleeding, the skin raw. And the sun is higher. Nine o'clock? Ten? The noise of the cicadas is beginning to build up, and squinting into the light, she forces herself onwards to the quivering silvery ribbon ahead, every step that bit nearer, that bit closer to home.

When finally she reaches it, however, it's deserted – a helter-skelter mountain road with no barriers between it and the cliff face on the other side. As far as the eye can see, forest-covered hills stretch out ahead, steam still rising from the canopy. Behind, the mountain towers overhead, the life within it a deafening industry of insects and hidden predators – intricate, individual works of art, some poisonous, all precious, all miraculous. But she would not survive another night in there, even without the threat of whatever had happened to the man left hanging in the trees. Or the poor young girls taken away in the four-by-four.

Below is a wide brown river, winding between verdant mountains with no sign of habitation, not a soul in sight. Not even the faint hum of a distant car.

She sets off downhill to the sound of her own lone footsteps. The heat is building now, the sun stronger, but the going is faster, the descent steep. Where is this place? It seems so deserted, so remote. Nothing but the sound of her own breathing, the padding of her trainers on tarmac, and the hypnotic, high-pitched screech of the cicadas. There has to be a town at the bottom of this hill. This is a route to somewhere.

On rounding a bend in the road, she comes face to face with a monkey sitting in the middle of it, eating something.

On spotting her, he pauses, holding onto his prize, a fresh melon. A curve of hard peel has been discarded and he's gnawing on the rest, some pulp strewn on the road. Her eyes widen as they stare at each other. The melon must have fallen off a truck, which means someone drove down here recently, and there could be more to follow. On their way to a town...

She skirts the monkey, aware he's watching her acutely, yellow teeth bared in a grimace, his eyes deep-set, crafty and sharp. He definitely isn't up for sharing and her stomach growls, her dry mouth salivating at the sight of the succulent melon pulp.

An hour or more passes to the dull thud of her own feet, and the dizzying sawmill of the cicadas. Eventually, the pain of raw flesh inside her trainers becomes unbearable and she sits on the tarmac to take them off, dismayed at the sight of torn skin and oozing sores. Taking the scarf from her head, she tears it in two and wraps each foot, tying the cloth at the ankles, before attempting to set off again. If there was a stream it would help. Anything. But the main thing is to get to the town. The melon truck had to be heading to market. And it can't be long now, even if she has to walk all the way there.

She clutches the bag containing Marion's cross, sticky with sweat against her chest, beneath the thin cotton jacket Noy gave her. Noy, who could have taken it, could have taken the baht, but didn't. Nothing of hers was stolen. Which is when it occurs to her, that if the tribe had been expecting a payment and didn't get it, then surely they'd have taken her money, because there's quite a bit. This occurs to her briefly. A wisp of doubt. A thread of knotted confusion. But mostly, rational thought has gone. And on standing up again, she momentarily blacks out, sways, and almost falls back again.

When suddenly, there's a whirring whoosh of air.

A man on a bike rounds the bend, appearing out of nowhere. Trailing a small cart of fresh fruit, he's careering down the middle of the road, pedalling fast, jet-black hair streaming behind him, and when he spies her, his eyes widen to saucer proportions. She's in the middle of the road, caught by surprise. He reacts by hard-braking, and swerving around her in a series of slalom moves. The trailer wobbles precariously, the whole thing snakes for a few seconds, and then he shoots straight past before she has time to even open her mouth.

"What the...? Oh, God – are you blind? Can't you see I need...?"

She raises her hands in despair. Surely, it's obvious she's staggering in the road with bandaged feet! But then, incredibly, wonderfully, it seems the cart has ground to a halt further down the road, has skidded at an angle.

She hobbles towards him, already reaching for her bag with fingers grown numb. She will pay. For one piece of melon. Or water. Anything. Water.

He shakes his head, staring at her as if he's never in his life seen such an apparition. As if she's quite insane.

Drawing nearer, she opens her bag, scrabbles for coins, points to the melons, forgetting her manners. Immediately, she corrects herself and makes the *wai* greeting, a slight bow with her palms pressed together.

Her mouth is dry and the words croak, "*Sawadee*!"

He stares.

She points to the fruit on the back of the cart. "*Chai*."

Still he appears confused, but then behind his eyes

there's a flicker of understanding. He indicates the half-laden cart, mimes her climbing into it, a chivalrous gesture.

"Me in there? Yes, yes please. *Chai.*"

He picks up a watermelon, slashes it in half with one swipe of a knife, then halves it again, puts the quarter pieces into the cart and helps her in, waving away the baht she offers with her soil-grimy fingers.

It almost feels unnatural to sink onto a solid floor, for the unrelenting momentum of the journey to temporarily stop.

He points towards the river.

"*Panya!*"

"I don't know what you mean, but thank you. Thank you. Yes – *chai.*"

She is shortly, however, to find out.

***

Chapter Twenty-Six

Panya is the owner of the only shop in a tiny village by the river. Made of bamboo, it has a flat, corrugated iron roof and a fruit stall outside under an awning, the air sweet with ripe papaya. Inside, it is relatively cool, with a ceiling fan and a fridge containing cans of soda and plastic bottles of water. The shelves are stocked with tins and cleaning materials, and several men sit at Formica-topped tables drinking coffee from small cups, watching her, like bats from the gloom of a cave, as she hobbles into the café.

"Panya!" the woman behind the counter shouts.

She is tiny, diminutive and wizened, with shrewd bright eyes.

"Panya!"

He appears through a flutter of coloured ribbons that separate the shop from the living quarters at the back, reminiscent of 1960s Britain. A radio programme is on, the language rapid and urgent, the aroma of spicy cooking wafting on the air.

Someone, the man who'd given her a lift, hands her a bottle of water from the fridge and she gulps half of it down in one go, vaguely aware of being helped, of arms under her elbows, to a table, onto a seat.

A conversation is bullet-fired over her head.

She starts to speak, to use the few Thai words she

knows, but Panya shakes his head.

He bows slightly, pressing his palms together.

"No good. Listen, un? You lady, you lost?"

She returns the greeting, dizzy and nauseous.

"Thank God, you speak English? My Thai is not good, you're right. Sorry, sorry..."

"No, not Thai. Where have you come from?"

The water swills in her stomach and she takes another sip, aware now of how much her head is pounding and her face is burning from the sun.

"Many days ago. An attack. My husband has gone. It was over there." She points to the mountains. "I was captured by a tribe. I think they were going to kill me. I escaped. Walked all night, all day."

"American?"

"No, English. I need to speak to the British Embassy."

"What happen to husband?"

"I don't know. We were somewhere near here when we were attacked."

He places a hand on her shoulder. "Drink."

"Thank you."

"What is name of place where you are attacked?"

Shall we walk the plank?

For a moment, the memory of sitting on the rocky ledge with nothing but clean, empty air all around and for hundreds of feet below, flashes before her. Floating in a liminal space where time, briefly, had stopped.

Shall we walk the plank?

"Lady?"

She smiles, points to her chest. "Louise. My name is Louise."

"Louise."

She drinks more water and her stomach cramps.

"Where you are attacked?"

The name flutters around the edges of her mind. Vic had repeated it enough times. But now it's gone. She shakes her head.

"Near Nam." Then it shoots to the surface. "Phu Hua Loan. That's it! Phu Hua Loan. Not far. Near here."

Panya frowns. "No. Long way. This is not Thailand. This is Lao Soung!"

"Lao Soung?"

"Laos. This is Laos. Different country, un?"

"Not Thailand?"

Her senses begin to blur. The room pitches and rolls like a galleon on a high swell.

Where on earth is she? How did she get here? It doesn't make any sense at all. They had been sitting on the rocky ledge, had come down the side of the hill, and that was when they were attacked. Woke up in a tribal village. But… so… how the hell did she end up in another country?

More rapid-fire words are being exchanged with the old woman, who then brings a dish of cooked rice from the kitchen and places it before her. Automatically, she reaches for her purse, but Panya holds up a hand.

"No. Eat."

Coffee is then brought in a small cup, very hot, black and strong.

"You drink."

And afterwards, she's led to a small room behind the ribbons to have her feet bathed and dressed, to be helped onto a small sofa.

"Which road down mountain?"

She looks up at him through a fog of drowsiness. A fan

breezes across her face, the whir of it hypnotic. He has kind eyes, sitting there watching her, the old woman standing behind. He could be thirty or he could be fifty, but he has the air of someone who's going to take care of things, and she feels the sudden catch of having lost consciousness then regained it a second later. A jolt.

"Down the mountain? Um, a man on a bike–"

He nods. "My son. Yes."

"Ah. I'd been walking a long time to get to the road. Many hours. Nine or ten. The track to the tribe in the mountains, joins it further up. I came out there. The first tribe is on the left. I saw a white van there this morning, with two men."

His eyebrows raise. "This morning? You see two men?"

"Yes. I passed that one. But the one where I was being held is much higher up. At the top, in the mountains. I walked downhill through the forest, all night. It was very different to the one lower down. Very different."

"Yes. You know Noy?"

"Noy? Um, yes!"

"Good. I take you back."

"What? No. You don't understand. I need the Embassy."

"I speak to Noy."

"No, listen. They want to kill me. She said in three days' time. Showed me a death."

Alarmed, she struggles to sit up, describing everything she can remember, from being ambushed to waking up in the longhouse. How Noy had smiled and told her they were going to sacrifice her.

"I cannot go back, don't you understand?"

But to her dismay, Panya is smiling.

"Louise! It is a good thing I speak the language of the tribe. They have three days for a funeral. A pig sacrifice. Three days of feasting. The elder die and it is in his honour."

He laughs, and the old woman laughs too, smiling with no teeth.

"Three days to clear bad spirit so man go into world of spirit clean, out of world of man, back to animal and spirit world. Into forest."

She stares at him, his words slowly permeating the barriers of fear. If those people had wanted her dead or to rob her, they could have done it any time. Instead, they had fed her, washed her, even clothed her, every item handwoven. But why did they drug her and how had she got there?

Panya shrugs.

"I fetch Noy."

Again she shakes her head. "No, no, please"

He smiles. Stands up.

"I go now! Before dark."

He turns to the old woman, giving her instructions.

Then back to Louise. "Rest."

She has no choice because all the fight suddenly leaves her, and she's already falling into a dreamless, timeless, void of exhaustion. His image swims before her for a few moments. And then it is gone.

Later that evening though, when the truth arrives with Panya, it is a beautiful if brutal thing, laden with stabs of shame and regret. How could she have misjudged Noy and the tribe so badly? Got it all so horribly wrong?

"Oh, God!" she says. "Oh, God!"

Panya pulls up a chair, his face kindly but grave. She's

been in a deep, heavy slumber, is still drowsy, only surfacing at all because he shook her awake. Now eleven o'clock at night, it's an effort to sit up, to take hold of the small cup of scalding tea he hands her.

"Noy," he mimics tears. "Crying. You have been there many weeks. Have become a dear friend."

She almost drops the cup. *Many weeks?*

"What? No, only days. A few days."

"Many weeks." He points to a calendar on the wall. "Today – November second."

She struggles to comprehend.

He points to the back of his head. "You hit very hard. They find you... in very deep sleep. Would not wake."

"November the second? That's today's date? But that must be..." She does a quick calculation. "Nearly six weeks?"

"They find you in a place not used for many years. It is being used for bad things. Gangs." He shakes his head.

A sudden memory. Of a clearing, and a figure spread-eagled in the branches, huge rats scurrying out of a disused longhouse, of blankets and rags on the floor. A large bird with red eyes is hopping towards her, a shriek of alarm in the jungle as she runs through the gates to the lane...

"They find you there. One night there is a fight, shouts, gunshots. Then all quiet. Very quiet." He shrugs. "They say after this they go to the place, and there is a woman on the floor not living, but very still, lying on the face, hands and feet tied, and in mouth..." He mimes having a gag. "But they go to lift her and find a heart. So after this they take her and heal her, and she comes alive. They do not want the men to find her, so they hide her."

They'd doped her to stop her from panicking, to stop

her from running into the kind of men she'd seen that morning.

"A man?" she asks. "Did they find a British man there, too? I need to know if my husband is still alive?"

He shakes his head. "No."

She frowns. So, how had she got there, to that place, into another country?

"It is, as you see this day, a business."

"Business?"

"You see the white van. This is what we are watching. You see for yourself. Today. You see they take children, girls."

Her stomach clenches. "So, you know about that? But–"

"It is big problem if people take money. But very poor people. Very poor. Big money to sell girls. They go to Bangkok or to other place, oversea, to very rich men."

Louise stares at him. Now there is a totally different dynamic. Another possibility. Maybe they let Vic escape because it was she who was wanted? She who was worth money to them? A lot!

"So, what went wrong? Why was I left there in the hut?"

"Noy says they do not know. Sometimes there are fights between gangs. There was blood on the floor and maybe one was killed and put into the trees to die a terrible slow death. It is known to do this. Maybe they did not have the money agreed?"

"I saw a man in the trees, just the bones, and ties on his ankles and his wrists."

Panya nods.

"But you say something went wrong?"

So, this gang saw a couple heading off alone to a remote beauty spot, let the man go and just took her? It was her they'd wanted?

But all she can see and all she can hear is the frantic revving of an engine and whirring of tyres, as Vic reversed out in the Jeep. And left her there. He just abandoned her and saved himself.

"I wonder where Vic is?" The sound of her voice, to her own ears, is cold and harsh. "Do they know? I need to find out."

"I have made call on telephone," Panya is saying. "A contact – he comes tomorrow."

"A contact? Who?"

She'd begun to relax, but is now less sure. There is the same flicker behind his eyes she'd seen earlier, when she'd mentioned the two men and the missionary van. He seems kind, but perhaps that's what she'd wanted to see? Perhaps he is coordinating everything and is just pretending?

This is what we are watching… Big money to sell girls…

Panya smiles and nods. "Sleep, Louise. We talk tomorrow."

***

Chapter Twenty-Seven

But now she cannot sleep. Instead, she is lying wide awake, staring into the black, velvet darkness.

A contact – he comes tomorrow.

And six weeks. She was with the hill tribe for six weeks! It must be true, though. Her own body is evidence enough. And she's taken a hit to the head, been left for dead, then sedated. Still, it's a shock.

A memory surfaces, of Noy, shyly putting her palms together in greeting each morning, placing a small share of their food before her, leading her to the waterfall to wash; of the old lady saving her from the poisonous butterfly. And lying back on the straw in the longhouse, sunlight slanting through the bamboo walls, the only sound cicadas and children playing outside.

Her eyes brim with quickly blinked-away tears. If only it was possible to go back in time and put things right. Those people had brought her back to health and kept her safe. But she cannot go back there now. The question, though, is what to do next? Can she risk trusting Panya?

He's left a dish of noodle soup. She takes a sip of the hot liquid, then puts down the spoon. What if it contains sedatives? But it is good, spicy and salty, and her stomach growls for the rest. To trust or not to trust? What if, just what if, Panya is part of the whole racket? And the contact who's coming tomorrow is going to return her to the gang who abducted her?

Was it worth the risk of hanging around to find out?

Of course, he and his mother would have fed her and bathed her feet. They'd need her in reasonable shape, as well as lulling her into a sense of security. On the other hand, he'd been to see Noy, ridden his scooter all the way up into the mountains, and reported back late at night, explaining the world of difference between the tribe that had taken the money, and the ones who lived in integrity and honour. But what if he'd gone up there purely to find out about her, to get information? A battle rages between her mind and her heart, until exhaustion claims its prize. And when she next wakes, to the sound of a cockerel crowing loudly outside the window, it is with a stab of alarm. Someone is coming to see her today. A contact. What if it's the police? And what if they're corrupt? Maybe Panya gets a cut?

She sits up in a lurch of panic.

Maybe it will be a pleasantly smiling man who tells her to get into a car, that he'll take her to the British Embassy, but instead it will be to some other place? She'd fallen through the net but would now be recaptured. If she got into that police car, she might never go home again. And no one would ever know. No one is looking for her. No worried relatives back home. No relatives, at all… Other than Vic. And where is he? What happened to him?

In the room upstairs there are sounds of movement.

She thinks quickly. Where is there likely to be a bathroom? She must have been seriously dehydrated not to have needed it in all this time. Maybe it's in the yard outside? There's no time to linger anyway, to be a sitting duck. Who knew the true motives and intent of others? Best then, to find the bathroom, and leave as soon as possible.

The blisters on her feet are now hard, shiny sores. There are plasters in the shop. And then there might be a bus or a taxi on the main road. As a plan begins to form, a sense of urgency grips her. Leaving before the rest of the household is up is paramount. The most important thing is to get to the British Embassy. To let them know she's alive, to go home.

Then find out what happened to Vic.

It takes less than ten minutes to prepare. The bathroom is a lean-to outside, with a small sink. In the poky cupboard space and murky light, she closes her mind to the myriad of spider webs, and washes in a thin spurt of cold water. Reflected in the round, rust-speckled mirror hanging on a string above the sink, a barely recognisable face peers back. Hurriedly, she does the best she can with the remaining lip salve and eye pencil, then ties her dampened hair back again. What on earth, she wonders, fastening on her cross-body satchel, is Vic going to think when he sees her like this? Or anyone? But soon the light will begin to pierce the dawn mist, and it will be too late if she doesn't get a move-on and get out of here in the next few minutes.

Bare-footed, she creeps into the grey half-light of the shop, takes a bottle of water from the fridge, then a packet of plasters from a shelf, and some rehydrating powders. Overhead, a bed creaks and groans as someone turns over, and for a fleeting moment it seems a pair of dark eyes are watching from beyond the curtain of ribbons in the back room, maybe the old lady's? But she leaves enough Thai baht on the counter to cover everything, then swiftly lets herself out and closes the door.

Once outside, she hurries down the road in bare feet for several minute, before stopping to put on the plasters and slip the trainers back on, all the while checking over her shoulder. The village is deserted, silent, apart from the crow of the cockerel, and minutes later she's on her way, vanishing into the mist and heading down the highway.

It is crucial not to get this wrong. Not to get into any car, but hopefully catch a bus or hitch a ride on a cart. But there is nothing on the road heading west towards the Thai border. Not a sound for at least an hour, maybe longer; until the light begins to lift, and a small town, a tumble of shacks, appears on the horizon through a soft white haze. Behind it, a wide river stretches out, brown with mud, turbulent in the middle. It can be no other than the mighty Mekong, as seen from the top of the mountain, and on the other side will be Thailand. She speeds up.

On the outskirts of the town, a man is setting up a stall of fruit, and she pauses briefly to buy bananas and rose apples, not stopping again until there's an old disused shack to hide behind. Here, she eats the fruit, tips a rehydration sachet into the bottle of water and drinks half. The smell of the fast-flowing river is on the air, the energy of a busy market town. She could be on a plane home by tomorrow. What if Vic has been looking for her all this time? If she'd thought the worst of him? What if he'd thought she was in the Jeep when he accelerated off, but then couldn't go back when he realised she wasn't? Or, what if he'd been badly injured and is still in hospital? Or worse? She tries not to think. Today could bring anything. All she has to do is get to a phone, a hotel perhaps, and ask for the Embassy. One step at a time. Then all of this will be over.

It won't be much further now, she tells herself, wincing from the pain of the blisters as she stands up. A mile? Maybe less. A truck passes, and then another. One or two cars. And then on the other side of the road is a line of women waiting at a crossroads. One of them, the one at the front, is stepping into the road with her hand out, and Louise glances over her shoulder. A grey single-decker bus is shimmering in the early morning sun.

If she runs she can make it.

The road is dry and dusty, and she hurries over, to where the women with brimming baskets eye her surreptitiously. The atmosphere changes instantly, from convivial and chatty, to quiet and unsure, but the bus is slowing and she climbs aboard.

It is only as the Mekong nears, however, and a giant golden Buddha sitting on a large moored boat floats into view on the opposite side, that the thought comes to her. She has nowhere to go. What if Vic is no longer alive? If the Embassy flies her back to Heathrow, where will she go?

The full impact is a blow. How absolutely reckless she's been with her life. No job. No family. And then to depend on Vic, a man she barely knew… for everything.

Swallowing down the alarming thought, she blanks it from her mind. Vic will be looking for her. He will have reported the whole thing. No one would be looking in Laos, they'd be looking in Thailand. That would explain everything.

But please, please, please… let Vic be alive!

***

Chapter Twenty-Eight

There's only one hotel in the sprawling riverside town.

"I want to phone the British Embassy. Can I use your telephone, please?"

The girl at the reception desk regards Louise without expression. She is told to wait. The manager will come.

Overhead, a ceiling fan whirs, the interior of the building gloomy, and the smell of frying garlic, sesame oil and spices wafts in on the downward draft of the river. There are no western tourists here, just locals busy loading and unloading boats, buying and selling at the wet market. The Mekong could be a half a mile wide, maybe more, the golden Buddha atop a moored boat on the opposite side, rising over the mist. Looking around for somewhere to sit, Louise flinches at her reflection on a large mirror. With her hair scraped back and having lost so much weight, she is barely recognisable. And then there are the clothes…

"Miss? You are to come with us."

It's a shock. Out of nowhere, two uniformed police officers are suddenly standing in front of her. Why? Instinctively, she shakes her head.

"No, no. You speak English? No, I just need to use a phone. I asked to use a telephone!"

"Miss. You come with us."

There is no getting past the stone-walling expressions

and, no matter how many times she refuses, they aren't budging. In the end, there's little choice but to allow herself to be escorted through the market stalls, with one officer either side of her. Local people stare then avert their eyes, as if they've just seen something they shouldn't have. A small child smiles and she tentatively smiles back, frightened now, because there isn't a good, reassuring feeling coming from the men in brown uniforms. Both carry guns. Both are walking at a smart pace.

The police headquarters is down a back street – the office small, unlit, furnished only with a desk, a phone, and two wooden chairs.

The larger, older one, with stubby fingers, lights up a cigarette and motions for her to take the opposite chair.

"Speak again. Why are you here?"

The interview feels like an interrogation, as if she's a criminal.

"English," she says, making a concerted effort to keep her voice calm. "My husband and I were attacked six weeks ago in Thailand, near Nam. I woke up here in a mountain village, and I do not know how I got there. Look, I really do need to speak with the British Embassy. I want to go home to England."

A curl of smoke rises into the air, pluming into a mushroom cloud, both men observing her with poker expressions.

She tries again. "My husband will be looking for me. Vic Landry. I am Louise Landry. There will be a search party."

A further hour passes while the older officer fills in forms, by which time the ashtray on the desk is full of cigarette ends, his fingers pudgy and stained. The other stands ramrod straight, back to the wall, as the hand of the clock on the wall nudges eleven. From outside comes the bustle of everyday life, shouts of people bartering at the market, a child wailing. And she wishes with all her heart she was one of them, that her life was as simple and natural as theirs. A roll of hunger turns over in her stomach and she closes her eyes. These men cannot be this heartless. They just can't be.

A phone rings in another room, on and on and on.

Then suddenly, the one filling out forms picks up the pile, taps them into a neat stack and slots them into a folder. Motions to the other one, snapping out orders she hasn't a hope of understanding. After which she's taken from the office to an even smaller room and left there on her own.

Strangely, after the bolt has been shot on the other side, it is a relief to be on her own and away from the suspicious glare of the two officers. In one corner is a small iron bed with a mattress on it. It stinks but she drops onto it anyway, draws up her knees, leans against the wall and closes her eyes. Now there is nothing, just the rush of the river, occasional footsteps outside the door, and the muted shouts of people outside. Time drifts in this cell of silence, and she finds her mind does, too. There are few choices now.

As midday approaches, the light intensifies, becoming brighter, harsher; the sounds of the street more subdued. There is the lap of the water, the hurtling tide, the soft whirr of boats, petrol fumes on the air. This is how an animal in a cage must feel, to be trapped, to have to wait, to be still and quiet.

After a while, footsteps quicken down the corridor,

sharp and purposeful, heading towards her door. The bolt is shot back and a different, but still unsmiling, officer puts a tray down on the floor, holding coffee and a bowl of spiced rice.

And later still, as the brilliance of the day begins to fade and shadows lengthen across the wall, there is a visitor. This one, however, meets her eyes, bows slightly, then pulls up the sole wooden chair and sits down.

"Louise Landry?"

"Yes."

His English is fluent, the accent American.

"We had a call from Panya, but when we arrived you'd vanished!"

Her heart slams like a rock into her ribs. Blood rushes to her face.

"Panya?"

"There's someone looking for you."

For a moment her mind blanks. This is the man Panya called. Not to be trusted, at all. And who is looking for her? The gang that kidnapped her?

She inches further back, as far away from him as possible. "No."

"No?"

She shakes her head. "I'm not going anywhere with you. I want to call the British Embassy."

He frowns. "You are definitely Louise Landry? Do you have anything, anything at all to identify..."

She shakes her head, points to the bag around her neck. "Only what's in here, a pearl cross of my grandmother's, some money–"

"A pearl cross. That's good. Look, Louise, someone from England is looking for you. We got Panya's call. But you'd gone."

Through a fog of incomprehension, she stares at him. Is he saying Vic is with him?

We got Panya's call!

Does that mean Vic's in the next room?

"Are you…" she says eventually, "are you the Thai police, or do you work for the Embassy or… I mean, is he…?"

He shakes his head.

"No, nothing like that."

The man is short, stocky, dressed in beige slacks and a white polo shirt. Watching her intently, his eyes burn into hers, a faint waft of lemon-fragranced cologne on the air. He smells clean, of soap, and she cringes inside a little that she doesn't. What if Vic is in the next room? This changes everything. What if he walks in here in the next few minutes?

She tries hard to keep her voice measured and calm.

"Well, who are you? I don't understand."

"My name's not important. Let's just say I work with men like Panya, and we're trying to stop what's going on with the children."

"Oh God, so I can trust Panya? I didn't, you see. That's why I escaped. I couldn't trust anyone, I didn't know who to trust–"

He stops her with a hand held up. "It's okay, Louise. We guessed what had happened. Luckily, we guessed you might have come here, too. Although, it might not have turned out so well for you if we hadn't."

"You mean they didn't call you? The officers here didn't call you? So, you just…"

He nods. "Yeah, we figured there weren't too many

places you could go to and our first punt proved right. And no, they didn't call us. My guess is they called their superiors and probably would have had you transferred somewhere, should we say, more secure. There's also a high probability they might have called the guys from White Clover. You're lucky it would take them a long while to come back."

The enormity of his words barely register, a shock that will not fully sink in for days.

"But who are you? You haven't said. Are you an undercover agent or something? And who is it that's with you?"

"Are you well, Louise? Have you been looked after?"

"I'm okay, thanks. I'd like a shower though, and some water. But—"

"That can be arranged. We'll check you into a hotel as soon as possible."

"You keep saying, 'We'? So, who is it that's with you? Are they here in this building?"

"Yes, yes. They are here."

***

Chapter Twenty-Nine

Louise stares at a woman she's never seen before in her life. She stares wide-eyed from her position on the stained mattress, with her back still against the wall, bare feet grimy and covered in plasters.

The woman coming towards her with a hand outstretched, has sleek black hair tied in a high ponytail. She wears a crisp white sleeveless dress and sandals, her limbs are lightly tanned, and she has startling blue-green eyes enhanced with cat-flick eyeliner.

"Hiya, Louise! I'm Ingrid. Ingrid Houseman," she says, in an unmistakeable Yorkshire accent.

Louise shakes her hand.

"Um, hi!"

"Don't worry, I'm not an official. I'm not even a journalist. Well, I was, but not at the moment. Long story."

Suddenly, it is all too much. This woman is not Vic, hunger has become a hollow ache inside, and the tiredness is overwhelming. Her eyes swim with tears. Just what the hell is going on? Can this man not just get her out of here, to the hotel, to the airport? Anything…

Ingrid sits next to her.

"I wouldn't, it's filthy."

"It doesn't matter. I've been looking for you for weeks actually, Louise. I come from the same town as you."

Louise has her eyes squeezed shut, knees drawn up, head back. Too disappointed to speak, tears course down her face.

"I'm sorry, I can see you're plain exhausted. Look, how about we get you to the hotel? It's on the other side of the river in Thailand. And then we can talk tomorrow – make plans and take it from there?"

The man, nodding in agreement, pushes back his chair and stands up.

"We need to go."

"I'll be staying there with you," Ingrid adds, "and then tomorrow I'll tell you all I know."

Sighing heavily, Louise opens her eyes and shoots her a sidelong glance.

"Right, okay. I still don't understand who you are, though."

"No, I know. But you're too traumatised at the moment, so let's just get you looked after, all right?"

It happens quickly after that. The man, who seems to have some jurisdiction over the officials, nods curtly at the guard, after which they walk smartly out to a white SUV parked in the street.

With the sun on her back, just before she gets into the car, Louise looks over her shoulder at the road she came down on the trundling bus that morning, squinting into the cool, glassy aqua sky. The deafening rise of cicadas fills the air, the swirl of the river behind. Miles of jungle-covered mountains stretch out as far as the eye can see, and just for a moment, the most fleeting moment, her heart swells. It had been deadly. But oh, so very, very beautiful.

The drive over to Thailand is a fast one, the journey a blur. In the back seat, Louise drifts in and out of sleep, noting first the muddy expanse of the river as the man accelerates at alarming speed across it, coming to with a start as the SUV then bombs south along a highway, and then again when they hit a pothole. Ingrid seems to be dozing, the man silent. But ahead, set into a hill overlooking the river, is a small spa resort hotel. At the front is an infinity pool fringed with swaying palm trees, the terrace empty.

"I'm going to leave you two ladies here," the man says, parking outside the main door. "Ingrid, I will see you later this evening. Just look after her, okay?"

Inside, the floor is cool beneath her bare feet as she hangs back while Ingrid checks them in. A man in a white suit takes them to their rooms, adjacent to one another, and when the door is opened to her own, Louise can hardly believe her eyes. A large double bed surrounded in white nets, a marble-tiled bathroom, a balcony with a view of the Mekong and the Laos mountains beyond. A toucan sits on a branch outside, as surreal as a painting.

"I'll be just next door, Louise. Knock if you need me, all right?"

"I will, thank you."

"We'll be quite safe, no one knows we're here. And don't worry about the bills, it's taken care of. Order what you need. Have what you want. Oh, and there's a bag coming up in a minute for you – just a few bits."

In the end, Louise sleeps for nearly twenty-four hours without waking, and when finally they meet again, it's late afternoon next day, on the outside terrace by the pool.

Ingrid is reclining on a lounger, sunglasses on, but facing the main entrance.

Smiling as Louise comes towards her, she says, "You've

had a long sleep. Feel better? Do you want something to drink? I've got a Tropical Sunrise, it's gorgeous."

"Yes, that'd be nice. Thank you." She sits down next to her. "And thanks for the toiletries, as well. It was kind of you, Ingrid. And the clean clothes. God knows what I'd have worn if you hadn't. Everything was filthy."

"I tried to think of what you might need," she says, as the drinks are brought over. "I'm just sorry everything's a bit too big. Janice said you were a UK size ten, but that dress is an eight and it's hanging off you. I guessed you'd have lost weight, but as you're my height I thought an eight would be–"

"Janice? Janice Case? You know Janice?"
"Yes, I interviewed her originally, and she rang me again later."

"Oh, I see. When you were a journalist, did you say? I'm sorry, I forgot you said that. Anyway, yes – I'm skin and bone. It was heaven to wash my hair with shampoo last night, though. Thank you for that. Tea tree was perfect."

"You're welcome."

"I washed it again when I woke up this afternoon."

"Don't blame you. I would have."

"Mind you, I think I'll have to scrub and wash several times a day for weeks before I feel properly clean."

"How are your feet?"

"Not too bad. As long as I'm barefoot!"

"I see you're wearing your pearl cross! A roadside stall holder remembered seeing a blonde woman with a pearl cross around her neck. It's how we knew for sure it was you."

She holds onto it, clasping it within her palm, and for a while they sit in companionable silence, sipping fruit juice, watching the swimmers, enjoying the warm, silky breeze beneath the palm trees.

"Shall we order an early dinner? We can eat out here."

Louise smiles. "Definitely."

They choose the house special – Malay beef rendang, pak choi, and spiced rice served in a bamboo basket.

"Has Ayrton Senna gone?"

"He was quite a fast driver, wasn't he? Bit hairy at times, especially on the bends."

"He never actually said who he was."

"No, he wouldn't. I don't know either, really. But from what I understand when we travelled up here together, there's a racket going on in the whole area. Men posing as aid workers offer the hill tribes huge amounts of money for their young girls. Then they're sold to brothels in Bangkok, even overseas. Panya's an informant."

"A spy."

"Yeah, putting his life on the line, apparently. The tribe you were with are, too! But they have to be careful. It's big business and the gangs are armed."

"So, you know all about that? And do you know what happened to me? Did the mystery man tell you?"

"Yes. He spoke to Panya in his native language, but from what he told me in the car on our way over to find to you, the tribe saved you. I gather you saw some girls being taken from another tribe?"

"Yes, they were really young. It was the day before yesterday, I think. I'd been walking all night. The men were English–"

They stop talking when the waitress arrives with the meal, waiting for her to set it out on the table.

"The tribe sedated me in order to protect me from the

gangs, but I didn't know that, I thought they were going to kill me so I escaped."

"I heard, yes. It was a shame you couldn't say good-bye to Noy, though."

"Or even thank her."

"I know. But you aren't to blame – you didn't speak each other's languages and you were traumatised. It's ironic we assume our own kinsmen are trustworthy though, isn't it?"

"The so-called aid workers, yes. I nearly ran up to them for help!"

"Thank God you didn't."

"I don't know why I held back and hid. Just… I don't know, something about their voices, their manner."

Ingrid frowns. "Well, the good news is, I know Panya has explained everything to the tribe elders. They understand. They're just happy you're safe."

"Thank you for that. I was feeling bad about it. I just wish I could go and thank them personally. So, has Panya been back again? He must have if he went to explain."

"Yes, our man with no name came back last night for an update. He's there again today, and they've gone to the other tribe, too. I think your story might have helped them connect a few more dots. They went back there quite urgently."

"I wonder if they've gone to the abandoned site I found? Did they tell you about the corpse I saw in the clearing?"

"Yes. I just hope it wasn't…I mean…"

Ingrid's face flushes as she bites back the words. Louise must surely have considered it could be Vic?

"I think he was probably one of the gang members. It was pretty horrible."

"Yes. Yes, you're probably right. Maybe a traitor?"

They drift away into their own thoughts for a while, lulled by the balmy breeze and the soft rippling of the pool. On the lea side of the hill, the sun has dropped behind the trees, and from deep within the forest, the faint rhythm of drums and the eerie, unmistakeable echo of wind chimes carries on the air.

"It's very beautiful here," Louise says softly.

"Mystical, exotic, a work of art. Look at the brushes of colour in the sky, the tangerine, the rose pink, the violet…"

"Yet, it has such a dark underbelly. Poverty, dirt, drugs and guns."

"Sex trafficking."

"Yes."

They order coffee and desserts, little parcels of fruit wrapped in deep-fried pastry.

"I'm sorry I'm quiet, Ingrid. I think my head's only just beginning to clear. I could go back to sleep again, to be honest. So, you said you'd been looking for me? A journalist, but not at the moment? Have you been sent to bring me home? I mean, here I am accepting your hospitality–"

"It's not quite like that."

Ingrid smiles at the waitress bringing dessert, fussing with coffee cups.

"How is it then? I mean, are you with the Embassy? Because I can't afford a hotel and I do have to get home, even if just to Vic's flat. I don't know what else to do until I find out what happened to him. That's the priority now, I think. I mean, where is he?"

Ingrid frowns again, stirs her coffee.

"Can you take some really hard truths, Louise? Are you

ready?"

"How do you mean?"

"Okay, well for a start, I'm definitely not from the Embassy. I'm just me, flying solo. I came to Thailand a week ago and went straight to the police in Bangkok, started asking a lot of questions, and I went to the media. But they just stonewalled me. Every department, every individual. And there's no way I'd go to the Embassy, which is something I'll also have to explain. Anyway, I was getting nowhere, so I thought I'd fly up to Chiang Rai and go to the hotel you'd been staying at. I had a few ideas to follow up and one of them was hiring a private detective. But the night before I was due to leave, there was a knock on my hotel door and it was our friend with no name."

"Ayrton Senna."

She smiles. "He'd had a phone call from Panya, describing a woman fitting your description, and he'd heard about me looking for you."

"So, what brought you to Bangkok? I mean, you met Janice – so were you working on the story? Were you a mainstream journalist?"

While Louise finishes dessert, Ingrid relates her interviews with Janice and Karl, taking her through each disclosure carefully.

"I'm skipping quite a bit of information, Louise, but I'll come back to it all later, I promise. For now, suffice to say I wrote an article after interviewing quite a few of your friends and family, but most of it never made it to print. And that's just what I submitted, which was only a fraction of what I actually found. Thing is, Karl had given me a couple of leads, and on my way back from following up on one of them, I overheard a conversation at one of those old

Mayfair clubs, a gentlemen's club?"

"Oh?"

"It must have been about eleven at night, pitch dark. I was walking back to the hotel and I was completely alone, when I heard two men talking outside in the grounds. And one of them quite clearly said the name, 'Vic Landry.' So, my ears pricked up because I was working on the story, and it turned out to be a guy called Nigel–"

"Nigel Scott-Renard?"

"Yes. I couldn't believe it. They were actually discussing Vic. I slowed down to listen, but they sensed someone was there, so I hurried away, but when I got to the corner of the street one of them leapt out of the gate, and basically slammed me into the railings. Like it was a dare or a joke."

"Oh, my God! Were you all right?"

"Yes. Pretty shaken up, but I was more determined than ever by then, to try and get to the bottom of what was going on. Everything about you and Vic was being hushed up, you see? By the press, the police, right across the board; and so after talking to some of Vic's friends and after the incident with Nigel and his friend, I wasn't going to be put off. So, long story short, I decided to kind of doorstep Vic's sister-in-law at her gym in Oxford because–"

"Samantha?"

"Yes. But I never got there, Louise. I was halfway down the steps to the tube, when a woman pushed a note into my hand, telling me to stop asking questions and that they knew exactly who I was."

"But why? I don't understand. Why was our disappearance being hushed up?"

Ingrid shakes her head. "I'm not a hundred percent sure. But when I got home to my flat, I found it had been turned over."

"This gets worse. But I don't get it – why didn't you just leave it at that? I mean, you're not police and it sounds like you were in danger."

"I will tell you all of it, Louise. But there's quite a bit you don't know yet, and it's pretty shocking. There's such a thing as controlled disclosure for a reason. We have to process things."

She hadn't meant to blurt anywhere near as much as she had on the first day, but in the end, dancing around the inconvenient truth wasn't going to help either of them, and she can't protect Louise from it for long. There is no London flat for her to go back to. Even Janice knows more than Louise. She deserves the truth and she deserves the chance to deal with it.

There is a pause. It stretches for what seems like an eternity. And then when she speaks, Louise's voice sounds overly loud, piercing. And the question lingers in the air long after it's been asked, like an echo.

"Do you know where Vic is?"

Ingrid holds her gaze. Shakes her head.

"No, we're going to have to find him together. But, I do know a lot more than I've told you and it is about him. Do you want to hear it now?"

"Yes, I do."
"Sure? Because you've been through a lot and–"

"No, I want to hear it, Ingrid. I'm okay, I promise."

Incredibly, Louise listens calmly to the entire story, exactly as Ingrid had uncovered it herself, occasionally throwing in a question until it's perfectly clear in her mind.

"I don't understand where Vic was going every day in Singapore, then," she says eventually. "I mean, he left every morning and came home late in the evenings. Worked most weekends."

Katty, Ingrid thinks, but doesn't say it. Besides, she cannot be sure.

"Kind of makes sense now, though"

"Does it? It doesn't to me. Not yet, anyway."

Dusk is settling over the valley and a single long-legged mosquito hovers between them, its whining buzz the alarm call they need to go inside to the bar, where a guitar is being played, and lamps are lit.

In the lounge, beneath the whirring ceiling fan, they order more coffee.

"There was this woman called Katty, you see?" Louise says.

Ingrid drops her cup into the saucer with a clatter.

Katty is the one person she's avoided mentioning. Was Vic's Thai girlfriend even relevant at the moment, when Louise's emotions are so raw already? She has watched her face, noting every reaction, treading softly around her feelings. Marsha had been easy to cover, an old family friend, and definitely not a lover. In fact, it would have helped Louise to know Marsha was gay, because of the newspapers she will see later, because of the inference in all of them.

But Katty…

"Oh, so you know about her, then?"

***

Chapter Thirty

Louise blanches briefly, her eyes registering dismay. So, she was right about her hunch, is the unspoken message. Had fished and caught something she didn't really want.

"Sort of. It was just a bit odd, that's all. She was his ex-girlfriend, long before he met me, of course. But she was the one who told him about the last place we went to, you see? Phu Hua Loan. And there was also someone called Katty at the hotel reception in Chiang Rai, who he saw but I never did, and I think it was her who drew the map he had that day. It just bugged me. Probably nothing. I don't know, bit of a coincidence."

"A map?"

"A detailed one for how to get to Phu Hua Loan, where we were attacked. The people in the village there even seemed to be expecting us. So, how did you know about her?"

"Karl. He was telling me about a holiday he and Vic had in Bangkok. Apparently, Vic had a tattoo done by Katty's brother. Karl didn't go in but waited outside, and when Vic came out he was behaving really oddly."

"Ah, so it was a holiday, then!"

"Sorry?"

"It's okay, it's not important. Carry on."

"Well, according to Karl, when they came back from the

trip, Vic started to change. Up to then he'd been very easy going, a bit of a lad, they'd had a lot of fun. But suddenly he was gambling, insider trading, basically behaving like there was a decaying oil painting up in the attic. Spending like he had no limit, and sorry, but going out with a hell of a lot of different women. And sometimes, this woman, Katty, would just reappear out of nowhere. She was a bit spooky. There'd been an occult ritual, or something."

"Yes, he told me. So, Karl said he changed afterwards? Specifically after that?"

"Yes. A lot."

"How weird! And then he saw Vic out with Katty in London, as well? So, it wasn't over after one holiday? It wasn't just a brief fling? So, how recently was she in London?"

Ingrid looks at Louise's stricken face, recalling Jan Lozensky's words, about how this time last year she would wait and wait for Vic to show up; and Janice telling her Louise would be all dressed up ready to go out but Vic wouldn't show. Maybe he'd turn up a few days later? Maybe a few weeks. And then there was the fact that Karl didn't even know Louise, but he certainly knew Katty.

"I'm not altogether sure when she was in London."

"He told me the affair with Katty was years ago. Then changed his story to just before he met me. One time, he said he met her through work, then it was a holiday. And then there just happened to be a woman with the same name at the hotel who knew exactly where that beauty spot was and could even draw a bloody map of it. Now I find out she was in London with him."

Ingrid bites her lip. How can she tell her Katty was with Vic at the family skiing holiday just weeks before telling

Louise he couldn't live without her? There's only so much Louise is going to be able to take. It was heartbreaking.

"Going back to Vic being sacked then," Louise says, eventually. "Why would the press cover that up?"

"Oh, I think confidence in the bank, image, big names…"

Louise nods. "Plausible. But, if he was in that much trouble, maybe in fear for his life, then why would he take on a wife? Especially someone penniless like me? It wasn't like I could help him out. It seems… odd."

"Doesn't it?"

Louise pours them both more coffee, emptying the pot.

"I don't drink much but shall we have a brandy in it?"

"I think you need one," Ingrid agrees. "I won't, but we'll definitely get you one."

While Louise digests both the brandy and the new information, Ingrid goes to the bathroom, sits on one of the chairs by the dresser, closes her eyes and prays. There is a lot more to tell her before this short stay is through. A lot more. It could go one of several ways.

When she comes back, however, Louise seems steady, contemplative.

"I wonder if it was escapism? The reason he married me, I mean. A chance for a new life with someone who knew very little about him? But his enemies caught up with him anyway?"

"Possibly."

"I wonder where he is, Ingrid? I suppose I'll just have to get home and… oh, you said his flat isn't really his… In that case, I don't even know where I'll go when I get back."

"I don't know where I'll go, either."

"How do you mean?"

"I can't go back to my flat, Louise. I told you it was turned over. Someone was having Karl watched and they had me watched, too. Remember, I told you about the white van outside the café when I was interviewing Karl? I thought we'd thrown them off the scent, but by the next day they knew everything about me. Must have followed my every move."

"Nigel Scott-Renard? Do you think he's behind it? From what you said–"

"Possibly. Or someone else in this secretive club they all seem to be in."

"So, what did you do when you found your flat had been broken into?"

"I went to stay with Mum and Dad. And this is what I've got to tell you, Louise. I've been working up to it but there's been such a lot for you to take in already, I thought it would be too much. In fact, I'd decided to leave it for a while. A day, anyway. I thought, tomorrow…"

"Tell me what? Is it about Vic?"

"No, it's about you. Me. Actually, I've only recently found out myself. It really might be best left 'til tomorrow, you know? You need another really good night's sleep."

"I need another month of really good nights' sleep. To be honest, though – I'll probably be waking up at four or five in the morning for the rest of my life until I know what's happened to Vic. So, you might as well say, Ingrid."

"All right, if you're absolutely sure."

"It can't be that bad. Besides, you haven't really said why you're here, helping me. You came all the way out to Thailand at your own expense, brought me clothes and paid for the meals. I suppose I've been too absorbed listening to everything you found out, but I've got to ask, why?"

Ingrid takes a deep breath.

"Okay, here goes. Right... Well, I went to stay with Mum and Dad because I didn't feel safe in the flat, especially with the lock damaged. I had to give them an explanation, of course, because I haven't lived at home for nearly ten years. So, I told them I'd been writing a feature on you and Vic, and it seemed I'd asked questions other people didn't like. My mother asked pretty much what you've asked – why I put myself at risk and went ruffling feathers. 'Not a policeman', she said."

Louise smiles.

"Basically, I told them I'd smelled a rat, the truth had been covered up, and how would they like it if I was written off as dead and no one even bothered to look for me? You were from the same town, your friend's story wasn't published and neither was Karl's. All of us were very concerned. Anyway, my mother suddenly snapped, and Louise, she really doesn't have a temper, so it was completely out of character. But she practically exploded – 'For the love of God, will you bloody well shut up about Louise bloody Draper!' Then she stormed out to the kitchen, slamming the door so the whole house shook. And later on, I know they had words, the atmosphere was terrible."

"Oh, my God! Louise bloody Draper?"

"I know. And it came out of nowhere. It wasn't like her, at all. Normally, she'd be really upset about a missing girl. Especially a local one. Anyway, she really laid it down. Enough about that family. Enough. I don't want to hear another word.'"

"That family?"

"Yes. Anyway, I didn't want to sit in the lounge with my dad, and it was raining, so I went up to my mother's sewing room, just a little box room overlooking the garden at the back. And I started leafing through all the old photo albums. I hadn't seen them since I was a teen and it was bit of a distraction – took my mind off things. Anyway, that's when I came across this photo, dated 1969 on the back. It was taken in Rhyl, and there's Mum and Dad, me as a little girl, and a few others. A day out, I guess. My mother had both her hands on my shoulders, and on her left is my grandmother, and next to her is my dad. And next to Dad, very close, is a woman who looks a dead ringer for you. Seriously, I had to look twice. And then I couldn't take my eyes off it."

"Me? In 1969? But I wasn't even born."

"Not yet, no. But she looks just like you."

"My mother?"

"Her name was Barbara, yes?"

"Uh-huh. Well, I suppose it would be very feasible. Small town. Same age."

"Hmm." She takes another deep breath. "Only my dad and your mother were dead close in that photo, Louise, as in their fingers are touching; and Barbara is looking at my dad in a way you cannot fake, and you cannot hide."

Louise's eyes widen and keep on widening.

"Look, it was just a guess, a wild guess. But when I interviewed Len Draper, he told me your mother was already pregnant and that, 'no one else would have her'."

Louise's eyes suddenly register the impact. And it's too much for Ingrid. She looks down at her fingernails, picking at the quicks.

"I challenged my dad outright, Louise. And he told me

never to mention it to my mother. Not ever. I'd only have been three years old when it happened. The affair with Barbara. And Barbara had a little girl nine months later, called Louise."

Still, Louise doesn't speak.

"Respectability was really important back then. Gossips and condemnation could make people's lives hell. We have to understand that. A small town, big disgrace. My dad was married."

"She let Len Draper, that horrible man, lock me up, smack me across the head."

Ingrid reaches out and takes her hand.

"Louise, I know you can't see this yet, but something kept telling me I mustn't give up on you, that you were alive. And as soon as I saw you yesterday, I knew you were my sister. We both look like my dad. Same eyes."

Eventually, after several long agonising minutes, she returns the squeeze of Ingrid's hand.

"My sister. I have a sister?"

"Yes. Yes, you do. And we're going to find out what happened to Vic, and we're going to look after each other from now on. Okay?"

But Louise can't talk. Because she's crying.

***

Chapter Thirty-One

The following morning, news arrives from the man with no name. He's waiting on the hotel terrace at one of the breakfast tables, gazing over the infinity pool at the mountains on the other side of the river. A low white mist hovers over the valley, with only the tops visible, the heat of the day yet to rise.

As soon as Ingrid appears, he motions for her to join him.

"Breakfast?"

She smiles. "Thank you. Louise will be with us soon. She's up and about."

"Have you told her everything?"

"Yes."

"Nothing left out?"

"Umm… Only Katty being with Vic last Christmas. It seemed a bit too much, too cruel. She's taking everything unbelievably well, but I just thought, well, I'll be honest – I couldn't do it."

"You're a very kind person, Ingrid. But we don't have a lot of time, and I need some information from her."

He pours them both coffee.

"Thank you."

"Thing is, there could be news of Victor in the not-too-distant future."

"Really? Is he still alive, then? How do you know?"

He pushes a card across the table. "We're going to need to keep in contact. This is an office number if you need me, but I will call you first. As you will see, it's a florist's. They will contact me, and then I will find you."

"You're a private detective, aren't you?"

"You can say whatever you wish. But in truth, I am a florist."

He smiles and she smiles back.

"So, this is for emergencies only?"

"Correct. But you must understand it could be weeks, or even months, before I have definite news, so I will need a way of contacting you."

"Actually, I've decided to stay in Thailand for a while. Bit of breathing space. A few weeks on the coast near Phuket. I had a holiday there years ago, and Louise is going to stay with me. We both need time out, to talk and decide what to do next. I'm probably going to sell my flat and start over. We've got some ideas, thoughts floating in, but it's too soon yet."

"Louise has somewhere to go? When she gets back to the UK?"

"Not really. Apparently, her grandmother left her the house, but of course, her step-father's in it. Eventually it will be hers, but not for a long time yet. When I knocked on his door, he'd been dancing round the living room by the sound of it. Not that she'd ever want go back there."

He nods.

"And now she knows Vic's flat isn't his, so she can't go there, either. And she doesn't have a job. So, you know – we need to thrash out what to do next. I've enough money for a while, but not for long."

He darts a glance towards the hotel door.

"Okay, can you give me the details of where you'll be staying, and also that of your parents? Do you have a mobile phone?"

Ingrid checks over her shoulder, just as Louise appears, quickly jots down the information and hands it over. "Yes, a Nokia. I only got it a few months ago but this is the number."

"Ah, now I see the resemblance," he exclaims, slipping the paper into his pocket as Louise approaches. "Same eyes, same expression. Just different hair. One blonde, one dark –or you could be the same girl!"

During breakfast, they chat about travel plans and the best route to take.

"I can drop you in Chiang Rai," he offers.

But despite Louise's best efforts, he tells them nothing about his findings with Panya the previous day.

"As soon as I know, I will tell you, Louise. You have my word of honour. Remember, I would not be here if this wasn't important, but it's somewhat bigger than you might realise. Much bigger, and much more dangerous. Some things it's better not to know at the moment, and some things you will never know because it wouldn't be safe for you if you did. Can you understand that?"

"I think I'm beginning to. But I do want to know what happened to Vic. Whatever the truth is, I want to know."

He nods, then looks at his watch. "You have my promise. We're going to need to leave soon, ten minutes. But first I need you to help me, Louise. With a missing piece of the puzzle."

"All right."

"Deep breath, because I can't sugarcoat this!"

She nods.

"Okay. Did Victor ever tell you anything about a woman called Katty?"

For a second, she closes her eyes, one hand clasping the pearl cross around her neck. "Her again."

"Yes, I'm sorry."

"Right."

After a quick glance at Ingrid, she repeats what she'd told her the night before.

"And that's pretty much all I know.... well, that's relevant."

"Okay. Well, I'm going to tell you now what Ingrid didn't tell you last night. And she didn't tell you because you'd had enough shocks already. But Victor was with Katty last Christmas, at the family holiday in Klosters. But before you become too upset about it, you have to know this woman is not what you think. So, I want you to hold onto that, okay?"

Barely perceptibly, she nods for him to go on.

"Did he tell you anything else about her? Think hard because it could be important. Anything else at all, that you didn't tell Ingrid last night?"

Louise's face is burning. Her mouth opens and closes. *Vic was with Katty last Christmas, when she was breaking her heart, and hadn't seen him for weeks and weeks...*

"There's something I didn't mention to you," Ingrid tells him. "I don't think I thought it was relevant, but actually Louise knew all about it, too. So, I suppose it could be. Karl, his best friend, told me about an occult ritual Vic took part in while he was in Bangkok, and that he was really different afterwards. I didn't think to say before because it sounded... you know... silly."

"Tell me."

"Well, Vic met this girl, Katty, in Bangkok, and one night they went to her brother's tattoo parlour. Karl waited outside because he had a bad feeling about it. And when Vic came out he was shaking and delirious. That night in the hotel he was freaked out, jumping at shadows. And apparently, he said something about having a spirit with him now. He said they'd conjured up a dark entity, and it would get him whatever he wanted, but in return he would pay a price.

"Karl said he thought Katty had some kind of hold over Vic, and after that he changed – took more risks, spent huge amounts of money, went to casinos and dodgy clubs, became hugely promiscuous. Literally self-sabotaging, and just… not himself. She was in London a lot, anyway. He said she was always around."

Ingrid turns to Louise.

"I'm sorry. But I agree with our man here, I don't think it's what we think. We've got to find the truth. Unless–"

"No, I want to know. It's just… yes, it's okay. I'm okay."

The man leans forward, speaking in a low voice as a young couple sit down at the table next to them.

"Louise, did Vic ever tell you about that night he had the tattoo? Is there anything more about Katty you can think of?"

"Yes. It was the day before the attack. We'd taken a day trip into the hills, and got into a conversation about shamans and voodoo. Vic was pretty knowledgeable, and I asked him how he knew all that. He said from a woman he once knew, called Katty. She had an amulet on a chain, with letters on the front she was always touching.

Sometimes, she'd have her eyes closed, holding onto it, murmuring. Apparently, it contained the ground bones, teeth, and bits of hair from a human sacrifice, and the seal on the front attaches the wearer to a spirit entity. It's done with a binding ritual, a contract.

"Anyway, one night she introduced him to her brother and he had a tattoo done, just like Karl told Ingrid, in the back room of his house. But I can tell you a bit more. He said it was really late at night and there were lit candles, joss sticks, all this incense floating around, and the table was set out with offerings. I'm trying to remember exactly – I think he said the brother put on a gold mask and started chanting, pounding on a drum, summoning what they called a grandmaster. He said he went into a trance because it went on for ages. Then it stopped and he woke up abruptly. After that, he had to say what he wished for, his deepest desires, and a spirit was brought through for him. Then he drank corpse oil made from bodily organs. Illegal, he said it was all illegal. And he had to keep chanting particular words over and over, and not to resist whatever came. Then he had the tattoo inked, and all the while they were continuing to chant these same words.

"He said there would be consequences, but he thought it was rubbish and very funny. He never mentioned all that stuff about shaking and jumping out of his skin, though. He told me he found it amusing."

"Do you think any of this is actually relevant, though?" Ingrid asks him. "I mean, to the attack on Vic and Louise?"

The man, a man with the kind of looks that would make him invisible in a crowd, shakes his head slightly. Then shrugs, and again looks at his watch.

"We must go. Look, Louise, I might know what's

happened to your husband. And it is possible I know what happened to you, but I want to be absolutely sure first. Once an idea is in the mind, it's difficult to dislodge it again. So, we must be sure."

Ingrid nods. "Absolutely. So, then. We're going to have to wait. Might as well make it enjoyable."

Louise smiles faintly and reaches for her hand.

"Thank you, Ingrid."

"And then," she smiles, "my sister and I will decide what to do."

"I wouldn't mind staying out here permanently, actually."

"Louise? Really? Are you kidding?"

"No. I prefer the weather, I love the polite, gentle people, and it's so beautiful. I just need to learn Thai. I also want to come back here one day and visit Noy."

"What would you do, though? For a living?"

"I don't know. I haven't thought yet. But, first I have to know if Vic's alive or not. There will be things to sort out. And I think we need to know about Katty. Because I'm convinced she is involved in all of this. Even if she just sent him mad. I just don't know why."

"You're right, we do need to know. And we will. But for now. Here's to us!"

Ingrid holds up a glass of juice, and they clink glasses.

"To my sister!"

"To my sister!"

"And now we must go," says the man whose name they will never know.

***

Chapter Thirty-Two

Housemans' Bespoke Travel Agency
London, May 1993

He is the man who blends into the crowd, the man who isn't seen, and yet he is everywhere. At first she doesn't recognise him. But then he takes off his sunglasses and their eyes meet.

"You've got news about Vic!"

He nods, turns, and flicks the 'Open' sign on the door to 'Closed'.

"Is there somewhere we can talk, Louise?"

Above the shop floor of the London travel agency she and Ingrid now run together, is a modest two-bedroomed flat.

"Come on up. Ingrid won't be back for a while, though."

He follows her up two flights of narrow stairs. "That's fine. It's you I need to talk to first. Nice place. How's business going?"

They reach the top, and she unlocks the door into a light, airy room with long sash windows overlooking a park.

"Well, we've only just started but it's very promising. And as you can see," she gestures to the watercolours hanging on the white walls, "Ingrid's started painting again."

"She's really good. Is this one of Yorkshire?"

"Yes. Beautiful, isn't it? The light on the purple heather."

"I'm seriously impressed. And this one must be of my home country?"

"She calls it, *Mist over the Mekong*."

"I love it."

"Would you like a coffee?"

"Please. Thank you."

While she makes the drinks, he sits on one of the deep, comfortable sofas either side of an old-style iron fireplace, and gazes out at the park, at the cherry blossom flowering on the trees, and the sunlight chasing on the breeze, rippling across the grass.

"We're organising bespoke trips to Thailand," Louise says, handing him a cup. "The first trip is in July for a group of single professionals."

She sits on the opposite sofa, tucking her legs underneath her. "We wanted to do something together, but in a way we would each be happy with. So, Ingrid sold her flat to help pay for this place, and she likes to go out to Thailand looking at hotels, talking to guides, writing everything up; and I wanted to stay here, to make this a home, and talk to the customers, tailor their holiday so it would be perfect for them. I also go out for lunch with Janice now and again, and…" She picks up her coffee, takes a sip. "Sorry, I'm rambling on. So, am I ready for what you're going to tell me?"

"Are you?"

"Yes, I think so. Well, last time, on the phone, you told

Ingrid you'd found his body, so that has to be the worst bit."

"It is, and it isn't."

"Oh, God!"

"I can't sugarcoat, you know that. Truth is truth."

She takes another gulp of coffee. "Okay."

"His body's going to be released and the news will be in the press. But the truth will not be published. There will be a story. So, just know that's what will happen."

She nods.

"I've pieced together a lot of information, but most is still shrouded in secrecy, even for me, so there's a fair bit of guesswork. I don't think I'm far off, though. I just wanted you to have, should we say, resolution. So you can move on in life, not be left wondering."

"Thank you."

"All right, well we have to go back to Katty. She's not who or what you might have thought. She wasn't some woman Vic met on holiday or anything else. She was planted. Katty's father's in the same secret society as Vic's. You've heard Karl and Ingrid tell you about this, so we don't need to go into how powerful or how dark this club is. But, from my insider source, Katty's what's known as a high priestess. And she was asked to seduce Vic into the ritual he told you about in Bangkok. It was not her brother who did the tattoo, but a fellow occultist."

"Planted by who?"

"It seems Vic wasn't playing the family game. Never had and didn't want to. But he knew what was going on, what they did, and because of that he basically dropped out, kept the family at a distance, hopping from job to job, disappearing with his friends. He wasn't, should we say, of strong character, but then again he wasn't an evil one, either. Like them. He hated what he came from but they weren't going to let him off the leash. Every now and again he'd be summoned, told what to do and what was expected of him. And every time he'd refuse. Nor would he be drawn into anything nefarious, because first of all he didn't want to be, and secondly he knew darned well what happened to people later. He could have been in any powerful position in the world, especially with his looks and charm, but he chose not to sell out. Unfortunately though, wherever he went, they found him."

"I never knew any of this."

"No. So, they sent Katty to use black magic on him, to lure him into a ritual that bound him with a dark entity, which is real, Louise. Don't be under the illusion that it isn't. I've seen people who've been involved in this kind of evil shit and they're definitely not themselves anymore - they can change before your eyes. And then she set about playing with his mind, placing compromising photographs of herself in his apartment, and…"

Louise gasped. "Oh, that was her!"

"She gave him things to wear with symbols painted on the back, would ring him using different voices, telling him to do this or that, and before long his behaviour began to change, and a lot of people noticed. Suddenly, he was gambling heavily, drinking heavily, taking cocaine, playing around with women whether they were married or not, and ultimately, fraudulently, siphoning off other people's money to the tune of millions."

"Sabotaging his own life, just like Karl said."

"And when he was in enough of a mess and they had enough photographs and evidence to prove it… when enough people were coming after him who'd been done over, they gave him the ultimatum they give to all those caught in the net of iniquity."

"Do what we tell you to do."

"And what was that, do you think?"

"I've racked my brains on this one. Whatever he was sent out to Singapore to do. But something went wrong and we were kidnapped or they murdered him…"

"Singapore was just a holding bay, a cover. Katty rented a flat there, and that's where he went each day. While she gave him instructions and the whole deal was set up."

"Yes, that makes sense. Okay."

"Okay so far?"

"Yes."

"It wasn't what you thought, though. She may well have seduced him but he was not in love with her. He was terrified of her. And by that time there were a lot of photographs of him, remember? All sorts of compromising photos he didn't even remember being taken. They'd have thrown him to the wolves if he hadn't agreed to what I'm going to tell you next. What they wanted him to do was head up their disgusting business over there, and that was trafficking drugs, arms, and people. Not from Singapore, of course not. From the mainland. But first, in order to prove they could trust him, there was an initiation. And that was you."

"Me?"

"All those who join the club must pass an initiation. It binds them. And his was to find an innocent, a woman with no ties, young and pretty. And then to sell her."

At first, she doesn't understand. The words replay in her head several times. And then it hits her in the gut. The truth. And now it's seen, it's so blindingly obvious.

"Katty was in the hotel, and she gave him explicit instructions. There was an initial attempt to abduct you on the day you went up to the first hill tribe, but believe it or not, the tribe you probably saw as threatening, refused to co-operate. I have spoken to the guide. And the two guys on the motorbikes you saw on the day of the attack? I've spoken to them personally, too. Their job was to make sure you got there. You were the deal, you see? Not Vic. He just had to get you to trust him. After that, he'd be in the club and they had their man for life."

Louise sits straight up, puts her cup down, then covers her face with her hands. Of course, of course… Everything is falling into place. But at the same time it is too terrible, too repugnant, too painful, to believe.

"Only something went wrong," he adds.

It is the faintest wisp of hope, something to grasp onto.

"What? What went wrong?"

"He came back for you."

It takes a long time, minutes, for her to take her hands from her eyes, to be able to speak.

"What? What do you mean?"

"He couldn't do it. He wasn't an evil man, Louise. There'd been a hold over him from the moment he was born into that gilded cage. No one knows the power of dark arts and mind control, unless it happens to them personally. And no one knows about dark entities unless they attach to them personally, either. But they finally caught up with him, and after that he changed. His best friend saw it. Many saw it. He was tricked. But deep inside, he wasn't like them. He really was just tricked."

"How do you know he came back for me?"

"Because one of the local gang members told us, eventually. Vic escaped in the Jeep as planned, but it looks like he followed them over the border. Two of them had been left to guard you, but he surprised them and there was a fight. We don't know exactly what happened next, but the two guards gave chase, one was injured and the other raised the alarm with the rest of the gang. And when they came back, you'd gone and Vic was nowhere to be found."

"So, when was Vic killed?"

"We're not sure, because his body hadn't been there long. It's possible he'd been searching for you for weeks. Maybe living rough for a long time."

"So, they caught up with him?"

"In the end, yes."

"But he came back for me."

Automatically, her hand reaches for the pearl cross around her neck, and the man looks into her blue-green eyes, at the shock and innocence in them.

"He came back for me," she says again.

"Yes, yes he did. Despite the power of the attack on his mind, I truly believe they did not get his soul."

"He knew about all that dark stuff, you know? I just don't think he believed it was real."

"No, he probably didn't."

For a while they sit in silence.

Eventually, Louise says, "So, that really was him, in the trees, then?"

"Yes."

The haunting image sits with her for a while, hovering over a white morning mist, the black drongo bird with red eyes standing watching.

"Will there be a funeral here in England?"

He nods.

"I don't think I'll go. I don't want anything to do with any of them. They don't know where I am and I prefer to keep it that way. Or do they? Do they know?"

"No, they don't know. Ingrid and I made sure of that. You're not a threat because you don't know anything, do you?"

"No."

"You were attacked by a gang and you were found by locals. You have nothing else to tell anyone and it is my best advice that you don't. You will not be able to change anything on your own, it would be best left to others. That will always be your choice, of course."

"And your work? Yours and Panya's?"

"It goes on. We will unpick everything they do, block them at every exit, and return the girls to their villages one by one. Things are changing, and the more help we have at ground level, the better. In actual fact, if it was not for you, there is a lot we wouldn't have known. For example, the three girls you saw that morning have all been returned to their village. And that was because of you."

She smiles. "That's good to know, really good."

"And now I must go, although it would have been nice to talk to Ingrid."

Right on cue, there is the sound of a key in the lock downstairs, and they stare at each other wide-eyed at the sound of clattering footsteps on the stairs.

"Oh, hi!" Ingrid says, "I didn't know anyone was here."

The man laughs, stands up, bows slightly. "The other beautiful sister. It's good to see you, Ingrid."

Today, she is wearing a crisp white shirt with black jeans and heels, her hair loose around her shoulders. Today,

Ingrid is radiant.

"You've been out with Karl," Louise says, still wiping away the tears from her face.

"Might have."

They both laugh.

"So, what have I missed?"

"He came back for me, Ingrid. Vic. Can you believe it? He came back for me. He could have been free and rich and in their horrible club. But he came back for me instead, and because of that he died."

Ingrid folds her in her arms and hugs her.

"I have a feeling he won a far bigger battle," she says, softly. "Whatever it was he got into, he kept the light in his heart."

"Yes, he held onto his precious soul. I feel better, a lot better, thinking of it that way. But it also sets me free, too. I'd thought I was so worthless, so utterly dispensable and unlovable. And now I have a beautiful new life. I have you. I love you. And I loved him."

She holds onto the pearl cross.

"I think he loved you too, Louise. My guess is he saw in you something he probably never had before, just pure love. I would go so far as to say you saved him. Perhaps you were meant to."

At that moment, a cool breeze passes over them both and they pull apart, suddenly remembering, at exactly the same moment, the man with no name.

But he's gone, has silently vanished, the door to the apartment gently closing behind him.

"I wonder if he's a guardian angel," Louise says.

"I don't know. But I'd say they're everywhere, wouldn't you?"

Louise looks into her eyes, thinking back to the kindness of strangers, to the wise words of passing friends, to the selfless courage of her own sister, and nods.

"Yes. Yes, I definitely would."

***

References

The Lonely Planet: Hill Tribes Phrasebook
Wildlife of South East Asia by Susan Myers

More Books by Sarah England

Father of Lies

A Darkly Disturbing Occult Horror Trilogy: Book 1

Ruby is the most violently disturbed patient ever admitted to Drummersgate Asylum, high on the bleak moors of northern England. With no improvement after two years, Dr Jack McGowan finally decides to take a risk and hypnotises her. With terrifying consequences.

A horrific dark force is now unleashed on the entire medical team, as each in turn attempts to unlock Ruby's shocking and sinister past. Who is this girl? And how did she manage to survive such unimaginable evil? Set in a desolate ex-mining village, where secrets are tightly kept and intruders hounded out, their questions soon lead to a haunted mill, the heart of darkness… and the Father of Lies.

***

Tanners Dell – Book 2

Now only one of the original team remains – Ward Sister Becky. However, despite her fiancé, Callum, being unconscious and many of her colleagues either dead or critically ill, she is determined to rescue Ruby's twelve-year-old daughter from a similar fate to her mother.

But no one asking questions in the desolate ex-mining village Ruby hails from ever comes to a good end. And as the diabolical history of the area is gradually revealed, it seems the evil invoked is both real and contagious.

Don't turn the lights out yet!

***

Magda – Book 3

The dark and twisted community of Woodsend harbours a terrible secret – one tracing back to the age of the Elizabethan witch hunts, when many innocent women were persecuted and hanged.

But there is a far deeper vein of horror running through this village, an evil that, once invoked, has no intention of relinquishing its grip on the modern world. Rather, it watches and waits with focused intelligence, leaving Ward Sister Becky and CID Officer Toby constantly checking over their shoulders and jumping at shadows.

Just who invited in this malevolent presence? And is the demonic woman who possessed Magda back in the sixteenth century the same one now gazing at Becky whenever she looks in the mirror?

Are you ready to meet Magda in this final instalment of the trilogy? Are you sure?

***

The Owlmen

If They See You, They Will Come for You

Ellie Blake is recovering from a nervous breakdown. Deciding to move back to her northern roots, she and her psychiatrist husband buy Tanners Dell at auction – an old water mill in the moorland village of Bridesmoor.

However, there is disquiet in the village. Tanners Dell has a terrible secret, one so well guarded no one speaks its name. But in her search for meaning and very much alone, Ellie is drawn to traditional witchcraft and determined to pursue it. All her life she has been cowed. All her life she has apologised for her very existence. And witchcraft has opened a door she could never have imagined. Imbued with power and overawed with its magic, for the first time she feels she has come home, truly knows who she is.

Tanners Dell, though, with its centuries-old demonic history… well, it's a dangerous place for a novice…

***

The Soprano

A Haunting Supernatural Thriller

It is 1951 and a remote mining village on the North Staffordshire Moors is hit by one of the worst snowstorms in living memory. Cut off for over three weeks, the old and the sick will die, the strongest bunker down, and those with evil intent will bring to its conclusion a family vendetta spanning three generations.

Inspired by a true event, *The Soprano* tells the story of Grace Holland – a strikingly beautiful, much admired local celebrity who brings glamour and inspiration to the grimy moorland community. But why is Grace still here? Why doesn't she leave this staunchly Methodist, rain-sodden place and the isolated farmhouse she shares with her mother?

Riddled with witchcraft and tales of superstition, the story is mostly narrated by the Whistler family, who own the local funeral parlour, in particular six-year-old Louise – now an elderly lady – who recalls one of the most shocking crimes imaginable.

***

Hidden Company

A dark psychological thriller set in a Victorian asylum in the heart of Wales.

1893, and nineteen-year-old Flora George is admitted to a remote asylum with no idea why she is there, what happened to her child, or how her wealthy family could have abandoned her to such a fate. However, within a short space of time, it becomes apparent she must save herself from something far worse than that of a harsh regime.

2018, and forty-one-year-old Isobel Lee moves into the gatehouse of what was once the old asylum. A reluctant medium, it is with dismay she realises there is a terrible secret here – one desperate to be heard. Angry and upset, Isobel baulks at what she must now face. But with the help of local dark arts practitioner Branwen, face it she must.

This is a dark story of human cruelty, folklore and superstition. But the human spirit can and will prevail… unless of course, the wrath of the fae is incited…

***

Monkspike

You are not forgiven

1149 was a violent year in the Forest of Dean.

Today, nearly 900 years later, the forest village of Monkspike sits brooding. There is a sickness here passed down through ancient lines, one noted and deeply felt by Sylvia Massey, the new psychologist. What is wrong with Nurse Belinda Sully's son? Why did her husband take his own life? Why are the old people in Temple Lake Nursing Home so terrified? And what are the lawless inhabitants of nearby Wolfs Cross hiding?

It is a dark village indeed, but one which has kept its secrets well. That is, until local girl Kezia Elwyn returns home as a practising Satanist, and resurrects a hellish wrath no longer containable. Burdo, the white monk, will infest your dreams… This is pure occult horror and definitely not for the faint of heart…

***

Baba Lenka

Pure Occult Horror

1970, and *Baba Lenka* begins in an icy Bavarian village with a highly unorthodox funeral. The deceased is Baba Lenka, great-grandmother to Eva Hart. But a terrible thing happens at the funeral, and from that moment on everything changes for seven-year-old Eva. The family flies back to Yorkshire but it seems the cold Alpine winds have followed them home... and the ghost of Baba Lenka has followed Eva. This is a story of demonic sorcery and occult practices during the World Wars, the horrors of which are drip-fed into young Eva's mind to devastating effect. Once again, this is absolutely not for the faint of heart. Nightmares pretty much guaranteed...

***

Masquerade

A Beth Harper Supernatural Thriller
Book 1

The first in a series of Beth Harper books, *Masquerade* is a supernatural thriller set in a remote North Yorkshire village. Following a whirlwind relocation for a live-in job at the local inn, Beth quickly realises the whole village is thoroughly haunted, the people here fearful and cowed. As a spiritual medium, her attention is drawn to Scarsdale Hall nearby, the enormous stately home dominating what is undoubtedly a wild and beautiful landscape. Built of black stone with majestic turrets, it seems to drain the energy from the land. There is, she feels, something malevolent about it, as if time has stopped…

***

Caduceus

Book Two in the Beth Harper Supernatural Thriller Series.

Beth Harper is a highly gifted spiritual medium and clairvoyant. Having fled Scarsdale Hall, she's drawn to the remote coastal town of Crewby in North West England, and it soon becomes apparent she has a job to do. The congeniality here is but a thin veneer masking decades of deeply embedded secrets, madness and fear. Although she has help from her spirit guides and many clues are shown in visions, it isn't until the senseless and ritualistic murders happen on Mailing Street, however, that the truth is finally unearthed. And Joe Sully, the investigating officer, is about to have the spiritual awakening of his life.

What's buried beneath these houses, though, is far more horrific and widespread than anything either of them could have imagined. Who is the man in black? What is the black goo crawling all over the rooftops? What exactly is The Gatehouse? And as for the local hospital, one night is more than enough for Beth... let alone three...

***

Groom Lake

A Dark Novella

Lauren Stafford, a traumatised divorcee, decides to rent a cottage on the edge of a beautiful ancestral estate in the Welsh Marches. But from the very first day of arrival, she instinctively knows there's something terribly wrong here – something malevolent and ancient – a feeling the whole place is trapped in a time warp. She really ought to leave. But the pull of the lake is too strong, its dark magic so powerful that it crosses over into dreams... turning them into nightmares. What lies beneath its still black surface? And why can't Lauren drag herself away? Why her? And why now?

***

The Droll Teller

A Ghostly Novella

1962, and on Christmas Day at precisely 6pm, a mysterious old man by the name of Silas Finn, calls on the new owners of an ancestral home in Devon and asks which they'd prefer to hear – a story or a song. Ten-year old Enys Quiller is adamant they must have a story, just as Cousin Beatrice instructed.

'You'll be sure to tell me dreckly, won't you?' says Beatrice. 'What the droll teller says?' But the strange and macabre tale of Victorian poisoning and madness that follows, has far-reaching repercussions for Enys and her family, and after the droll teller has finished, any notion of staying there, or even together, is shattered.

***

Creech Cross

A Paranormal Mystery Thriller

'Thirteen in number... It is my belief my daughter danced with the devil...'

As soon as Lyddie crosses the old stone bridge into Creech Cross, there's a strong feeling of stepping, not so much back in time, as out of it. Ancient magic overlaid with dark witchcraft and superstition bleeds into the present day, events and people as woven into the fabric of history as the age-old tracks traversing the land itself. Local people barely acknowledge her, and the incomers are that bit too friendly, until gradually it becomes clear she and her husband are in danger.

Who to trust? Who not to trust? Before the situation becomes alarmingly, inexplicably... unsafe.'

The Witching Hour

A Collection of thrillers, chillers and mysteries

The title story, *The Witching Hour*, inspired the prologue for *Father of Lies*. Other stories include *Someone Out There*, a three-part crime thriller set on the Yorkshire moorlands; *The Witchfinders*, a spooky 17th century witch hunt; and *Cold Melon Tart*, where the waitress discovers there are some things she simply cannot do. In *A Second Opinion*, a consultant surgeon is haunted by his late mistress; and *Sixty Seconds* sees a nursing home manager driven to murder. Whatever you choose, hopefully you'll enjoy the ride.

***

www.sarahenglandauthor.co.uk

Printed in Great Britain
by Amazon